T0208850

JIMMY THE GEEK

James Buckley Heath

JIMMY THE GEEK

cover by Harrison Orr, Timothy Heath

iUniverse books may be ordered through booksellers or by contacting:

iUniverse
1663 Liberty Drive
Bloomington, IN 47403
www.iuniverse.com
1-800-Authors (1-800-288-4677)

ISBN: 978-1-4917-7680-3 (sc)
ISBN: 978-1-4917-7681-0 (e)

Library of Congress Control Number: 2015916538

Print information available on the last page.

iUniverse rev. date: 11/9/2015

I am indebted to my editor and brother, John Aloise Buckley. Without his counsel, infallible "ear," and tireless, creative, and so often brilliant work, *Jimmy the Geek*' would still be "Sophomore Year" and not worth your time.

Since 1990 when I completed the first draft, many others patiently read the manuscript and offered their unfailingly good counsel: my Aunts Patricia Bozell, Jane Buckley Smith, and Priscilla Buckley, all of whom are now deceased. My Aunt Carol Buckley, my former colleague, Julia Cowans Wilhelm, my quondam agent, Elizabeth Backman-Potter, and one of the first sophomores I taught in my public school career, Lee Gotheimer.

And finally, my greatest and best friend, my wife, Edie, who very likely could recite much of the book by heart. Thank you, thank you, thank you.

For aught that ever I could read
Could ever hear by tale or historie,
The course of true love never did run smooth,
But either it was different in blood.
Or else misgraffed, in respect of years.
Or else it stood upon the choice of merit.
Or if there were a simpathie in choise,
Warre, death, or sickness, did lay siege to it;
Making it momentanie, as a sound:
Swift as a shadow, short as any dreame,
Briefe as the lightning in the collied night
That (in a spleene) unfolds both heaven and earth;
And ere a man hath power to say behold,
The jaws of darknesse do devoure it up:
So quick bright things come to confusion.

William Shakespeare
A Midsommer nights Dreame, First Folio
Act I, scene i

Foreword

The tenth reunion of my high school graduation will be in June of 2016. Because I was editor of our yearbook, I suppose, the reunion committee asked me to write a class history. I wanted very much not to do that, and I tried as hard as politeness would let me to beg off, but the head of the committee, Joe Sider, who had been president of our class three of four years, said if I wouldn't do it, he'd do it himself.

Since I haven't seen Joe in nine years, I can't be sure he's not still the jerk he was in high school. He could have changed in that time, enough, I mean so he wouldn't embarrass himself and everyone else who might read his version of the History of the Class of 2006. On the other hand, if he hadn't, then I'd have to sit listening to him, and the last time I did that was more than enough. So, I agreed.

Joe sent me the filled out questionnaires which not much more than a quarter of our classmates submitted. Forty out of a class of 157. Of those, exactly nine provided more information than you'd need to include just to tell yourself you did it: address, phone numbers, email, spouse (not too many of those), children (even fewer), colleges, degrees, employment (not so much on that front either).

To write something that didn't sound like the worst history lecture you have ever heard in your life based on what Joe sent was not going to be possible. Unhelpfully at all, Joe had enclosed a note saying I should contact the guidance department at the high school if I had any questions about anyone. I was pretty sure the obsession with privacy we all are subject to these days would make that a dead end. What I did, though, was call home and ask my mother what she thought.

She suggested contacting old friends. I asked her if she had anyone in mind. "Oh," she said. "You haven't kept in touch."

"No," I said, "I haven't."

I'd done my undergraduate work in New Hampshire. Graduate school (archeology for no better reason than it interested me and my interest in journalism had waned) in Pennsylvania. At the moment, I am teaching science at a boarding school in New Jersey. "Anyway," I said, "I never had many friends to begin with."

She didn't respond to that, and we were both quiet for a while. I would have thought the call had been lost except I could hear her breathing. "You need something to jog your memory."

"Gee, Mother, I knew you were the right person to call. What a great idea! Something to jog my memory."

"Brian. You may be almost thirty years old and the teenagers you teach call you Mr. Lister, but you will never be old or important enough to be snarky to your mother."

She was right, of course, and I apologized. She accepted and went on. "As it happens, I was not simply speaking for the sake of filling the silence. I have something in mind that will, I am certain, do the job. I shall send it to you."

A day later a FedEx overnight envelope was stuffed uncomfortably into my campus mail box. I knew right away what it was. Nevertheless, I waited until I was back in my apartment before opening the envelope. I carried what I needed for my classes, and anything else I thought I might want during the course of the day, in a back pack which I used instead of a briefcase. The school's campus is large and the dormitory my apartment is part of is distant and three flights up.

The apartment opens into a small foyer, small but large enough to fit a short bench against the wall across from the door. I put my backpack down and removed the FedEx envelope, opened it and removed the very old manila envelope. Leaving the backpack on the bench, I took the envelope with me into my living room / dining room / study.

I had one very comfortable chair my father had given me, leather, with a footrest that could be extruded with a lever. He imagined me, Mr. Chips-like, reading winter afternoons away, chatting with adoring students sitting round me on the floor, napping occasionally.

The reality was different. The chair became my office. I corrected there, prepared classes, read enough earth science and biology to stay a few weeks ahead of my students, and, on the rare night completely free of other responsibilities, read for pleasure and drank a beer or three. Each of my classes had a spot of floor within reach of my chair. The two freshman classes (earth science) were on my left, the two first year biology classes on my right, thus mercifully leaving no room for enthralled students.

I brought the envelope to the chair. On the back, in black, faded magic marker, I had written Sophomore Year. Inside was a manuscript I had begun to write late in my sophomore year, and didn't finish until summer vacation was almost over.

It did jog my memory and then some.

1

Jimmy Was Really Special

I can't tell you I wanted to go to Jimmy's funeral. Now I say that, I guess nobody really wants to go to a funeral. Of course, Jimmy's wasn't the first I'd gone to, but it was the first one for someone even close to my age.

I didn't completely make up my mind to go or not to go, either. That decision got made for me by Harry. He refused to go. I found that out from my mom. Harry's mother called her to ask her to ask me if I would be willing to say something at the funeral. When she told me that, I got completely scared and was about to say no, but she saw that coming and held up her hand to stop me. "Here's why you have to do this. The Rosens called Harry to ask him to speak. Harry can't do it."

"Is he going to the funeral?" I said.

"He is not. Mrs. Landis is very concerned. She said…well, she said he's having a very hard time with Jimmy's death. So that is why you have to stand in for him. He is your best friend and even if honoring the Rosens' request were not the right thing to do, speaking in Harry's stead is the fair thing to do."

So I really didn't have any other choice.

You probably know that if you're Jewish, you have to be buried right away. Tuesday was too soon because it was pretty late Monday night when Jimmy died, but the funeral happened first thing Wednesday morning at the Kennedy Funeral Home.

Most of the people there were adults. The chapel they held the service in was the biggest they had, but still it was so packed a lot of people who came too late had to stand basically out in the lobby and try to hear what everybody said.

Not that many kids went to the funeral, but that was okay because Dr. Frank had already made plans for a memorial assembly at the end of the week. Supposedly the funeral was going to be mostly for Jimmy's family and their friends, but as I said, many people showed up. After all, everybody in Afton, in all of Connecticut probably, knew about what had happened to Jimmy: about his being taken away in the ambulance, again, about his dying in the emergency room later; about the demonstrations and the people trying to stop him from being able to go to school. There was a story in the paper Tuesday morning, and TV trucks from the local stations were parked in the funeral home's parking lot. They wanted to talk to the Rosens, of course, but that didn't happen. They didn't have any trouble finding people to talk, though.

I wasn't the only kid who stood up to say something about Jimmy. Two other guys from student government were there. John Battistoni, the president of the Student Council, was honest. He said he hadn't known Jimmy, but he remembered him from the time John had visited Jimmy's homeroom to ask kids if they had any suggestions for improving our school. Apparently Jimmy had made a suggestion and the other kids gave him a hard time; but John told Jimmy he thought it was a good idea and promised the student council would give it serious consideration. Then John mostly talked right to Jimmy's parents and told them how sorry the whole student body was about Jimmy's death. He told them about the money the student council was going to collect for some sort of memorial for Jimmy.

Then Joe Sider got up. He was president of the sophomore class and a prime jerk. I guess what they say about sophomores is true because Joe certainly wasn't elected for being sensitive or hard-working or a good student or anything else you could possibly imagine would be a good idea for voting for someone to be the president of your class. He was elected because most sophomores are jerks. I'm sorry to say that, but it's true. So voting for Joe felt very familiar. Joe is also, however, very smooth. He stood up at the podium, hair all neat and combed, wearing a new dark suit his parents probably got him just for the occasion. He looked solemn and sincere, and that was the only time I thought it was a good idea Harry wasn't there. If he had been, we would have looked at Joe, then at each other, and started to laugh, funeral or not.

Joe said he had stayed up late last night thinking about what he should say. He said deciding was so hard because Jimmy was the kind of kid you could say so much about; he just couldn't decide where to start. Then he reached into his vest pocket and pulled out a piece of paper. As he did, he said, "I finally decided I couldn't hope to say anything on my own even close to adequate" – I remembered to remember that exactly because I knew Harry would want to hear that; he would say that at least Joe said *something* true. "So, if no one minds," Joe continued, "I'll read John Donne's "Death" because for one thing I know Jimmy really respected and admired John Donne." The ironic thing was he was probably right, but he didn't have any idea. He just made that up. But at funerals, people are in a mood to feel sad, and good about anybody who helps them feel that way, too, so he got away with it.

Then it was my turn, and I still didn't know what I wanted to say. Well, that's not true; what I wanted to say was nothing at all, but here's what I did say, as nearly as I remember:

"Mr. and Mrs. Rosen, I'm really sorry Jimmy had to die. I feel sad about it for Jimmy's sake and for mine and for my friends; but mostly I feel sad for you. I know you loved Jimmy a lot. All of us could tell by the way you three talked to each other. I think it's too bad you guys didn't move here sooner than last summer 'cause then we would have been able to get to know Jimmy better, but from the little time we did get to know him, I can tell you one thing for certain: Jimmy was really special; we never knew anyone like him before.

"I wish Harry had been able to come here today. You know, he knew Jimmy better than any of us, and he would have been better at this than I am. Anyway, there really isn't too much for me to say except that we'll miss having Jimmy around, and everybody in his class will never forget him, ever. As I said, he was really special, really an individual."

After me, some adult friends of Jimmy's parents got up, and finally Jimmy's father. He didn't make much sense. He kept jumping around from when Jimmy was a baby to how he nearly died once already this year, then to how tough the move from Ohio was on everybody but especially on Jimmy. He told a lot of stuff about Jimmy and what he enjoyed, but I knew that already; I think most everybody did. Finally, when Mr. Rosen got to talking about how Jimmy had always wanted to grow up to be a conductor like Marin Alsop or Gustavo Dudamel, he started to lose it, so the rabbi went over and helped him back to his seat. The funeral finished up pretty quickly after that.

Even though I didn't want to, I went to the burial, and then I went back to the Rosen's house afterwards, but the only other kids there were Joe and John. I wouldn't have hung out with Joe no matter what, and John was more or less kept occupied by adults. I didn't know him that well anyway. After about a half-hour, Mom came over to me and said I could go now if I wanted to, but make sure I said something to the Rosens before I left. I found Mr. Rosen in the kitchen with his business friends. He shook hands with me and thanked me and said I was welcome to come over anytime.

Mrs. Rosen was in the dining room. She just hugged me and said, "Bless you! You're such a good boy. Such a mensch. Jimmy loved you, too." Then she hugged me again, and I said thank you or something lame. I started to go, but she wouldn't let go of my arms. "Please come some afternoon for cookies. I'd so much like to see you. And if you can, ask Kathryn and Harry, and Melinda, too. All right?"

I said I'd try.

Then I left to go to Harry's house because I needed to see him and talk to him.

2

Harry ♥
Kathryn Sittin'
In a Tree

Harry hated his name, or at least he used to. His real name, Harold Orpheus Landis, wasn't the one he hated because he never used it. "Look," he'd say, "if your name is Harold, everybody's going to think you're a dork no matter what you really are." Anyway, he said Harry was the name he hated because it sounds like a name for a little kid.

He started hating it when we were getting ready for ninth grade, first year of high school. He said every time he heard his name, it felt like somebody's mom calling out the backdoor, "Ha-ree! Time to come inSIGHeed. Your DIN-DIN'S redee!"

That summer, Harry tried out a bunch of new names. The first: "Har." One morning when my folks were already gone to work, Harry just let himself in the back door and came up to my room. I was already up even though I usually slept later than Harry did. He held out a piece of paper in front of me and asked me what I thought. He had the name all written in capital letters – like this: H-A-R. At first I had no idea what he wanted. "What's this? A secret code?"

"No, jerk. It's my new name. What do you think?"

"Har?" (I pronounced it the way it was spelled so it rhymed with tar.)

"No, fool. Har, like the way you'd say the first part of arrow, only with a H. Say it right, say AR, and then say it with an H in front."

"Okay. Ar. Ar with an H in front." I thought that was pretty funny, and I couldn't help laughing. I can usually crack me up. Even Harry laughed a little.

"You are such a jerk. Come on, say it right. And if you say, 'It right,' I'm going to waste you."

So I called him Har the way he wanted me to. At first he thought it sounded all right, but by the end of the day, Harry decided Har was more like for someone who sold used cars to people who can't speak English. That was the end of Har. The rest of the summer he ran through about a dozen new names. I can't remember them all. A lot of them didn't last much more than a few hours, but two came pretty close: Dutch and Stab. I have no idea where those names came from. Harry's ancestors were mostly English and German. They definitely did not come from Holland. Harry just said he'd heard the name Dutch in a movie or something. And Stab? Harry couldn't even begin to say how Stab came into his brain. He just liked it, liked the way it sounded.

Stab lasted the longest. Harry really worked on getting that to be his name. He made me call him every night, not on his cell, and ask to speak to Stab. He always knew I was calling, but he never answered the phone. He figured this way, we could get his parents used to calling him by his new name, but they never did. Mr. or Mrs. Landis would answer the phone, and I'd ask to speak to Stab. They'd say, "Just a minute Brian, I'll call him. HaREE! Brian's on the phone."

Right up until the first day before we had to go to school for Freshman Orientation, Harry was insisting I call him Stab. We both lived close to the school, so we walked. I met up with Harry on West Afton Road, about a half-mile from the high school.

"So," I said. "What are you going to do when they take attendance?"

"What are you talking about?"

"The teacher is going to say, 'Landis, Harry, not Landis, Stab.' What's your plan for that?"

"No plan. I'll say, 'Here.' I'm wasting Stab. I don't like the way it sounds anymore."

Harry gave up on trying to find a new name. He didn't like his old one any better, and at least once a day he'd say to someone, "Don't call me that! I HATE that name!" But he never told anyone what to call him instead. So, mostly people didn't use his name unless absolutely necessary, like if he was standing with a bunch of guys and you needed to say something only to him. That was pretty much the way it was until about Thanksgiving when Harry started going out with Kathryn.

Of course, I knew something was up before anyone else did, but it didn't take long for people to notice. He and Kathryn started hanging out down by the library every morning before homeroom. Not exactly a private place. Pretty soon nobody could think about anything else to talk about. It was so lame. First some guy would say, "That'll never last!" Then someone else would go, "They won't make it to Christmas." Then the girls would start in, "How can she even *like* him?" or, "How can he even *like* her?"

Me, I wasn't really surprised. At first, you'd think Kathryn and Harry didn't seem to be too alike – I mean, they didn't really like the same things much. For instance, Harry loved fishing and Kathryn doesn't even like to eat lobsters. Or Harry wouldn't miss watching the New York Giants during football season, and Kathryn still says football doesn't make any sense. Or Kathryn takes ballet lessons after school, and Harry used to say you'd never get him even to try it – but they really were alike in the way they were.

Look at it this way: Harry was one of those people that everyone likes, but they couldn't really tell you why. He was pretty cool looking, but not like a movie star or anything. He's probably still a pretty good athlete, but he was never top scorer or most valuable player or anything like that. Well, except in baseball and that was on account of his being able to hit pretty much any pitch anywhere you'd want, lefty or righty. Harry had this amazing bat control so, for instance, when the coach told him to try to hit the ball behind the second baseman, mostly he did. Or, maybe his team had a runner on third and only one out and the score was tied, and the coach had noticed that the right fielder was playing pretty deep. He's just tell Harry to try to drop one into shallow right, and he would do that, too.

Harry mostly always did his homework, and he got *B*s and sometimes a few *A*s so he was usually on the honor roll, except nobody ever called him a brain or a poin. But here's the thing: he was friendly to just about everybody (not like best friends; I was probably his only best friend unless you counted Kathryn which I guess you could, and for a while there Jimmy was at least close to being like a best friend), and he would listen to more or less anything you had to say.

Also, he had this really good sense of humor that saw something funny in a good way in almost anything, even if it was like a kid who was caught copying somebody else's homework and then sent to the office. Harry would say to him, "Don't worry. Your dad is definitely going to tell you how proud he is of you. Wouldn't surprise me if he even gets you a new belt to replace the one he's going to wear out on your sorry butt." I know that doesn't sound too funny, but if you saw the really straight face Harry used when he would say it, you'd know what I mean. Anyway, the guy he'd have said it to would laugh, and you could see him relax a little.

In those kinds of ways, Kathryn was the same. Harry and Kathryn liked other kids. If people wanted to hang around with either one of them, that was cool, but if they didn't, that was cool, too. Harry and Kathryn liked *being* with other kids, but they didn't *need* to be with them, if you see what I mean.

Another way they were alike was that Kathryn also had a best friend she'd been best friends with ever since first grade. That was Melinda, and she was okay, except she was about as different from Kathryn as you could imagine. Also, until toward the end when she changed completely which I'm not going to talk about now, she was reliable. I mean, you could count on her, and she always said what was on her mind, so you could trust her.

One really good thing that both Harry and Kathryn did was never try to get me and Melinda together, which come to think of it, was also an important thing they had in common. They would let other people be whatever they wanted to be. If Melinda and I had wanted to go out, that would have been cool; but since we didn't, that was cool, too.

So, freshman year from about Thanksgiving on, Harry stopped minding about his name. He never said so to me, but I could tell he liked the way his name sounded when Kathryn talked to him. I guess when your girlfriend calls you your name, you stop thinking it makes you sound like a little boy.

3

Being Fair

Peer pressure. If I had five dollars for every time an adult told me how hard it is to resist peer pressure, I wouldn't have to worry about paying for college. I'm not saying it's not a real thing. I'm just bringing it up so you can see this other way Harry wasn't like most kids. He didn't get peer pressure. He didn't believe in it. He didn't feel it. He didn't see it. He actually didn't know what it was because he always made up his own mind, and it never mattered enough what anyone else thought.

Let me try to explain it this way: I know I told you Harry got good grades pretty much all the time. Even so, once in a while, he wouldn't do an assignment for some class. That's not a big deal or anything, I'm just pointing that out to show you Harry's reason for doing homework wasn't because he was worried about getting into trouble; he'd do it because he *decided* to, because it made sense to; because, as Harry would say, "It's the fair thing to do."

Harry got his idea about fair from his parents who are pretty cool. There was only one rule at Harry's house: Be Fair. Harry and his brother could do anything they wanted as long as it was "Fair." If Harry were here, he could explain it better, but here is how it worked:

"Fair" is whether or not what you do hurts anybody else. Take homework. Harry played music while he did his math. He'd heard all that stuff about how much better you do if you don't have distractions while you're working, but you couldn't convince Harry of that because he always had an A in math — always since first grade. But if Harry's brother Michael, who was older, ever got bothered by Harry's music, then for Harry not to turn it down wouldn't be fair. Harry would call that a *significant* example, but the rule worked in other, not so significant situations, too. For instance, once I was at Harry's house for dinner. Mrs. Landis made some fancy vegetable dish to go with the pot roast. Vegetables are not my favorite thing, and Harry isn't their biggest fan, either; and with this dish, you couldn't quite tell what was there because of the sauce and some kind of crust. What I wanted to say was just, "No thanks on the vegetables, Mrs. Landis," but that wouldn't have been Fair. Since Mrs. Landis worked hard to make the dish, you had to give it a try, otherwise you'd be hurting her feelings by acting like what she did didn't matter. (And, no, the vegetables weren't terrible, but I didn't rush right home and beg my mom to make me some, either.)

For Harry, things that a person did were always fair or unfair. I mean, if he saw two kids fighting and one of them was bigger than the other, that wouldn't necessarily mean anything. How the fight started would be, for Harry anyway, more important. Harry would think the fight was unfair if one of the kids hadn't done anything to make the fight happen. You know how for no reason there's a kid almost nobody likes? And then some guys will start teasing him and making him mad and maybe that's why the fight starts? Harry would say that was unfair, and it was like his job to try to fix it.

So that's what ended up making Harry's second high school year — and mine and Kathryn's, too, for that matter — the worst one of his life.

4
Wonderland

I had to go away to camp at the beginning of the summer after our freshman year. It wasn't like a regular camp, a go there and play games and make moccasins kind of place; it was a four week long canoe trip in Canada. My dad went on something like it when he was a kid, and for years I told him I wanted to do it too. He went the summer after his freshman year, so that's when he'd been telling me I'd get to go. When it actually got to be that year, I only half wanted to, but I went anyway. I had a good time; I liked it, but I wasn't around when Jimmy moved to town so I didn't get to know him as well as Harry did.

According to Harry, the way they met was a couple of days after I left, Harry went for a run. He and I had this route we'd follow together sometimes. He'd run over to my house, then together we'd go over to the high school, do four miles — that's sixteen laps on the track — then head back. That day though, Harry didn't stop at four miles. He said it was because he was missing me so much, he couldn't think of anything else to do. He just kept going until he was at seven. Between the high school and Harry's house round trip was another three miles, so that's ten. Ten miles, Harry said, appealed to him. The only thing was, I guess it was really hot and humid, and when he got back to his house, he was pretty wasted.

All the coaches tell you not to sit down after you've done a hard work-out, especially on a really hot day, because you'll start to cramp up. So Harry kept walking, down to the end of his street, then around the block down onto the next street. When he got to the end and was turning around, this voice comes out of nowhere and says. "You look as if you could stand a drink of water." As far as Harry knew, he was standing in front of the old Robinson house that was still empty since the Robinsons moved away six months before. You can't see much of the house from the road because it's really thick with pine trees.

Harry said hearing the voice was like being Alice and hearing the Cheshire cat. He said, "Is this Wonderland? Are you the Cheshire cat?"

That's when Jimmy Rosen stepped out from the trees. He goes, "How unusual to hear literary allusion from a runner gasping for breath."[vw1]

So Harry used his "unwasted mind" line. He said, "I'm not just a good looking, well-built, dumb jock, you know. I've got an unwasted mind." Anyway, Jimmy offered him a glass of water up in the old Robinson house which the Rosens had moved into. By the time I got home almost at the end of July, Jimmy and Harry had been hanging out for a little more than three weeks. Harry told me Jimmy was okay. Me? I wasn't so sure.

Jimmy was strange looking. He was sort of in the shape of the moon just before it disappears. He wasn't all that tall, but because he was shaped in that funny way, you thought of him as being fairly tall and skinny. And he *was* skinny. You're probably thinking he wore glasses, too, right? Well, he didn't, but he probably should have; anyway, that's the way you'd think about him.

For a medical reason I'll explain later, Jimmy had to be really careful. He couldn't do too much in the way of the kinds of things

---

[vw] I'm not a fan of footnotes, but Jimmy used words I'm going to call Vocab Words. You will find definitions for them at the end of the book, if you're interested.

that Harry and I used to do practically every day, all summer long. First of all, Jimmy played no sports. What was wrong with Jimmy meant he had to worry about falling down or getting hit, and he would start wheezing like crazy whenever he had to move around any faster than a really slow walk. Believe it or not, Jimmy had to work pretty hard to get up and down stairs without running seriously out of breath. He could have gone fishing, especially if Harry or I baited his hook for him and took his fish off for him so he wouldn't have to worry about getting stuck or pricked or anything that might have caused an infection or anything, but he said he couldn't stand the idea of seeing anything suffer. And other stuff, like going to the mall or hanging out once in a while with just some of the other guys — whenever doing something like that would come up, Jimmy changed the subject.

What Jimmy liked was playing chess or cards — games like whist and bridge and cribbage. He also loved going to see plays or listening to classical music or even opera, or watching dancing, ballet and like that. Harry and I had been to school plays, and my parents took us to see *Phantom of the Opera* when it came to Hartford; once in a while if it was a bad rainy day or snowing or super hot and humid, Harry and I would play cards – rummy or crazy eights. And music, mostly some kind of rock, was always playing if we were in one of our rooms. But what Jimmy liked... well, if it hadn't been for Jimmy's moving to town, I'd be willing to bet everything I own that Harry never would ever have listened to opera until he was about sixty years old and living out on a farm. And I *know* I never would have.

For most of August, Jimmy and his family went on a trip back to Ohio, so I only got to know him a couple of weeks' worth. Then he came back a few days before Labor Day.

In about no time at all, Jimmy's life got interesting. That's the word Jimmy used. I would have put it differently. If we'd been in middle school, I would have said Jimmy was being picked on, but that phrase isn't nearly strong enough for what can happen in high school. Sometimes in middle school, one kid would tape a sign onto another kid's back saying "Kick me!" And it didn't take very long at all for somebody to try to do it. That's basically what happened, but there wasn't any sign.

Jimmy wasn't in our homeroom since his last name, Rosen, is in the part of the alphabet after ours, Landis and Lister. Who *was* in his homeroom were Carl Rawley and Gerry Roan. Imagine guys with the intelligence of a dumb puppy. Now take away any idea at all that would make you think the puppy was cute. Now imagine the puppies are dirty and sort of greasy looking. Plus, they do what they feel like doing all the time, and what they feel like doing is always terrible. That gives you a good idea of Carl and Gerry. What I think is, Jimmy walked into the room on the first day of classes, and they started to drool.

Now, what you need to try to understand about Jimmy is that while he was a wuss physically, he wasn't intellectually. What's not a good plan with kids who have made up their minds that they're only going to feel good if you feel bad is to confuse them.

Jimmy was funny, he was witty, and he knew how to say things that would make people laugh. While he was in homeroom, Carl and Gerry couldn't stop themselves from trying to provoke Jimmy, but what would happen instead is that the rest of the kids in the homeroom always ended up laughing at what Jimmy said in reply. I don't mean the other kids were on Jimmy's side or anything, just that they appreciated the distraction and getting to laugh at Carl and Gerry was a bonus. As long as the homeroom teacher was there, nothing physical ever happened so Jimmy always won.

All that didn't surprise me much, and it really shouldn't have surprised Harry. You can't get to be a sophomore in high school without knowing that kids who look like they're easy to pick on are going to get picked on. Maybe Harry wasn't actually surprised, but it did bother him a lot, and to be honest, it bothered me, too.

Also, I guess I was a little jealous. Guys have friends, but they only have one best friend. Harry and I had been best friends since as long as I could remember. I guess what happened was that since Harry was pretty much the only person who knew Jimmy well at all before school started, he saw himself as Jimmy's only friend. Plus, the way Jimmy was being treated was definitely not Fair so Harry figured he had to do something to fix it. That was hard for me, as well as for Kathryn. In the end, though, it was even harder for Harry.

5

Jimmy's Way

By the time we got close to Thanksgiving break, the feud Jimmy was having with Carl and Gerry had gotten boring. Harry and I, Kathryn, and Melinda pretty much always ate lunch together from the beginning of our Freshman year. So this year, Jimmy just joined us. The first day, Harry brought him over to our table right from the lunch line. I think for about the first month or maybe more, Jimmy would tell what had happened in homeroom with his two BFs. Then one day he didn't. One of us asked, but you could tell from the way he answered Jimmy was losing his sense of humor about it. Anyway, Jimmy's homeroom just stopped being anything we talked about. Then two things happened that were that were more than disagreeable for Jimmy, but for all of us, they were also harmful.

On the Monday before Thanksgiving, Melinda got her braces off so she didn't get to school till just before lunch. She was already sitting at our table when I got to the cafeteria. Kathryn, Jimmy, Harry and I had all just been in Chemistry, but Jimmy wanted to stay behind to ask Mr. Bartow a question about valences. Harry decided to wait for him, and Kathryn waited for Harry. I saw them when they finally got to the cafeteria. Harry waved and said something to Kathryn. She headed over to the table while Jimmy and Harry went to the lunch line.

All the time Melinda and I had been sitting there, she was super fidgety. If she wasn't texting, then she was whipping through stuff on her phone, not to mention constantly looking at the door to the cafe. Apparently she never got texted back, 'cause she'd sigh and say, "Come on! Where are you?" about a dozen times.

I didn't bother to ask what was going on. With Melinda, it's better to follow her lead no matter what kind of mood she's in. If she'd wanted me to know, she'd have told me. When Kathryn got to the table and put her books down, Melinda said, "Where were you? I've been waiting so long." That cleared it up.

Kathryn said, "I know. I'm sorry. They called down just before the end of Chem so we had to stop at the office. I've got a dentist appointment Mom forgot to tell me about. She's picking me up after school."

That was not what Melinda wanted to hear. "Thanks a lot! You said you'd help me shop today." When Melinda was unhappy, she said every word with the same emphasis – hard, sharp, and a little too loud.

"I know. I'm really sorry, but what can I do?" Kathryn waited. Melinda sulked and breathed. "Can't we shop tomorrow?"

Melinda was not in a cooperative mood. "Tomorrow we need to do the history report." Kathryn looked puzzled. "History? Report? Like, it's due Friday!"

If I'd been Kathryn, I would probably have reminded Melinda how many days there were between Monday and Friday. Then again, if I were Kathryn, I don't think I would've been best friends with Melinda.

"Mel, we'll go shopping tomorrow. It won't take long, then we can start on the report after."

"When has shopping ever not taken like two hours?"

"Tomorrow. We'll be in an out in twenty minutes."

"How?"

Kathryn smiled. "I'm so glad you asked. Let me tell you. Instead of walking all over the mall, we'll skip that and go right to Abercrombie so you can get something you like. And the good part is, you won't have to get upset when you can't find anything you like at any other store."

Apparently that was true because all Melinda could come up with was, "Whatever."

Then Kathryn said just the right thing to take Melinda's mind off of shopping. "Your teeth are gorgeous!"

I can't say I'd actually noticed. But when Kathryn said that, Melinda smiled. It was true.

"Hey, what's taking Harry so long?"

You might not be surprised to know that Melinda was not Jimmy's biggest fan; she tolerated him, though. She looked over at the lunch line to see how far they'd gotten. "There they are. " Then she did one of the things we called Melinda-isms. She put her hands flat on the table, squinted her eyes and tilted her head a little in Kathryn's direction. "Hey!" she said. That was Melinda shorthand for *OMG! I just thought of something I never realized before this second and it's epic!* "How come Harry's always hanging around with that geek?"

"He's not a geek, Melinda."

"Yeah he *is*. Look at him. He's too tall, he's way too skinny. He has too long hands. And he talks funny." She looked from Kathryn to me. "So why does Harry even like him?"

"Because he's a nice kid," Kathryn said. She didn't want this conversation to go on. Melinda did, though.

"How can he be? He's so queer."

Kathryn was on the edge of getting upset. She said, "The only thing *queer* about Jimmy is he comes from Ohio, and doesn't know hardly anybody. And he looks a little different."

Melinda sat back in her chair. She opened her mouth in this over the top way. "A little! He's a lot more than a little. Kathryn, that kid is…"

Which was exactly when Jimmy and Harry walked up. "Oh, Melinda. I'm so flattered," Jimmy said. "One so loves to be the subject of conversation."

To her credit, Melinda blushed, a little. "No, no," Jimmy went on. "Don't let my humble presence deter you from continuing your chat."[2] He put down his tray in the space next to Melinda. "Is this seat taken?

Melinda got all flustered. "What? Oh, um, no."

So Jimmy goes, "May I have the pleasure?"

"Hunh?"

"May I have the pleasure of sitting next to you?"

"Sure, help yourself. It's a free world."

Jimmy pulled out the chair in front of his tray. "I am truly honored. Although it really isn't."

"What?" Melinda said it as if she was accusing Jimmy of something.

He ignored that part of it. "Honored. Privileged. It is my great pleasure to bask in the aura[3] of your loveliness in this small portion of the world which enjoys the relative freedom denied so many of our fellow travelers."

Melinda went into her thinking trance, another Melinda-ism. Jimmy had never seen this before. He looked at Harry who was now sitting next to Kathryn. Harry just raised his eyebrows, sort of not saying anything one way or another.

Kathryn said, "It's O.K. She just does that. She's thinking about what you said. It'll take a minute, but she'll be back."

Melinda more or less shook her head, looked at Jimmy and said, "You know, I wish you wouldn't do that. It's really annoying."

Jimmy had no clue. "I'm sorry. Do what?"

"Talk like that. Use all those big words. What are you trying to prove?"

That really bothered Jimmy, which surprised me. "Oh, dear, I beg your pardon. I don't mean to offend. What 'big words' did you mean?"

Melinda said, "Like you really don't know?" My guess was she couldn't remember.

Jimmy said, "No, I really don't, and I really am sorry. It's just my way, I guess."

"Yeah? Well, don't be that way with me, O.K.?"

Jimmy looked confused and maybe embarrassed. He said "Yes, O.K."

That was when Jimmy's favorite homeroom buds appeared at our table. A junior named Broom – nobody I knew had any idea why – had sort of adopted them, I guess is the way to put it. Carl and Gerry were like Broom's followers or apprentices. They weren't really alike. I mean, you could see that Broom was heavily into weight lifting; but the only muscles Cal and Gerry exercised were the ones they used to light their cigarettes. Broom wore sweat pants and muscle shirts. His boys belted their jeans across the middle of their butts and displayed their taste in underwear – thank God they wore underwear.

Anyway, Broom walked behind Jimmy, clapped him on the back in this way that was supposed to look friendly but really was too hard. "Jimbo, my man! What's up?"

Jimmy was barely able to stop his head from smacking the edge of the table. As it was, he spilled his milk onto his salad.

Harry said, "Broom, you are such a fool!"

And Broom came back with, "Oooh, Harry, not nice to call people names. Careful, or I might have to wash your mouth out with soap."

Before that interesting idea could go anywhere, Carl said, "Geez, Broom, look what you made Jimbo do to his food. His milk got spilled all over his salad."

Broom leaned over and stuck his face down next to Jimmy. He looked at the salad, then straightened up. "Yeah, I see that," he said. "But, you know what? That's actually good 'cause now he'll have a lot of calcium and protein with his vitamins. Hey, Jimbo. I'll bet you're gonna thank me for this. I'll bet you're gonna like your salad way better now. Maybe we could get famous and rich. *Broom and Jimbo's Milk Salad.* We'll be like Paul Newsome and his spaghetti sauce or whatever, you know?"

One thing you're going to notice a lot is Jimmy did not have a knack for making things better. He said, "That's such a blitheringly inane[4] idea, it might just work." Of course, Broom and his buddies all thought Jimmy had called them insane so they got all puffed up and outraged. "Hey, watch out who you're calling insane, dork!"

At this point Melinda leaned forward and said directly to Broom, "Do you mind if we finish our lunch in peace?"

"No, I don't mind," he said, "but let me check with my good buddy, Carl. Carl, do you mind if they finish their lunch in peace?"

"Geez, no, I don't mind a bit," Carl said.

"Oh, good. Well, that's two so far. How about you Gerry?"

"Nope," Gerry allowed, "I don't mind either."

"Well, babe, I guess you've got your answer. We don't mind. But another question is, do you mind if we watch?" And with that, Broom, Carl, and Gerry all grabbed chairs from the next table, turned them around, and sat down so they were leaning on the chair backs, staring at us.

About then I was thinking it might be a good idea if we gave up on lunch for the day. "You know what, guys," I said, "I don't know about anybody else, but I've just lost my appetite."

"I can't imagine why," Jimmy said, "unless it's that curious odor of swine that has only recently begun to pervade the air."

Suddenly Broom lost his sense of humor, if you could call it that. He stood up. Naturally Carl and Gerry did, too. He was all red in the face. He said, "Now you've hurt my feelings, Jimbo, and I'm pretty sure you've hurt my friends' feelings, too. I don't think we're going to feel better until you apologize." Jimmy was about to say something when Broom added, "On your knees."

Melinda giggled. Then Harry stood up. Everybody got really twitchy because nobody knew what he was up to. He moved around the table until he was standing right in front of Broom. Then he started talking in a pretty loud voice. "Oh, mighty and terrible Broom. Those of us at this humble table entreat your forgiveness." Broom started to smile. So did Carl and Gerry. Harry went on.

"When you sat to grace us with your presence, we mistakenly thought we detected the odor of pigs. But we were wrong; so, so wrong. So we beg your pardon for our hasty evaluation, for now we realize our mistake. It was not pig we smelled, but dung beetle."

That caught Broom by surprise. He wasn't expecting Harry to turn things around on him, and it took a second for the words to catch up to him. By that time, the kids at tables close enough to hear were laughing. When everything came clear for him, Broom sort of exploded forward a step saying, "You are going to wish you had never said that, Landis!"

Before Broom did anything, Gerry said in a really exaggerated voice, "Hi, there, Mr. Buell!"

Mr. Buell was one of the teachers on duty in the cafeteria. He said, "Were you giving a speech, Harry?"

"Yes, sir," Harry said. "I was practicing for English. You know, a speech to persuade?"

"And Broom was just giving you a standing ovation? Was that it, Broom?"

"Right!" Broom said. "Later, Landis. Count on it!" And then he, Carl, and Gerry left the cafeteria.

Next day, just about three minutes after the bell rang for the first lunch wave, Harry and I were putting our books away and waiting for Jimmy to come from P.E. so we could go to lunch. Jimmy didn't do anything there except watch, but it's like a state rule, or something, that everybody has to take P.E.

Just about when we were expecting to see Jimmy, a slimy little kid named Derek Mistovich came sliding up to us. "Hey, Landis, if you want to say anything to your geek buddy before he dies, you'd better get your butt downstairs to the bathroom." I was all set to make Derek explain what he was talking about, but Harry just took off. I wasn't in a mood to join him on a rescue mission, so I kind of dawdled over my books for a minute. I found out later what I missed.

When Harry stepped into the boys' bathroom, Broom and the

Broomettes had Jimmy suspended in the air. Broom was holding Jimmy around the knees, and the other two were grabbing his arms. What they were trying to do was lower his head into one of the urinals.

Now, I know I told you Harry really isn't that big, and next to Broom in fact he looks small. But what he did was move quietly up in back of Broom and grab him by the hair on the back of his neck. Broom wears the hair on the back of his head in a mullet. That's one of those pony tail kind of things that's a lot longer than the rest of his hair. The mullet was what Harry got a hold of. He yanked down on that tail as hard as he could, and Broom gave out with a squeal. At the same time, he let go of Jimmy's legs. With his feet on the floor, Jimmy could start twisting his body around some. He wasn't about to get away, but at least he wasn't in any immediate danger of getting drowned.

That's when I got to the bathroom. I didn't know what I should do, I mean apart from calling a teacher, which in one way would have been smart but in another, really dumb. I took a couple of steps toward Harry and Broom, but by this time, the guys holding Jimmy had his arms up in back of him. They said if I helped Harry they'd break both Jimmy's arms. Maybe they wouldn't really have done it or meant to, but Jimmy was such a scarecrow, I was afraid his arms might get broken by mistake. Meanwhile, Broom kept trying to get his hands on Harry, but Harry kept hauling down on that ponytail and moving backwards and from side to side. Broom couldn't grab anything. I could see what Harry was doing. He kept moving Broom backwards toward the closest stall. Once he got Broom inside the stall, he sat on the toilet, put one foot in the small of Broom's back, and yanked for all he was worth with both hands.

With all the struggling going on, saying anything wasn't all that easy. Harry said, between yanks and breaths, "Tell your. Dork friends. Let – Jimmy – go. And – get out. Then l. Let. You go."

Broom didn't say anything; he just kept squawking and squeaking. Harry started to pull with each hand in opposite directions, and it didn't take more than a couple of seconds for Broom to decide he didn't want any more of that.

"Okay, okay, okay! You guys. Leddim go and geddowda here!" Broom's buddies acted as if they didn't want to leave him alone so Harry gave another yank. That did it. "Get the fuck outta here!" Broom screamed.

As soon as Carl and Gerry were gone, Broom thought Harry would turn him loose, but that's not what happened. Harry slipped by Broom and began dragging him out of the stall toward the door. He said to me over his shoulder, "Look outside. See if those idiots are still there." Of course, they were. Harry didn't have to say anything more than Broom's name before he had Broom screaming out through the open door. "Take off, you assholes."

Even though the other guys were really gone this time, Harry still didn't let Broom go. Instead he told him to undo his pants and drop them down around his ankles. Broom didn't exactly want to do that — "You're out of your mind," he said — but Harry didn't exactly give him a chance to say any more about it. He just tried to haul that pony tail right out of Broom's scalp. Broom didn't waste any more time.

Once his pants were down, Harry gave him a little shove — not to make him fall, but enough so he had to pay strict attention to keeping his balance. By that time, I had Jimmy over with me next to the door, and the three of us took off — if you can describe any movement Jimmy could make even at the best of times as taking off — and headed for the cafeteria.

To put it mildly, Jimmy was not in good shape. He was wheezing so badly his breathing sounded more like whistling. We kept having to stop on the way because Jimmy was feeling light-headed. "A moment, mes amis, if you please, to give the fog a chance to dissipate."[5] We'd go ten or twenty more feet, and he'd say that again.

About twenty minutes later, we saw Broom and his buddies come in and get into the lunch line. Harry said he'd be right back. He walked across the cafeteria, through all the tables, over to the line. Harry was outside the rope, but he moved up even with Broom. I saw him motion to Broom like he wanted to talk to him privately. Broom must have said something exceedingly dumb because his buddies broke up laughing. Harry seemed to repeat what he had said before. Broom gave everyone a look that was supposed to say, "Well, this is going to be *good*!" — but he did lean across the rope close to Harry. What Harry had to say didn't take him very long, and Broom didn't give the kind of reaction you'd have expected. At first he straightened up and smiled in a mean way and said something. Then Harry said something back. This time Broom didn't say anything, and he didn't have the smile on his face either. In fact, he didn't have much of any expression on his face. Harry came back over to the table.

By now most of the school knew Harry and Broom had been in some kind of fight. I doubt anybody other than Jimmy and I and the Broomettes knew exactly what had happened. When Harry walked over to Broom in the lunch line, and for the whole time he was there and as he walked back to our table, almost everybody paid attention in a kind of sneaky way. When Harry sat back down, the noise level slowly got back to normal. "What did you have to say to Broom?" I asked Harry.

"Not much," Harry said. "I just wanted to make sure he and his goons don't try that trick again."

"Come on, Harold! Enlighten us. How ever do you think you'll be able to guarantee Master Broom and his pet troglodytes[6] will keep their distance?" Jimmy talked that way; it was normal for him but not my favorite thing.

Harry poked at the rest of the potato chips on his plate. "I told Broom that if he didn't leave us alone, I'd find him and split his head open with a baseball bat." I started to laugh and Jimmy began to get a good giggle going. Then we both noticed Harry wasn't smiling. "Broom didn't believe me either, so I said, 'You know I'd have to pay you back, Broom, to be fair.'"

6

The Milk
of Human
Kindness

Broom saw himself as a combination heavy metal rock star and professional wrestler. You might have seen *The Wrestler* with Mickey Rourke or just enough of it till you got nauseated. Anyway, I'd bet anything that was Broom's favorite movie. In addition to his pony tail, he wore a string of safety pins through his right earlobe, and the hair on the right side of his head, which he sprayed or dyed a sort of black gold color, was shaved high and tight. Probably a big difference between Broom and Stone Cold Steve Austin (I don't really know who that is. I just Googled *professional wrestler*) was that Broom was capable of feeling fear. Anyway, evidently Harry scared Broom enough with the threat about the baseball bat so Broom and his buddies had to be satisfied with huffing and puffing and saying incredibly nasty and disgusting things to Jimmy and Harry and sometimes me, too. Other than that, things quieted down for a while, and three weeks after Thanksgiving, Christmas vacation started.

Almost for as long as I can remember, the day after Christmas Harry and I, his mother and father, sometimes his older brother Michael and my older sister Beth, and my mother and father would go skiing. We'd drive up to Stratton or Mt. Snow or once Killington.

We'd leave early the day after Christmas, get up to the mountain in time to ski, stay the night, ski most of the next day, then drive home. The truth is we had a really good time, and our parents always said, "We should do this more often." Of course we never did. I think saying that was actually part of the excursion, as my mother called it. If we ever had "done this more often," we wouldn't have had such a good time, and maybe we would have stopped going altogether. I think going up only once a year, the day after Christmas, is a lot of the reason we enjoyed ourselves so much.

Well, you've probably guessed. Our excursion that year wasn't quite the same. The last day before Christmas vacation, not much happens in school, at least not the kinds of things you normally expect to have happen like quizzes and tests, labs, lectures, class discussions — that sort of stuff. When the bell for first period rang, Harry and I got up to leave homeroom. Just outside the door we found Jimmy. As we came out into the hall, he handed Harry and me cards. "Season's greetings, Gentiles. May your Yule logs burn merrily this holiday fortnight."

I thanked Jimmy and put his card with the other ones I had already. I needed to get to my English class. Mr. Field was an exception to the rule. The days before vacations were his favorite for giving tests. He said it was the only way to make sure something meaningful was accomplished on those days. As I left, Harry was opening his card and looking at it. He said something to Jimmy, but I was thinking about *The Illiad* and didn't pay much attention.

The test wasn't too bad. The rest of my classes were pretty much normal for that day so by the time lunch rolled around, I was completely bored. Harry and I waited for Jimmy as usual. When we got to our table with our food, Kathryn was already there. Harry, Jimmy, and I sat down, and everybody started to eat. Then Melinda arrived with her tray. She was obviously upset. She sat down, looked hard at Jimmy and said, "Do you expect to live a long time?"

Jimmy's face got all flat. "I beg your pardon?" he said.

"It's not like a hard question: I said, 'Do you expect to live a long time?'"

For once, Jimmy was confused and didn't quite know what to say. "I suppose that I do. Or at least I hope I do. Might one inquire as to why you ask?"

Melinda said, "Yeah, in a minute." She stared down at her tray for a while, getting herself back together. Then she said, "Why does he do that? I mean, why does he even care? Besides, I wasn't even doing anything, I was just in there."

Kathryn seemed to know what Melinda meant. "Is it about Dr. Frank?"

"Well, yeah! What do you think?"

Then she told us the whole story. Dr. Frank, the principal, was running mostly a one man campaign to stop kids from smoking in the bathrooms. You had to admire the effort, but it was pretty much a lost cause. In each of the bathrooms, there was always a lookout so hardly anyone ever got caught really smoking. When teachers came by, whoever was watching the door said, "Not cool!" and all cigarettes got dropped into toilets. So, what Dr. Frank started doing was, he'd open the door to the bathrooms — boys or girls, either one. If the room was smoky, he'd call in, "Thirty seconds!" That meant he'd wait outside the door that long for kids to leave. When he went in, if he found anyone there, they'd be busted for smoking. If he found cigarettes in the toilets, he'd lock the bathroom for the rest of the day. That meant kids would have to go all the way down to the locker room bathrooms at the other end of the building which you'd have to get one of the P.E teachers to open for you.

Melinda had just been in the girl's bathroom on the first floor of the academic wing. According to her, three other girls had been there smoking, but they had just left. Melinda was still in the bathroom when the door opened a crack and she heard Dr. Frank call out, "Thirty seconds!" So Melinda went out.

"That's when he said to me, 'Do you expect to live a long time?' And I felt like really bummed."

Jimmy started to look more like himself. "So that's why you asked me that?"

"Sort of," Melinda said. "I just wondered if it would, like, bum out anyone else to get asked that."

"Oh," Jimmy said.

"Well?" Melinda leaned toward Jimmy.

"Well what?"

"Did it?"

"Did it what?" Jimmy said, getting confused again.

"Geez, come on. Did it like bum you out to have me ask you if you expect to live a long time?"

Jimmy started out slowly, not sure what the right answer was. "Not very much, no." Then he got completely back together. "In fact, I am too filled with the milk of human kindness and holiday cheer on this the last day before the Christmas hiatus."[7]

"Cool," Melinda said.

"Quite," Jimmy answered.

From there the talk moved on to how dumb the last day of classes always was. I said, "I cannot believe Mr. Field gives tests on the last day before vacations."

"That's better than my classes," Melinda said. "We haven't done anything all morning. And I bet we won't in Health either." She went on to say she thought they ought to just forget having the last day altogether. "I mean, it's such a waste of time. It's so stupid to just come to school and not do anything."

"So what should they do instead?" Harry asked in this really reasonable way that told me it wasn't just a casual question.

"Just not have the last day!" Melinda sounded as though Harry was a moron.

"So, you mean, today we'd all be on vacation already?" Harry wanted to know.

Melinda rolled her eyes. "Well, yeah! What do you *think*? If today wasn't the last day, then – duh! – we'd already be out of school. And we'd have more time for shopping and stuff."

Harry held his hands together on the edge of the table and leaned forward over them. "Melinda? If we were already on vacation, what would yesterday have been?"

That question caused the Melinda-ism where she had to stop being conscious of the outside world to give her mind a chance to figure stuff out. Her face went entirely blank for a few seconds while she mulled it over. When she came back she said, "Wednesday."

Harry didn't say anything. He had thought Melinda was following along. Actually, Harry couldn't say anything because anything he said would probably have sounded mean.

"I think what Harold was getting at, Melinda, was that no matter what, some day has to be the last day of classes. And if we were on vacation today, then yesterday, which was, as you pointed out quite percipiently…"[8]

Melinda arched her eyebrows. Jimmy apologized, then continued. "As you correctly said, Wednesday, would have been the last day and probably as boring as today."

Melinda shut down again. When she came back to life, she turned away from Jimmy and said, "I don't *think* so!"

No one responded.

Melinda looked back at Jimmy. "What's it like having a birthday the day after Christmas? Do you, like, get not as much presents on your birthday? What should we bring? Do you want something that's like a Christmas present or like a birthday present? This is so *confusing*!"

When Melinda said the part about what should we bring, I started to pay more attention. Jimmy said, "First of all, Melinda. You may not have realized it because of my remarkably WASP-like appearance, but I am Jewish and therefore do not attach the same meaning to Christmas as do you and most of your friends. In the Rosen household, the coming of Jesus has never been celebrated. Serendipitously,[9] my nativity gave my parents reason enough to celebrate at a time when all the rest of the world is celebrating as well. As for what you should bring — whatever small token of your affection you would care to grace me with will be immensely appreciated."

We all assumed Melinda heard what Jimmy said, but when she spoke, it was pretty clear her mind had taken a severe turn back there a while. She leaned forward toward Jimmy and scrunched her face up; that meant she was being serious, at least for her. "Do you know that if Jews have Christmas trees they'll go to hell if they don't call them Chanukah trees?"

"That's perfectly fascinating, Melinda," Jimmy said, completely straight. "No, I didn't know that. How is it that *you* know that?"

"Newspaper. At Stop & Shop. The Enquirer whatever? They had this interview with a priest that sort of died for a while? And while he was in this coma thing? He talked to these people who were really dead? And one of them was this Jewish guy who went to hell. It's true."

That would have put an end to the conversation for the time being, but by now I had some questions. "I think I missed something a while back," I said. "Did I miss something back there about birthday presents?" I asked Harry.

"If you'd read your mail once in a while, you'd be as well informed as the rest of the world," Harry said. I guess it was pretty obvious I didn't know what he meant. "The card Jimmy gave you this morning was an invitation to his birthday party."

"Celebration," Jimmy corrected.

"Birthday celebration, sorry. Jimmy's birthday is December 26th. He's invited us to be his guests at a performance of *The Nutcracker*." Harry took out his invitation and read the rest. "To be followed by a late supper at the Ashe Club." Harry turned his chair so he could look me square in the face to tell me more than he was going to say. "Now tell me that doesn't sound better than a routine ski excursion."

I got the message, but sometimes I can be more stubborn than even I think is a good idea. "I don't know how it sounds to me yet, but I'm pretty sure I know how it's going to sound to my mother.

I'd be willing to bet your parents won't be too thrilled with the way it sounds, either."

Jimmy looked concerned. Harry cocked his hands and waved them slightly back and forth. He meant Jimmy shouldn't worry about it. Naturally Melinda was confused, and Kathryn just watched. I was pretty sure I knew how this was all going to work out.

"Oh, dear. Have I caused trouble again?" Jimmy said. His distress was obvious.

"You tell him," I told Harry

"The day after Christmas, every year Brian's family and mine go to Vermont skiing." He looked at me; I raised my eyebrows. "And, actually, it's usually pretty fun; but not going won't be that big a deal. We'll just put it off a day."

I should have let it drop, but I didn't. "Harry, they send in their deposits for that condo place like in July or something. You can't change days at the last minute."

Jimmy dithered more and more. "Oh, I'm really sorry. Truly. Let me ask my father if he can exchange the tickets for another performance. When do you all get back?"

"That's just the point," Harry said. "We come back the next night. It's not like we go away for this long trip. And besides, it'd be just as impossible to change nights for *The Nutcracker*." Harry went on, trying to persuade me to stay behind as well. He even made it sound like a lot of fun when he suggested we two could stay at his house alone. "Your mom would let you if you told her it was like a really big deal. Come on, I'll get my mom to talk to her." But I guess I had gotten my feelings hurt again so I didn't cooperate.

The ski excursion took place as planned except for Harry didn't come. Our parents had sent in big deposits, and the deposits weren't refundable that late. Harry's parents weren't happy, but he convinced them his not going to Jimmy's birthday celebration wouldn't be Fair. They wouldn't let Harry stay in his house by himself, but that wasn't a problem. Jimmy invited him to stay over. I probably could have gotten out of going on the excursion as well, but to tell the truth, I didn't really want to try. I was mad at Harry for not telling Jimmy we always went skiing the day after Christmas; I was even mad at Jimmy for being born the day after Christmas.

Our parents enjoyed themselves. As far as the skiing went, it was pretty good, but other than that I didn't have much of a good time. I'm seven years younger than Beth; there really isn't that much we like to do together. She's cool enough. She and Michael asked me if I wanted to go with them when they went out after dinner, but I knew their feelings weren't hurt when I thanked them anyway.

We got back late the night of the twentyseventh. I was planning to sleep late the next day so I wasn't ready at all for Harry to wake me up at nine thirty the next morning. He brought an icicle into my room and was holding it above my head, letting it melt and drip onto my forehead. The cold drops of water made me have a really strange dream you'll be glad to know I don't remember at all. Harry was pressed up against the wall so I didn't see him at first. What I did see when I opened my eyes was this icicle hanging above my head, pointing at me. Then I saw it was being held by a glove. Then I knew it had to be Harry, and I forgot I was mad at him.

Harry told me about the celebration, and I was sorry I didn't go. Mr. and Mrs. Rosen hired a limousine to take them all to the Bushnell, the big theater in downtown Hartford where things like *The Nutcracker* happen. Then when the performance was over, the limo took them to the Ashe Club. That's a club for business people in Hartford.

Their late supper was served in a private room all for themselves with a waiter only for them and everything. Harry said it was really cool. They had Beef Wellington. And somehow, Mr. Rosen managed to get the people who run the club to serve them all a glass of champagne — just one — to toast Jimmy's birthday.

"Here's a really funny thing that happened 'cause you weren't there," Harry said. "Melinda and Jimmy were sort of like dates."

Harry was right. That was funny. I know I told you how Jimmy's not really comfortable around girls, but ballet and classical music and high class stuff like that get him really excited, so he kept trying to explain everything that was going on to Melinda. The more Jimmy went on, the blanker Melinda's face got.

"By the time we got to the club, Melinda was like in a trance. I don't think she'd said a word for almost an hour."

After they were all seated and served shrimp or fruit cocktail, whichever you wanted, Harry asked, "So, Melinda, how did you like the performance?"

"Okay. You know, I thought it was..." She didn't finish whatever she was going to say. "But you know what? How come there weren't any words? Wasn't that supposed to be a musical or something?"

"Jimmy was cool about it," Harry said. "He just said no, that *The Nutcracker* is a ballet and a ballet tells a story but only with dancing."

Melinda thought about that for a while. Then she said, "But how are you supposed to know what the dancing means?"

"Simply, my dear, by being in touch with your soul, by listening to the way the music makes you feel," Jimmy answered her.

"It didn't make me *feel* anything. I just thought it was like, you know, so queer that they wore such tight pants."

Jimmy hung right in there. "Melinda, *The Nutcracker* is a traditional ballet. Consequently, the costumes of the dancers are traditional as well, and as such not a matter of their choice or indicative[10] of their personalities or sexual orientation."[11]

Harry was almost laughing by the time he got to this part. He said, "You know the Melinda-ism where her mind goes on hold? Well, that's what happened when Jimmy said that about sexual orientation. It was like she had short-circuited. She was gone for a long time, Brian. I mean, you have never seen anything like it. Kathryn was starting to get worried, but Jimmy and I were having a major giggle attack. Finally the light came back on and she just said, 'Oh,' and everyone let it drop."

The rest of the vacation was pretty good. Harry and I went skating a couple of times. I went with him and Kathryn to the movies. And Harry and Jimmy and I spent an afternoon over at

Jimmy's house baking bread and listening to opera. Jimmy was the chef, and Harry and I did whatever he told us. The opera was playing on the radio. Jimmy wore an apron and a chef's hat. He held a wooden spoon like it was a conductor's baton. I was pretty sure we were going to get in trouble with Mrs. Rosen for just about covering their whole kitchen with flour, but when she came in later on, she just liked it that everyone was having a good time. To tell the truth, we *were* having a good time. I mean, I was really enjoying myself playing assistant chef, and Jimmy was like a different person. He called us Alphonse and Giscard, and ordered us around in time to the music.

When the bread came out of the oven, it was exceptional. I took a loaf home to my Mom. She thought it was exceptional, too.

That was about it. The day after New Year's Day, we all went back to school, and not long after that I knew Christmas vacation was going to turn out to have been the last fun I'd have for almost the whole rest of that year.

7
Get It Away

Our homeroom teacher that year was cool. She didn't just open her room in the morning and then go away somewhere else to hang around with other teachers. I don't mean she was in her room one hundred percent of the time like a recess monitor in elementary school. Lots of times there was stuff she had to do like meetings or using the copy machine, but when she left, she didn't kick everyone out and lock the door. If kids needed help with something, she'd give it to them even if they weren't in her homeroom or even in one of her classes. When we'd get too loud, she didn't have a fit; she'd just whistle. She had one that was loud, high, and thin; it would go right through your head, everybody's head, and you quieted down right away. Then in the quiet after, she'd just say in a soft voice, "Getting a little noisy, there, gang."

Her name is Miss Berry. She's a health teacher, and she's got a really, really great sense of humor. She and the school psychologist, who was new that year, were on some committee together. Practically every other day, Mr. Maslewski would come down to Miss Berry's room before school to ask her something or show her something. When she saw him coming through the door, she'd say, "What's up, Shrink Man?" Then she'd look over at us. "Watch out what you say around the Shrink Man, guys. He's got a tape recorder in his pocket. He listens to it later and does the old analysis on you while you're not looking." Mr. Maslewski would just smile and look exasperated, but I think he enjoyed it. It's really hard not to like Miss Berry.

Miss Berry arranged the desks in her room so they were all against the walls facing into the room. That's because in Health, having discussions is important, and it's hard to discuss things with each other if you can't look at the person you're trying to discuss with. Three of the room's walls were all posters about health issues: AIDS, of course; STDs (that's sexually transmitted diseases), alcohol and drugs, abortion, birth control, personal hygiene, fitness, diet, exercise, personal relations, date rape, adolescence, etc. On the fourth wall was a bulletin board. She marked it off into two parts — one half said *Class Clippings* and the other *My Clippings*. The idea was you'd bring in clippings from magazines and newspapers. They didn't necessarily have to be about Health, but you'd be surprised how many actually turned out to be Health related, as Miss Berry put it.

Miss Berry's homeroom kids brought articles in for the board, too. Naturally Harry was the first to do it. His father had showed him an article in the *New York Times* that was a report on research done in California about eighth grade boys. Did you know that the average eighth grade boy has a thought that has something to do with sex once every thirty seconds? No wonder I almost flunked eight grade math.

The morning we got back from Christmas vacation, Miss Berry was at the bulletin board putting up her clippings from over vacation. Just while she was reaching up, putting the last thumb tack in an article about a twentyfive year old woman who just found out she had gotten AIDS from having sex only once five years ago with some guy who turned out to be a drug addict, Mr. Maslewski came in. "Miss Berry, are you busy?"

"Hey, Shrink Man!" Miss Berry said, "How was your Christmas? You look a little tired. Stay up late getting everybody's presents analyzed?"

Mr. Maslewski put on his little smile and looked down at the floor. "Miss Berry. So sarcastic. How can you be so sarcastic so soon after Christmas?"

"That's the trouble with you shrink men, Shrink Man! You get all that heavy psychological training, and you forget your sense of humor. I'm never sarcastic. I'm just..."

A scream that was almost as loud and earsplitting as Miss Berry's whistle made her completely stop talking. Mr. Maslewski was closest to the door so he got out in the hall first. Miss Berry didn't bother to put down the rest of her clippings and thumb tacks. She just dropped them and got to the door next. Harry and I followed. The scream turned into screaming.

Down the hall, standing in the middle and close to the double doors you have to go through if you're going to the office was Jimmy. His body was writhing and twisting. He kept swiping his hands down the sides of his head, over his chest, and down the front of his thighs. Up closer, you could tell he was actually screaming words. "No, no!" he was saying, "Get it away, get it away from me! No! Get it away!" He pretty much just kept repeating that over and over, but running the words together so fast you could hardly hear the difference.

Broom and Carl and Gerry were standing a few feet away, laughing and saying things to Jimmy I couldn't hear. In fact, there was already a crowd gathering around them. Most were at least smiling, but a lot were laughing. Mr. Maslewski and Miss Berry got to Jimmy pretty quickly. Mr. Maslewski tried to take Jimmy by an arm. Jimmy's face jerked toward him. His eyes bulged, and he backed away a couple of steps. If anything, his screams got louder and the jerky movements worse. Miss Berry didn't try to touch him, but she started talking to him in this low voice so you couldn't really hear what she was saying, and I'm pretty sure Jimmy couldn't hear either. By that time, other teachers had come out into the hall. Mr. Maslewski sent one of them for the nurse. The rest did what they could to move the kids back away from Jimmy.

Miss Berry kept talking to Jimmy, very calm, very quiet. Harry came up and stood beside her, and I was right behind Harry. That close, I could hear Miss Berry. She was saying over and over again, "Okay, Jimmy. It's okay now. Take it easy. Take a deep breath. It's okay."

It didn't really matter what she was saying. It was her voice that was finally beginning to get through. Jimmy stopped that stuff with his arms, and he wasn't really screaming anymore, just breathing so hard he was making a weird rushing noise. He looked as if he was about to fall over, and Miss Berry started to reach for him. Just then, out of the corner of my eye, I saw something move in an open locker which turned out to be Jimmy's. Actually everybody saw it. The locker door was wide open, the only one that was like that. Everybody, including Jimmy, of course, turned toward the locker. A big, thick, black snake sort of leaned out from the locker's shelf. For a second it looked like it was going to go straight out into the air, but then it bent down and started to slide out. It got about a foot, maybe less, out of the locker, and then fell all the way out.

If you thought it might have been a little crazy in the hall before, that was nothing compared to what happened as soon as the snake hit the floor. It liked being in the hallway about as much as anyone else liked having it there, but the snake didn't have as much choice. Everybody, me included, took off, moving backwards away from the snake, running, yelling, squealing, piling into classrooms or through the door toward the office. Of course the snake didn't just stay put either, it started moving as well; unfortunately, it started moving toward the center of the hall, and that's where Jimmy was still standing.

I had moved through the hall door. On either side is floor-to-ceiling glass so you can see if anyone is coming the other way before you crash the door open. As soon as I got through, I turned around to see what was happening. Miss Berry, Jimmy, and Harry were the only ones who hadn't run away – Jimmy because he couldn't; Miss Berry and Harry because they aren't afraid of snakes, or maybe they were more concerned about Jimmy than they were afraid of snakes.

Looking at Jimmy, I figured that was probably it. He was in deep trouble, and I don't mean with the snake. The snake must have passed really close to him — Harry said later he thought it actually crawled over his shoes — but then it took off down the hall. I couldn't even see it anymore, but that didn't matter. It couldn't have done any more to Jimmy unless it had been a cobra or something.

First of all, Jimmy wet himself. All down the right side of his leg, his pants were soaking wet, and you could see his right sneaker was wet as well. His face was the kind of white of mushrooms or those asparagus they grow without any light. Pale doesn't really tell what his face looked like; Jimmy was more than pale. I'd never seen a dead person before, but to me Jimmy looked dead. Miss Berry and Harry stared at him for a second, then at the same time, they lunged forward, but they were too far away. Jimmy's legs just stopped holding him up, and he crumpled. His head bonked off the floor like some kind of heavy ball. It just bounced. Even through the window, you could hear it. Just behind me, someone said, "Oh, my God!" That was the nurse, Mrs. Coffman, standing in the doorway, holding the door open.

Miss Berry and Harry had gotten to Jimmy right after he collapsed. They were sort of semi-kneeling down next to him. Miss Berry pulled Jimmy's legs out from under him. Harry looked around, didn't see what he was looking for, then took off his sweater and put it under Jimmy's head. Mrs. Coffman stepped through the doors and joined them. First she felt Jimmy's neck, checking his pulse. Then she reached around to the back side of Jimmy's head to see what had happened when he fell. She found the place he hit and pulled her hand back to see if there was any blood on it. There wasn't. She pulled back his eyelids. Everything Mrs. Coffman could see checked out all right. Then they waited, Mrs. Coffman holding Jimmy's head, Miss Berry his left hand, and Harry essentially just close by and watching.

By this time, kids were starting to come back out of the rooms, and then Dr. Frank and the vice principal, Mrs. Gerardi, came down from the offices. They and the rest of the teachers made sure everybody stayed back away from Jimmy. Someone said Mrs. Burk, a science teacher, had caught the snake and put it in a tank in one of the biology labs. Dr. Frank said an ambulance was on the way. Until it arrived there was nothing to do but keep waiting. I wish it had arrived about five minutes sooner than it did.

In a couple of minutes, Jimmy started to stir and he began to make that funny noise with his breath again; then he opened his eyes. Right away, you could tell he wasn't any calmer because of having knocked himself out. His eyes bulged again, his legs started to move up and down as if he was trying to kick something away. Mrs. Coffman tried to say something to him, but Jimmy just jerked his head around so he wouldn't have to look at her. While he was doing that, he noticed Harry. He sort of froze for a second. Then with his feet, he started shoving himself toward Harry, and while he did, he was saying, "Oh, Harry, please take it away. Oh, my Harry, please help me, get it away."

What I should have said was, that's what I believe I heard him saying. Everything from when Jimmy first screamed till after he was taken away happened high-speed and loud and was impossible to keep track of. You couldn't think about anything – you could only be a part of it. So I'm only telling you what it was like for me. Ask Miss Berry, ask Harry. I'd bet what they'd tell you wouldn't really be the same. You need to get this is me writing about what happened a few months after it actually happened. The main thing is, what Jimmy was saying was incoherent and so fast the words blended together. I'm interrupting here to make sure you realize what happened next isn't any easier to get right than what happened before.

Jimmy kept scrabbling over toward Harry who, as I said, was down on one knee across from Miss Berry while Mrs. Coffman was checking Jimmy out. His momentum sort of knocked Harry into a sitting position on the hall floor. Then he just kept getting closer until he was actually curled up in Harry's lap. Jimmy put his arms around Harry's neck. All this time, he never stopped saying, you know, what I thought I heard him saying. Then – well, I wish there was another way to describe it, but if there is, I can't think of it – he started kissing Harry on the neck, on the cheek – pretty much all over Harry's face.

From where I was standing, I could see people had taken out their cell phones and were either taking pictures or video. And here's where Harry might have been able to save the situation, a least a little, if he had only pushed Jimmy off him. Instead, Harry put his arms around Jimmy, as you would around a little kid, which was really the fair thing to do because in this instance, Jimmy *was* a little, hurt kid. Nobody stopped to think of that at the time, including me. With one hand, Harry stroked Jimmy's head and said in a low voice like Miss Berry, "It's okay, Jimmy. It's okay. Take it easy. It's going to be okay."

Jimmy quieted down and because he did, I guess everybody else did too. I looked up from where Harry was caring for Jimmy. The cell phones were still out. The expressions on people's faces, kids and teachers, were all exaggerated. It reminded me of in a movie when they eliminate the sound after something extreme happens, like a car crash or a bomb going off. The camera pans over all the dead and injured and smashed up things, but all you can hear are your own thoughts. There were all these faces staring down at Harry and Jimmy; you could tell so much about all the people just by the way they were watching. Most of the teachers seemed as if they cared in a good way, if you see what I mean, but two had their lips curled up as though they were tasting something really bad. A couple of girls were crying. A few kids were smiling in that way people do when they're nervous, when they just don't really know how to react or how they're supposed to react. But the rest were watching Harry and Jimmy in the way you'd watch something you've never seen before, never could imagine you would ever see, and are afraid you won't get enough of it before it's over. Different from everybody else were Broom and Carl and Gerry. They were smiling; they were enjoying themselves.

Then the ambulance guys were there with a stretcher. Jimmy started screaming as soon as they took him away from Harry. Harry wanted to go to the hospital with Jimmy, but they wouldn't let him. Mrs. Coffman went instead. She took over where Harry had left off, stroking Jimmy's hair and telling him he'd be okay.

Then they were gone, and Miss Berry and Harry were left standing alone in the middle of the hall. Nobody said anything for the longest time, and nobody moved away either.

Then somebody said, "Fag!"

8

Peanut Butter Banana and Chopped Walnuts

The rest of that day in school was not much fun. After Jimmy was gone, and Dr. Frank and Mrs. Gerardi had herded all the kids out of the hall, Harry went down to the office to call his mother. By the time I got out of English, he was gone.

For the rest of the day, all most kids could talk about was what had happened. Kids I really didn't know stopped me to ask what happened after Jimmy passed out which was dumb because practically everybody saw the videos and pictures. So I'd give them a quick answer, then they'd tell me that wasn't what happened. And I'd go, "Okay, so you tell me."

They'd pull out their phones and hold them up. "It's all in the video. Look for yourself. Jimmy's mauling Harry, kissing him and hugging him and crawling into his lap."

Then I'd get pissed and say, "What did you ask for? Doesn't matter, does it? You're going to believe what you want either way."

The hardest ones to take that day were Broom and his buddies. I don't think one of them didn't pass me at least once and do a campy version of a gay guy. "Thay, thweety, howth your hanthome fwiend, Hawwy? He looked tho cute making out with Jimmy." Usually

I'm pretty good at ignoring jerks — Harry taught me to do that, I guess — but the thing is, in my mind I couldn't stop seeing Jimmy hanging onto Harry and kissing him all over and Harry not really doing anything to make him stop but just holding him and patting his hair. Of course, I didn't believe Harry was gay or anything like that, but to tell the truth, I really didn't know what to think. I still pretended I was ignoring the Broom group, but inside I wasn't.

When I got home that afternoon, nobody else was there. My Mom works for an H.M.O, and sometimes she's home by three thirty. It all depends on where she's been that day. Lots of the time she travels around to different businesses to tell them why they should switch to her company. Either she had to go somewhere that was pretty far away, or else it was one of the days she spent a whole day in her office. My sister was back at graduate school, and my father never got home much before six or six thirty anyway.

I went into the kitchen and put my books down on one of the stools that are lined up on the side of this counter that sort of sticks out into the room. That's where everybody in my family eats breakfast and sometimes lunch. I almost always have something to eat as soon as I get home. Eating first lunch makes 3:30 a long time away from having had any food, at least that's the way it is for me.

I got out bread, peanut butter, a banana, and chopped walnuts, but before I could start to put it together, the doorbell rang. That was a surprise. People who know us well just come in through the kitchen door, and the mail gets delivered in the morning.

I left my sandwich stuff on the counter and went through the hall to the front door. When I opened the door, I was totally surprised to see Kathryn. As far as I knew, she didn't even know where I lived. She must not have even gone home yet because she had her book bag still with her.

"Hi!" she said. Her voice sounded different. I said hi back. "Melinda and I are going to go to the hospital later to visit Jimmy. Harry's already there. You want to come?"

"Sure. I mean, I guess it'll be okay. I'll have to ask my mom, but she'll say it's okay." I was feeling uncomfortable and sort of nervous. I'd never really spent any time with Kathryn unless Harry was around. "So, what's up?"

"Not much." Kathryn smiled about a half a smile. We stood there for this really long time. I was thinking hard about what to say, but each time I thought of something, I'd wait too long, and then I couldn't say it. Then it was just too late to say anything, so I laughed instead and felt like such a fool.

Finally Kathryn saved me. "Look, can I come in for a second? I really need to talk to you."

Another surprise. "Oh, sure, of course. Sorry. Come on. I was just getting something to eat. You want something? Come on back to the kitchen. That's where I was."

Kathryn followed me to the kitchen. She put her book bag down on the stool next to the one I had used for my books. "Do you have a coke or something?" she said.

"Just diet stuff. My Mom's always on a diet. She says if we have any soda that's not diet, she'll drink it, so diet's all we have. I'm used to it. Is a diet coke okay?" I couldn't manage to say anything simple. I could either say nothing at all or way too much; and nothing I said reminded me of me.

"Diet's fine."

"Do you want a glass or is a can okay? I can get you a glass if you want. It's no problem. They're right here," and like a complete idiot, I pointed to the cabinet that had the glasses in it.

"Yes, a glass would be nice. I really like it better in a glass; it's not quite so fizzy, you know what I mean?"

"Yeah," I said. I turned away from her for a moment to get out one of my father's beer mugs. I always used them when I had a soda. I took the mug over to the refrigerator door. We have the kind that you can get ice or water from the door. "Do you like your ice in cubes or crushed?"

"Oh, no ice, please." You could hear the machine in the

refrigerator starting to send the ice out. "I'm sorry; I should have said so before. I don't like ice. Oh, unless the soda's not cold. Isn't it cold?"

Because of my mother's diet, we always had at least six sodas in the refrigerator all the time. "No, it's already cold. No problem." I stepped across the kitchen to the sink, tilted the ice into it, went back, got Kathryn her soda, poured most of it into the mug and put it on the counter in front of where she was standing. "Sit down on one of those other stools if you want. I'm just going to finish making my sandwich."

"Thanks," she said. Then it got quiet again, but this time I had my sandwich to make.

Before I tell you what Kathryn wanted to talk to me about, which you've probably guessed what it was already, I should tell you more about Kathryn herself. The day Kathryn came over to talk to me, I didn't actually know all that much about her. (I know a lot about her now, but that's because now we're good friends.)

I think when two people get to be friends, it's because somehow they decided sort of to open a special door or a window that they don't open up for just regular people they know. I mean the truth is, not everyone can be friends. Just because someone's a good guy or nice or friendly or good at some sport or great looking or is really funny or always tells you how wonderful you are — that doesn't mean you can be good friends or best friends, with that person. Take Melinda: Now, even though I knew a lot more about Melinda that day than I had a few months before, and I didn't think she was quite as much of a dip as I used to, I couldn't ever imagine being good friends with her. But Melinda and Kathryn were really good friends, and they had been for a long time. So if I'm right about friends, then they each had a door or window that matched up with one the other had.

Anyway, that day Kathryn came over, I already liked her okay, but mostly because Harry liked her so much. Everything I already said about her was true, and I liked her for those reasons, too; but if Harry hadn't thought she was special, I don't think I would have either. But now I like her for herself.

Kathryn sees stuff other people miss. Remember the time that Harry went up to Broom in the lunch line and threatened him? When I saw Harry do stuff like that, to me he was almost a hero. I wished I could be as cool as that, not be afraid of someone so much bigger and scary looking. To me Harry was like a real life Matt Damon (you saw the Jason Bourne movies, right?) – not too big, not too great looking, but cooler than anyone else could be.

Kathryn, on the other hand, didn't see that incident exactly the same way. She told me Harry was really scared of Broom. She said Harry's hands were shaking when he got back to the table, and the reason he didn't say anything much was his mouth was so dry he couldn't. That didn't mean Kathryn thought any less of Harry; actually, she thought what he had done that time was even more remarkable because of how scared he was. That's one of the things I learned from Kathryn: to try to see more of what's *really* going on when people do the things they do instead of thinking I know everything right away just from what I first see.

Here's something else about Kathryn. She's not really a brain. She works harder than anyone I know to get the grades she does. She works on homework for sometimes six hours every day. Now, I know that may not seem to be much of a big deal, but if you have to do that much homework, you don't have time to have a job. Having a job is one of the things that can mean whether or not you're cool. I work in Bristol's, a hardware store, on weekends and sometimes in the afternoons during busier times of the year. Harry works in a video store for a couple of hours almost every day. When you think about it, not having a job is a sacrifice and actually sort of brave. So anyway, Kathryn gets really good grades. She is always at least on the honor roll and most of the time on the high honor roll, but she never makes you feel she's better than you because of it.

Freshman year, Kathryn started a group in our school called Peer Tutors. (I knew about the group but I didn't know Kathryn started it. When you're a freshman, you automatically think that anything at the high school has been going on since before you got there.) I know many schools have groups like that, but what makes the one Kathryn started different is that her Peer Tutors go looking for kids to help.

For example, I'm in Kathryn's math class and so is Melinda. Now, you'd expect that since Kathryn and Melinda are such good friends, they'd sit together. They don't. Kathryn sits in the front row, all the way over on the right with a girl named Marilyn Langhorn. Marilyn has been living in our town at least as long as Harry and I have, and if you ask any kids who've known her for long at all, you'll find out Marilyn is a really sweet kid who doesn't get school. Some people have trouble with English or social studies, and even more people have trouble with math, but Marilyn has trouble with anything that happens inside a classroom. When Kathryn saw she and Marilyn were in the same math class, she just decided to be Marilyn's tutor. She tutors Marilyn in math almost at the same time as the teacher Mr. Rushman teaches the rest of the class. Kathryn has worked it out with Mr. Rushman so she explains what's going on to Marilyn and helps her solve her problems. Sitting all the way over on the right keeps them from bothering anyone else, especially Mr. Rushman who, if the truth be known, as my Mom says, isn't actually the best math teacher who ever lived.

When Kathryn talks to you, something about her face makes you think of a question. Her eyes and eye brows, her nose, and her mouth all look as if they're getting ready for her to ask you something about what you're saying. That's because Kathryn is really interested in what you have to say, what anyone has to say. She listens hard, and she's always ready to ask you to try to say something differently if she didn't understand it well the first time. That's for sure one of the reasons Kathryn does well in school. Teachers have no chance to get away with not explaining something really clearly if Kathryn is in their classes.

I guess the part that explains about Kathryn the best is her kindness, and that part of her more than anything else is the reason Harry and Kathryn liked each other for as long and as well as they did. What I think is that you can't be kind without being fair, and vice versa; just that alone made Kathryn and Harry an almost perfect match.

(You probably would also like to know that Kathryn is pretty great looking, but even though that's true, it's not anywhere close to the main reason people like her as much as they do, including me now. She's pretty tall for a girl. I don't know how tall exactly, but I'm just a fraction under six feet, and I don't think she's any more than two or three inches shorter than I am. She's in good shape. She plays field hockey in the fall, and softball in the spring, and she does enough running and skiing in the winter to stay in condition. Her skin is pretty fair and in the warm weather she gets freckles. Her eyes are mostly gray, but the kind of gray that changes depending on what colors she's wearing. The closest I can get to telling the actual color of her hair is it's the color they call burnt sienna in art. It's not really like the red hair you find on "red heads;" it's not that orange, and it's much finer than red hair usually is. And in the summer, strands of her hair turn blond. You can't believe how cool that looks. All around, Kathryn is really lovely.)

Anyway, the point is that by the time Kathryn and I finished talking, I knew her much better. I wasn't feeling and acting like the jerk who answered the door, and I had a new friend who was a girl. Oh, and one more thing. Kathryn, when she saw what I was having for a sandwich, asked me if she could possibly have a half a sandwich the same as mine. Anyone who knows that peanut butter is not just for having with jelly is, hands down, a truly great person.

Kathryn sipped her coke and watched me make my sandwich. I could feel her paying attention to what I was doing so without looking up, I asked her if she wanted one too.

"You know," she said, "I'm not really hungry, but the idea of peanut butter and banana is making my stomach grumble. Could you hear it?"

"Not really. I could just feel you getting jealous."

"Do you think you could make me just a half a one of those?" she said. "Just so I could see what's it's like?" So I did. I put her half on a small plate, my whole on a larger plate, and poured myself a glass of milk — they still haven't invented anything better to drink with a peanut butter and whatever sandwich than milk.

I brought the last empty stool around to the other side of the counter, and then we ate. Kathryn made these funny little noises while she was eating. She kept saying that she'd never had anything as good as this sandwich, so I started telling her about other things you could have with peanut butter. "You can also add raisins to this sandwich," I said. "Peanut butter with melted cheese is also good, but my favorite is bacon, tomato, peanut butter and melted cheese. That is the all-time best sandwich in the whole world. I only let myself have it once in a while, usually while we're on vacation. Harry loves that one, by the way, but he says he only has it here. That way it stays special." By mentioning Harry, I reminded Kathryn why she came to talk to me. The kitchen got really quiet while we both finished our sandwiches. Then Kathryn started.

"What was Jimmy saying to Harry after he fell down?"

I was pretty sure what she was asking about, but not completely sure, so I answered a bit vaguely. "You know, just sort of hysterical stuff. He was still freaked about the snake. He didn't know it was gone. I think he maybe thought it was still right there, and he wanted Harry to get it away."

Kathryn had that question on her face. "Brian, I just spent an entire day answering the dumbest questions and listening to the meanest comments, so I need you to be straight with me. Tell me the truth. Did you hear Jimmy say, 'Please love me,' to Harry?"

I waited a second, but Kathryn is someone you have to tell the truth to. "I think I did." She didn't say anything. "Yes. I'm pretty sure he did say that."

"Okay. That's what I thought, too," admitted Kathryn. "Now, please, tell me what you think that meant?"

For some reason, I felt my face flush. That or the question or both made me feel a little angry. "It didn't mean anything! Jimmy was freaking out. He was just babbling. I mean, did you see that snake? What would you have done if you'd found that sucker curled up in your locker?"

"Hey, Brian, I'm not Broom. I'm a friend: Harry's friend, Jimmy's, and yours, too. Don't be angry with me, and please, don't yell at me. I'm just trying to find out what was going on this morning."

Kathryn's voice was soft and firm and warm. "You know what happened was more than a skinny, nerdy kid being scared half out of his mind. Jimmy asked Harry to please love him, then he crawled into Harry's lap the way...well, I've done that the same way, almost exactly. I've done exactly what Jimmy did, only I wasn't terrified, and I hadn't just been knocked out."

I knew then that I had been pretty much thinking the same thing in a way, but without really knowing it, if you see what I mean. Sure, Jimmy had been scared and knocked out, but if he just needed to hang on to someone so he could feel better, why didn't he grab hold of Miss Berry? "So what are you saying, Kathryn? You can't possibly think Harry's gay or anything, can you?"

"No. No, I'm sure *Harry's* not, but I'm not sure about Jimmy at all. And now I'm feeling like I really want to know how Jimmy and Harry got to be such good friends last summer so quickly." I started to react again the way I had a minute ago. "Take it easy, Brian. It's only a question, a real one, but I'm not accusing anyone of anything. And don't tell me you didn't feel a little jealous when you got back from camp."

I didn't say anything. Kathryn pushed aside her plate and leaned toward me. "Well, didn't you?"

"Yeah, I guess I did."

"You're not the only one. I didn't really get to see much of Harry last summer when Jimmy was around, you know."

Then there didn't seem to be anything else we could say. Kathryn looked as though she was daydreaming. I asked her if she wanted any more coke or anything. She shook her head, not in the way of answering me, but just to get away from what she'd been thinking. Then she looked at me.

"No. No thanks." She got up off the stool and moved around the counter to my side. "So, listen. My mom is bringing me and Melinda down to the hospital around 6:00. Shall we pick you up on the way?"

"Six? Sure. That would be good." We walked back through the hall to the front door.

"Thanks, Brian. Thanks for talking to me."

"Yeah, that's okay." I really didn't know what to say. I felt good about Kathryn's coming by, but not really about our conversation. "Me, too. I mean, thanks for wanting to. Talk to me, I mean." I opened the door and Kathryn stepped out onto the front step and turned back toward me.

"See you around six," she said. Then she got that question look on her face, but instead of saying anything, she just smiled, turned around, stepped down onto the walk and headed home. And that's another thing about Kathryn which is not that big a deal but is part of what makes her nobody else: her smile.

I went back inside and went into what my parents call the Children's Room. It's a room they built on in back of the garage, a few years ago, when they got the idea that my sister needed a place she could have her friends come over and visit that wasn't her bedroom or the living room. They bought new living room furniture and put the old stuff, most of it, in the Children's Room. We've got a stereo in there and an air hockey game, and that's where we keep our skis and skates, field hockey sticks and softball equipment, soccer balls and Frisbees — all that kind of stuff — and, of course, a TV. That's why I went in there then. I needed to see *Cheers*. Channel 40 plays back-to-back reruns of *Cheers* every weekday starting at five o'clock. Sometimes *Cheers* is the only thing you can count on that isn't serious or sad or depressing or confusing.

9
Circle of Friends

The smell of a hospital does two things to me: makes me nervous because of everything that goes on there, and reminds me of Dr. Newberry. He's the pediatrician both my sister Beth and I go to. Beth is really too old to go to a pediatrician anymore, and she's pretty funny about how dumb she feels sitting around a waiting room filled with toys and games and books for kids at least twelve years younger than she is. On the other hand, I don't think she minds *too* much. For one thing, Dr. Newberry is about the only adult who has known us as long as our parents have, but he's definitely not a parent, at least not one of ours. When you go to see him and after he's examined you, he always asks if there's anything you might like to let him know about. It never matters what it is you might want to ask or say, he always answers you the best he can.

Anyway, the hospital smell is good that way, but the whole idea of a hospital also makes me a little scared. So much goes on in hospitals that you can't even begin to understand. People only go to hospitals when what's wrong with them is so bad they can't do anything about it at home anymore. So now they're in this huge, extra-bright place with nurses and doctors and technicians and laboratories, not to mention x-ray machines, MRIs, ultra-sound machines, and don't forget all those other tests they can do using radioactive material. Now, all of that is supposed to make sick people feel like they have a good chance of getting better? I don't think so. All that makes me think about Bromden, the giant guy they called Chief in *One Flew Over the Cuckoo's Nest* and his idea that a hospital was just a big factory run by nobody really knew what.

We took the elevator to the seventh floor, the pediatric floor. There were signs all over saying that children under sixteen had to be accompanied by an adult, but since Kathryn's mother was with us that wasn't a problem. Actually, Melinda was already sixteen, but I don't think she counted as an adult in this situation. Jimmy was in the last room at the end of the east wing, Room 720. When we got to the room, the door was about half open. Mrs. Mullen, Kathryn's mother, knocked. We didn't go right in, but we were all sort of leaning in the opening, trying to see Jimmy but without disturbing him. While we were doing that, Harry appeared on the other side, doing some leaning himself.

"Hi," he whispered. "Jimmy's asleep. Hi, Mrs. Mullen, thanks for bringing everybody down."

At that, we all stepped inside the door. It was a double room but with no one in the other bed. Jimmy's bed was next to the window which looked out over, as Beth put it when she explained why she didn't want to go to Trinity College, beautiful downtown Hartford. The bed was cranked up a little, about as much as it would be if you had two or three pillows behind you. He was wearing a hospital gown. He didn't have any bandage on his head, which I didn't really expect he would have but wouldn't have been entirely surprised if he had. He had an IV bottle hooked up to his right wrist which I felt the same way about. But what *was* a surprise was that he had one of those oxygen tubes that clip onto the end of your nose, and he was connected to a monitor. He also looked terrible. His normal skin color was really pale anyway, but now it was also a sort of grayblue.

We stood looking at Jimmy. Finally, Mrs. Mullen said she would go down to the visitors' lounge to have a cup of coffee. When she left, we moved the rest of the way into the room. Kathryn and Melinda sat on the other bed. Harry perched himself up on the window sill — it was more like a window seat except for being pretty high — and I took one of the chairs which I moved so it was between the two beds.

Harry said, "Jimmy just had his dinner about a halfhour before you got here. He didn't eat very much. Can't say I blame him; it looked pretty gross. Then he just went back to sleep."

"How long have you been here?" Kathryn asked. We weren't really whispering anymore, but we were talking very softly.

"Since this morning. When my mother picked me up from school, I had her bring me down here. Jimmy was in the emergency room for a couple of hours. His parents got here before I did. They just left to get something to eat."

"So how come they let you stay? You're not sixteen yet," Melinda said.

"Either because I act so mature, or because my mom lied for me."

Melinda did what she does that means she's thinking. When she came back, she asked Harry, "So which was it?"

"I'm not sure, Melinda. It's too hard to tell with nurses. They're very good at obfuscation."[12]

"Now you sound like Jimmy."

Harry was about to say something when Melinda apparently took notice of Jimmy for the first time. "Oh, my Ga-od! (She always made God a two syllable word.) Why does he have that thing in his arm and those tubes in his nose? And what's that machine supposed to be for? He has to have all this because he got scared of a snake?"

Harry held up his index finger. "Shh. He didn't just get scared, Melinda. No, all this *didn't* happen just because he got scared. When he banged his head, he got a concussion, a bad one. Plus, Jimmy has this, like…condition. What happened made it worse."

"What is it? What's wrong with him?" Melinda wanted to know.

"Can't say," Harry said. He looked at me quickly then turned away. He motioned us over to the doorway.

For the next few minutes, we told Harry about the rest of the day at school. We basically said how not nice people were being, Broom and company especially. A couple times Kathryn had to poke Melinda when she started to go into gory details. I could tell Harry knew there was more we weren't saying. But then abruptly, as though we weren't all pretty good friends, as though we didn't know what to talk about if we couldn't find anything more to say about Jimmy, we stopped talking. We just sort of sat there looking not at each other but at Jimmy; and, of course, as if he could tell he had everyone's attention, Jimmy opened his eyes.

"Ah, how splendid!" He looked deliberately at each one of us. He was trying to smile, but with each breath, you could see his chest lifting up and down so he couldn't quite do it. "My entire. Circle. Of friends, admirers. And wellwishers. Come to pay homage."[13]

Just because Jimmy had been hurt didn't mean I liked that way of talking any better. Kathryn didn't seem to mind. She acted like Jimmy had just walked into the cafeteria for lunch. "Hi," she said, "How are you doing?"

"Well. Not precisely certain. Can't stay awake long enough to find out." Then he looked puzzled. "May I ask a frivolous[14] question? What is the time?"

Harry looked at his watch. "Ten past seven."

Jimmy looked blank, "A.M. or P.M.?"

"Oh, wow!" Melinda put in. "You don't know? You just had *dinner* a little while ago."

"P.M. then. Thank you." He looked around at us again. "Well, splendid you came to visit. Thank you. Truly."

"No problem," I said. No one else said anything, for quite a long time.

Finally Jimmy spoke again. He was doing better, taking in long breaths through his oxygen thing. "Tell me. Vaguely aware I made spectacle of myself, but don't recall much. I remember my locker, reaching for my French notebook, touching something distinctly not my notebook. Then, seeing...a snake?" Again the look at all of us. "Large? Black, if I recall? After that, nothing clearly. Care to fill me in?"

Of the three of us, of course, Harry and I had been the closest to everything that happened from that point on, but Melinda was the first one to volunteer.

"Okay" she began, "right after you saw the snake or whatever, you...let me see…"

Kathryn took over before Melinda could get rolling, "You were standing in the middle of the hallway and began to yell. Almost every homeroom on the first floor came out to see what was happening. Before anyone could really get to you, the snake slid out of your locker and headed right toward you, and you passed out. The nurse came, someone called the paramedics. They came and brought you here." Kathryn smiled looking around at all of us. "All in all, a very unusual way to start the new year."

"Really," was all Jimmy said. You could tell Melinda was dying to add a few more details, and Harry was trying to decide what he thought about Kathryn's version. I was positive Jimmy was going to hear about what else happened whenever he got back to school. Obviously the question was not whether it was better if we told him first, but only should we tell him at all? What Kathryn did was decide we weren't going to tell him yet, not that evening, not while he was still in the hospital.

As it turned out, we couldn't have told him anyway.

While we watched, Jimmy's eyes began to droop. "Oh, dear," he said, "Afraid...drifting off again. Good bye, dear friends, till we…." And with that, Jimmy slept, and we didn't see him awake again while we were there.

We stayed in his room about a halfhour more, until his parents came back from getting dinner. We left them there and went down to the visitors' lounge to join Mrs. Mullen. Mr. Rosen came along a few minutes later. "He woke up again," Mr. Rosen told us. "He's visiting with his mama. We want you to know, children, how much it means to Mrs. Rosen and me that you came to sit with Jimmy this way. And even more how much it means to Jimmy. And thank you, Mrs. Mullen, for driving them."

"Please, don't mention it, Mr. Rosen," Harry said.

"Not at all," Mrs. Mullen said. "And please call me Irene."

"Yes, thank you. I will. Irene." Mr. Rosen smiled at Mrs. Mullen and then at all of us. We all smiled back.

"Mr. Rosen?" Kathryn asked, "Why does Jimmy have to have an oxygen tube? And why is he hooked up to that monitor? Do they normally do that for a concussion?"

"Well, no. At least I don't think so. But, you know, Jimmy is... and these doctors here in Hartford — so cautious, so careful. But, not to worry. Just a precaution, really, just in case. Just to be safe."

"Oh," Kathryn said, "I see." But she didn't see at all, and neither did I. Melinda wasn't even trying.

We sat around for a few minutes more. Mrs. Mullen and Mr. Rosen talked. We looked at the TV in the corner. I don't remember what was on. Then a voice on a loudspeaker said visiting hours were over. We all stood up to wait for Mrs. Rosen who came in just a few moments later. Her eyes were pretty red, and she was still blotting at them with a handkerchief. "He's sleeping again. He said to tell you he hopes you'll be able to visit again soon. I think he may be home tomorrow by the time your classes are over. Please, you must feel perfectly free to come over then, if you'd like, or any time. If Jimmy's asleep, we'll just visit until he wakes up. I'll make some cookies." We said we certainly would be over. Harry joked about how she didn't need to bribe us, but if she was planning on making the cookies anyway, could she make the ginger kind with the icing on top?

Mrs. Rosen said positively she would and enough to take some home. Then we all left. When we got to the parking garage for the hospital, Mr. Rosen offered to give any of us a ride. Mrs. Mullen rescued us. "Now, you two have had a long, hard day. You just get yourselves home so you can try to relax and get a good night's sleep." The Rosens said perhaps that was best, and actually, I think they were a little relieved not to have to go out of their way. We all rode up in the elevator together. Mrs. Mullen's car was on the fourth level, the Rosens' on the second. We said good night when they got out. Then we rode up to where Mrs. Mullen had parked her car. Driving back through the second level, we saw the Rosens still there, sitting in their car. We waved and headed on down the rest of the way out.

10
Fire Burn
✦ Cauldron
Bubble

Mrs. Mullen dropped Harry off first. As soon as the car was moving away, Kathryn turned around in the front seat and looked at me. "I want you to call Harry as soon as you get home. He should know what to expect at school tomorrow."

"Really!" Melinda said. Evidently she agreed.

I could see Mrs. Mullen look at me in the rear view mirror, but she didn't say anything. I said okay, but I wondered why she wouldn't just call Harry herself.

She was right, of course. Harry was going to be in for a paininthebutt day. All the questions kids had asked me and Kathryn, they were going to ask him and more. Not to mention how glad Broom and his buddies were going to be, making their comments directly to Harry himself. No question he'd be a lot better off with some idea what to expect.

I went into my house through the kitchen door. Mom and Dad were in the Children's Room watching TV. They did that sometimes. I walked through the kitchen, across the hall, and stopped in the doorway.

"Hi. What's up?"

"We'll get to that in a minute," Dad said, which was not what I expected. "What's up with Jimmy?"

I told them about our visit. They were surprised about the oxygen and the monitor, too. "What's wrong with that new friend of yours, anyway?" Dad wanted to know.

"I don't know, Dad. I mean, beyond the fact the snake scared him so bad he passed out and banged his head so hard, he got a concussion. He's just, you know, like not very strong; he's got like a condition that makes him a wimp, but an okay wimp if you know what I mean."

"Yeah," Dad said, "I, like, think I know, like, what you, like, mean, like." Dad wasn't overly fond of my saying like.

Mom cleared her throat. That usually meant she was in a serious mood. "Mrs. Hughes called earlier this evening. You know what that means. She said she was terribly worried about you and felt I ought to know since you and Harry are such good friends."

I walked into the room and sat down in the arm chair next to the couch. "Mom, I don't even want to hear what Mrs. Hughes said, whatever it was. The only thing Mrs. Hughes ever wants to do is get kids in trouble."

Dad nodded. He had known Mrs. Hughes since they were in high school together. He had at least a hundred stories from when before she got to be Mrs. Hughes, she caused all sorts of fights and arguments among different kids and groups of kids.

"I know that's true," Mom said, "and, believe me, I didn't let her carry on at any length at all, and I promise you I have not let myself think anything about what she told me one way or another. But what she said was too offensive to ignore." She waited for me to say something, but I didn't have much idea what I was supposed to say.

"Okay," I tried.

"Okay," she echoed. "I shall tell you what Mrs. Hughes said. You tell me what you think about it. Try not to react to the fact that Mrs. Hughes said it." She waited again.

"Okay," I said again.

"Okay. Mrs. Hughes first asked me if I knew what had happened with Jimmy this morning. I said you had filled me in before you went to the hospital. 'Oh, good,' she said. 'Then you know all about how this new Rosen boy and your Brian's good friend, Harry, were...' – Mom looked at me to warn me I should pay attention to this part — "making out, I think was the phrase, on the floor of the hall right in front of at least half the teachers and students in the school."

Mom could see I was getting angry. Actually, I had been getting angry as soon as she told me Mrs. Hughes had butted into this mess. Now I was more than getting angry. I am usually pretty good about not losing my temper; I almost never let myself get out-of-control angry, but that's really what I wanted to do.

"Brian!" she warned me. I nodded. " I agree fundamentally with everything you're thinking about Mrs. Hughes, but if you let her get you so upset, you start to yell, and then we all start to argue and fight, you've helped her do precisely the kind of things she is even now hoping will happen."

I knew she was right. Something like this happened before, more or less, and all of us, including Beth that time, had a huge fight. That time, it took almost a week for us to start to feel normal again. I don't have to tell you, Mrs. Hughes was not our family's most favorite person.

I looked at my mother and nodded. It took me a couple of minutes to stop feeling like I wanted to scream.

Then I told my parents what I thought.

I told them about the comments I'd heard all day long and that the worst of them had come from Broom and his friends. Mrs. Hughes's son Dan wasn't one of Broom's buddies, but every now and then he hung out with them, at lunch or after school. It was pretty obvious where Mrs. Hughes's information had come from.

After that I told Mom and Dad how I felt about what Jimmy had done which was weird and uncomfortable. I told them about Kathryn coming by that afternoon, and what we'd talked about.

"So you would not agree that Jimmy and Harry were making out?" asked my dad.

"Dad, Jimmy was *freaking out*. He was hysterical. He was so scared he peed his pants. Harry was just being Harry. He was helping someone who needed help."

That satisfied them; it almost satisfied me.

"I'll call Mrs. Hughes. Maybe I can stop her from spreading this any farther," Mother said.

I took out my cell phone. "And I'll call Harry? Kathryn and I think he needs to know what happened in school today after he left."

She nodded, but then said, "Why don't you go on ahead upstairs and get yourself settled, then call Harry."

Harry answered the phone before it rang a second time. The way he said hello, I almost didn't recognize him.

"Harry?" I asked.

"Yes, this is Harry." He didn't recognize my voice either.

"It's Brian."

"Oh. Sorry, man. I thought you were going to be somebody else. What's up?"

"What's up with you? You sounded pissed when you said hello."

"Yeah, well, that's probably because I was." Harry still sounded annoyed. "When I got home, my parents were a little worked up. Guess who called not one, not two, but three times this evening?"

"Old Lady Hughes."

"She called you guys, too." Harry knew he was right.

"You got it. Mom just got off the phone with her. She was going to try to get her to stop."

"Well, tell your mother 'Nice try!' for me, but she'd have a better chance getting spring to come early." Harry's voice was back to being a little sharp. "So, what's up? How come you called?"

"Now that Mrs. Hughes has spread her cheer over at your house, I probably really don't need to tell you what I was going to tell you," I said.

"I'm not sure I get it. Try it out anyway."

"It's just, Kathryn asked me to call you when I got home. She thought...well, we both thought, you ought to know what happened at school after you left. Just so you wouldn't be completely surprised tomorrow 'cause I'm sure they'll start up again with you."

"Brian, say exactly what you're talking about, okay?" Harry's voice was getting tighter. I'd heard it get that way before, but not when he was talking to me.

"It's just the stuff Mrs. Hughes was probably telling your parents about." Then I told him about the questions and comments that followed me around school all day. "And, you've got to know, man, they're going to start in with you the minute you get to school. And that's not even counting Broom and Carl and Jerry and those types. They'll be up all night thinking up stuff for you."

I stopped talking and waited. Harry didn't say anything for a while. "Harry? You okay? You still there?"

"Yeah," he finally said. Then, "Brian, what's going on? Why is everybody making such a big deal of all this? The bad thing that happened today was some incredible fool put that snake in Jimmy's locker. That was so unfair I can't even begin to believe it! How come no one wants to talk about that? How come everybody's so bent out of shape I was trying to calm Jimmy down? He could have freaked out totally. We're lucky they didn't ship him off to some shrink hospital for a long rest, know what I mean?"

"Yeah, I do, but, come on, Harry. I mean, don't you see? Jimmy was..." I didn't really want to say the words that came into my head, but Harry more or less dared to me to.

"Was what?" he said.

"He was acting like a girl." Harry didn't say anything so I went on. He was all cuddled in your lap, like a girl. And, Harry, he was kissing you! That's what everybody's talking about. That's why Broom and everybody is acting like that." I wasn't sure I should have said all that. I was even less sure when Harry spoke again.

"Right," he said, but his voice was flat and cold. "Okay. I get the picture. Thanks for calling. See you tomorrow." And then Harry hung up without waiting for me to say good-bye.

11

Cool Pizza

So we were right. Harry did not have a good time next day. Pretty much all morning long, one bunch of kids after another wanted to know all the gory details. If they hadn't seen the videos – hard to imagine – they'd heard some wild story but were afraid to come right out and ask him. So the questions kept on coming — "Then what'd he do?" "What did he say?" "Did he say anything?" "Did he, like, you know, do anything to you?" "Was he, like, holding on to you or anything?"

No matter what anyone asked, Harry said the same thing: "Jimmy totally freaked when the snake crawled at him. He fainted. He hit his head on the floor and got a concussion. He came to for a second and didn't know where he was. He was scared. I helped him. Period." By lunch time the questions tapered off. What took their place was worse.

In the fifth grade I found out what it's like to have no one like you. Recess in the winter was not my favorite. To go outside, you had to get all dressed in boots and parkas and hats and gloves and whatever else your parents made you wear; for fifteen minutes it was hardly worth the effort. Lots of kids tried not to wear all that stuff, but our teacher was always out in the hall checking. If you started to go out without putting on something you came to school with, she'd make you go back. Some of us tried anyway, but hardly anyone succeeded.

One day I tried not to put on my warmups. I was walking toward the door with two or three other kids, but the teacher stopped me. Typical of fifth graders, the kids I was walking with made comments. "Ooh, Brian has to wear what his mommy tells him." "Yeah, Brian, don't forget your, *nice, new, SNOW-PANTS.*" By the time I got the pants on and got outside, recess was more than half over, and everybody was already doing something so I was more or less alone.

I was looking for Harry when a snowball hit me on my shoulder. It broke apart and sprayed hard, gritty snow into my face. Almost right away, another snowball hit my back, then my stomach, then the back of my head. I looked around, holding up my arms in front of my face. A whole bunch of the boys had surrounded me, and they were all throwing snowballs at me. I didn't know what to do, but I knew what I wanted to do: sit down in the snow and cry. Eventually the teacher came over and made them stop. The rest of the day and for some more days after that, I was sort of separated from everybody. People weren't necessarily mean, but they didn't say much to me and wouldn't really answer me when I said things to them. The point is I've never forgotten how it felt to be the only one on my side.

I met Harry before lunch. He didn't have much to say. We walked down to the cafeteria and got in line for lunch. We hadn't been standing there twenty seconds when Josh Cunningham appeared outside the line ropes but right at Harry's elbow. "What's up, dude?" he said to Harry.

Harry looked at me, rolled his eyes, looked annoyed for a second, and then turned to Josh and said in a perfectly pleasant voice, "Not much, Josh, what's up with you?"

"Not much," Josh said, "but Harry, like I was wondering..."

Harry cut him off. "If this is going to be a question about Jimmy, let me save you the trouble of asking: Jimmy totally freaked when the snake crawled at him. He fainted. He hit his head..."

"Whoa, wait up," Josh said, "I heard about that already. No, I just wanted to know if you could help me with the science later, but if you're not up for it..."

"Sorry, Josh, no, that's cool. How's seventh period? I'll be in the library, okay?"

"Yeah, great, dude. Thanks a lot!"

Harry watched him go and then said to me. "That's the first normal question anybody has asked me all day."

I said, "I know, man, I'm sorry."

We got our lunch and went out to the table. Kathryn and Melinda were sitting there waiting for us. Harry and I sat down, and then nothing else happened. Nobody spoke, nobody ate, nobody looked at any anyone else. I was the only one foolish enough to have gotten pizza. I watched the cheese change from hot and runny to cool and crusty.

Finally, Melinda couldn't take it. "What is going on?" she said. "I'm like starving. Why aren't we eating?"

Kathryn turned to Harry, "That's why I asked Brian to call you. It's just that nobody has ever seen anything like that before. Everybody just wants to know what was going on? What did you expect?"

When Harry spoke, it was like he was talking to everybody, not just at our table, but in the whole cafeteria. The more he went on, the louder his voice got. "I don't know what I *expected*, but I'll tell you what I *didn't* expect.

"First off, what kind of an idiot puts a snake in somebody's locker?

"Second, I really didn't expect people to act like jackasses. Did you see them staring at Jimmy? What were they doing, hoping to see a little blood maybe?

"Third, I never in a million years would have expected practically every kid in this school to suddenly be so interested in Jimmy. Before Christmas nobody but the three of us gave a damn about him except maybe to make fun of him every once and a while."

By this time, Harry was practically yelling, and the whole cafeteria had gotten really quiet which Harry noticed. He looked me in the eyes, but I don't think he was directing any thoughts at me. He just had this very hard look. "Now I'll tell you what I *do* expect."

Harry stood up, thought about it for just a second, then stepped up on his chair. "Here's what I *expect*. I *expect* everybody will stop asking me what happened yesterday to Jimmy. As far as I'm concerned, you know everything there is to know. Here's what else I expect: Tomorrow or the next day or whatever day it is Jimmy comes back to school, I expect nobody – **nobody** – will bug him about what happened yesterday." Harry looked around the whole room. He stopped turning when he faced Broom who was sitting at his usual table in the far corner. "Nobody," Harry said again, "no matter how big an asshole he is."

Broom had been drinking from a chocolate milk container. He gazed over at Harry and, without looking back at what he was doing, he smashed the container down on the table. It made a very loud pop, like a small firecracker. Harry never blinked. Broom stood up and turned so he was facing Harry directly. For just a few seconds, he didn't move, Harry didn't move, and the whole cafeteria was totally noiseless. Even the two teachers who were on duty just watched. Then Broom rose and started walking toward our table. Harry stayed up on his chair. Broom was moving deliberately, not too slowly, and he wasn't giving the appearance of being mad. One of the teachers stood up from his seat near the cafeteria's main entrance, but he didn't come toward us. Nothing had really happened anyway.

Broom got to our table and moved until he was standing very close to Harry who was still up on the chair. Broom's face was about even with Harry's stomach. Broom raised his head slowly. He looked up at Harry and just stared. He didn't seem angry. He didn't seem anything. His face was just blank. Harry stared back at him. They stayed that way for maybe a minute or maybe not, but to me, it seemed like a *very* long time. Then Broom pushed his lips together, sticking them out, and he made this long, long, loud kissing sound.

What he did wasn't really funny, but, on the other hand, it wasn't even close to what you thought was going to happen. I guess that's really why everybody started to laugh, and I do mean everybody although Kathryn and Melinda and I didn't laugh as hard or loud as most everyone else.

Harry, of course, didn't laugh at all, and he never took his eyes off Broom. He and Broom still just stared at each other. When the laughter started to slack off, Broom said, only loud enough for Harry and us to hear, "Give my best to your boyfriend. Tell him I can't wait till he gets back to school." Then Broom turned and did a mini-double take. He looked down at Melinda and smiled. To be fair, I have to say he didn't look half-bad when he smiled. I could even believe Broom had human ancestors somewhere back in his family tree.

"You're cute," he said to Melinda, like he was partly surprised. Melinda turned bright scarlet, started to smile a little smile, and then recaptured her *I don't have time for jerks like you* look.

Broom walked back to his table. Every here and there, some kid gave him a high five, and of course, when he got back where he'd come from, all his buddies were lined up like baseball players in a dugout to greet the guy who'd just hit the game winning home run.

Harry stayed standing on his chair. He watched Broom all the way back, watched him being congratulated, watched him swell up with his victory. And Harry kept standing on the chair. We noticed. And as more kids looked over to see how Harry was reacting, they noticed, too. The cafeteria started to get quiet again – not silent like before, but quiet. Suddenly, out of nowhere and with no warning, in a voice even I was surprised to hear coming out of him, Harry yelled, "Broom!"

Broom turned around, surprised but still smiling. Harry waited till he had Broom's full attention. He brought his hands together as though he was holding a bat, getting ready to hit. He waggled the imaginary bat a couple of times in Broom's direction. He gave Broom this kind of sick looking smile and said, "Remember?"

As far as I know, nobody there but Harry, Kathryn, Melinda, and I, and Broom, of course, knew what Harry was talking about. Even so, Broom's face changed completely when Harry said that. It got red and ugly and puffed out. "Fuck you, Landis!" he screamed.

Broom took off back toward Harry, like he was rushing the quarterback in a football game. He knocked into kids, he kicked chairs out of his way. The whole time, Harry never moved, but the teachers on duty did. They got to our table just before Broom.

Everything stopped

"That's it!" one of the teachers said. "Mr. Huggar, you go back to your table. Mr. Landis, why don't you take up your tray and get ready for your next class."

Melinda, not one to ignore the basics, said, "We haven't eaten yet."

"Then perhaps just Mr. Landis should leave," the other teacher said, his tone of voice reasonable but not enough to put Melinda off.

"He hasn't eaten either. Look!"

"All, right, Mr. Landis," the first teacher said. "You and your friends have exactly seven minutes to eat your lunch. Is that clear?"

"Yes, sir," Harry said.

We poked at our food for a lot less than the seven minutes. My pizza wasn't something even my sister Beth could have eaten. We gave up on the idea of eating. We got up, dumped the food into the garbage, stacked our trays, then left.

About half way down the hall, Harry turned to Kathryn and said, "I hate it when teachers call you Mister. My name's Harry. Why can't he just call me Harry?" He paused for a moment, thinking. "Of course, in Broom's case, I think I'd prefer Mr. Huggar."

Kathryn wasn't being distracted. "Harry, are you okay?" she said.

"Yeah, I think so. Yes, I am."

"What are you going to do about, Broom?" Melinda wanted to know. She was curling a strand of hair around and around her finger.

"I don't need to do anything about Broom," Harry said He

stepped out in front of us. "I mean that. Brian knows that's true. Jimmy's the only one we..." Harry stopped for a second and looked at each one of us. "Well, me, anyhow. Jimmy's the only one I have to worry about. I, I guess *we*, are the only kids who give a damn at all about Jimmy. You know what I mean? The only thing Jimmy's going to hear about from now on is the snake and peeing his pants and passing out." I'm sure we all noticed what Harry left out.

"Yeah, but Harry," Melinda said. "What can we do? What can we say? Who's going to listen to me?" I didn't say anything, but I thought Melinda made an excellent point for maybe the first time in her life.

"You don't have to *say* anything. To anybody. Just don't leave Jimmy alone. Sit next to him in class, walk with him in the hall, stay with him in the cafe, wait with him for the bus. Don't let him be alone. I can't do it all by myself."

Kathryn and I looked at each other. "All right," she said, "we'll try."

"Got your back, man," I said, trying not to show how self-conscious saying those words made me feel.

"Not my back, *Jimmy's*!" There was a tone in Harry's voice I'd never heard before.

I said, "I know that, Harry. That's what I meant. Really, it's cool; we can deal with that."

Melinda said, "Okay! But I hope this doesn't go on too long. This could get to be a pain so fast."

"You're right, Melinda," Harry said, "it really could."

That's what I was thinking too, except I knew it was going to be a pain from the beginning. Plus, I wasn't so sure how well it was going to work.

12

Momma Rosen's Cookies

Mom was in the kitchen when I got home. She said Mrs. Rosen called. Jimmy had been released from the hospital, and Mrs. Rosen said if I'd like to drop by for a while after dinner, they would all be very happy for the company, but especially Jimmy would. She asked if I was going to go over. I said I thought probably I would depending on how much homework I got done before. I didn't really have all that much work, but I wasn't sure yet whether I was ready to deal with the whole thing about Jimmy again that day.

Just before dinner, while I was upstairs working on the homework I did have to do, my mother called upstairs to tell me Kathryn was on the phone. I had a phone in my room, but I usually muted the ringer when I was working or listening to music. I picked up and said hello.

"Brian," Kathryn started off, "did Mrs. Rosen call you?"

"Well, she called here, but I wasn't home yet."

"But you know why she called, right?," she said. "So, are you going?"

"I don't know, I haven't really decided. Are you?"

"Look, Brian, I said I would, but then Melinda called and said she wasn't going to go."

"Yeah, so?" I said.

"So, Brian, you have to. If you're not there I'm going to feel totally uncomfortable with just Harry and Jimmy. You know what I mean?" How she sounded, almost panicky, was a surprise.

"I guess so," I said.

"Please, Brian! You have to."

I really had to go after that. "Okay," I said. "I'll see you there around seven?"

"How about my mom and I will pick you up on the way over? Is quarter after seven okay? We don't usually eat till six-thirty."

I said that would be fine, and we hung up. I still wasn't really sure I wanted to see Jimmy, but it made me feel sort of good doing something to make Kathryn feel better.

At dinner, I gave Mom and Dad a quick, somewhat cleaned up version of the day. They didn't say anything much except for my mother wanted to know why Broom was called Broom. He had only moved to Afton the year before, I told her, and that was the name he showed up with. She wanted to know where he had come from, but I didn't know that either. My mother is the kind of person who figures that just about everything has a reason for being the way it is, and if you try hard, you can more than likely come up with it. For the rest of dinner, we all tried figuring out why Broom was called Broom.

Dad asked what he looked like and what kind of clothes he wore. I described the ponytail, the rest of Broom's hairdo, sweatpants, tank-top, etc. I didn't mention that Broom was lucky he still had the ponytail after the workout Harry gave it. I said he had kind of a big head, thick eyebrows, gray eyes, and he always looked like he needed to shave. Dad was disappointed.

"Too bad," Dad said. "I was sort of hoping he wore boots and a leather jacket, like Marlon Brando in *The Wild One*? Then the name would make sense."

I didn't know what he was talking about. I checked Mom out; she obviously didn't either. We both looked at Dad.

"Maureen," Dad said to Mom, "I'm ashamed of you. *The Wild One*, Marlon Brando, motorcycle gang?"

Dad was ready to give up. "Never mind."

"No, Dad. Come on. What's the connection?"

Dad sighed. "What's the noise a motorcycle makes?"

"Loud?" my mother tried.

"Broom, broom," Dad said, making it sound sort of growly.

"Oh. Good one, Dad."

Dad smiled as if he'd been really clever so Mom and I smiled back at him, but he could tell *we* didn't think he'd been as clever as *he* thought he had. "All right," he said kind of a little annoyed, "let's hear something better from either one of you."

Of course, the best explanation anyone could come up with was the obvious one, the kind of thing that was right up my mother's alley. "Well, this Broom fellow obviously sees himself as a powerful force, sweeping all in his path either along with him or out of his way. All well and good, perhaps he could achieve greater accuracy but retain the same generic quality by calling himself Blower?"

Both my father and I burst out laughing, but when we saw Mom didn't really get it, we toned it down. "Thank you," my mother said. "It is so gratifying to be appreciated by the ones you love."

By seven-twenty, which is when Mrs. Mullen actually turned into our driveway, we had the dining table clear, leftovers put away, and the dishes done. I was looking forward to telling Harry and Jimmy what Mom said about Broom's name. I told my parents I guessed I'd be back around nine or so, grabbed my parka on my way, and went out through the garage.

Both the Rosens met us at their front door. "Kathryn, Brian, please come in, come in. Jimmy will be so happy."

We said hello and how are you and stuff like that. Then Mrs. Rosen invited us into the kitchen. "We're just preparing a tray of cookies and hot chocolate to take upstairs. Harry's here already. He's up with Jimmy. You'll help us put the tray together, then we'll all go up for a little look-in." Mr. Rosen took our parkas and began to hang them in the front closet. We followed Mrs. Rosen.

The Rosen's kitchen wasn't any different from any other kitchen in the way it was laid out except for Mrs. Rosen didn't like overhead lighting so she used lamps instead. She put lamps on just about every surface you could think to put one. They weren't tall living room type lamps. They were mostly short, squatty ones so they could fit on the counters without getting in the way of a cupboard door opening up. When you walked in there at night, you felt you were walking into an old fashioned house before they had much electricity. It took some getting used to, but once you did, being in that kitchen felt cozy and quiet and safe. And this night it had the bakery smell that makes you want to go in and buy one of everything that looks good, which is usually just about everything I see.

"Kathryn, you and Brian sit down and keep me company while I finish with the hot chocolate. Take a cookie from the plate while you're waiting if you want. Take all you like." The plate was piled with at least four different kinds of cookies. Some of them were still warm from the oven.

"Mrs. Rosen, I'm going to get fat just sitting here smelling these," Kathryn said. "If I were Jimmy, I'd be a little butterball."

"Oh, no," Mrs. Rosen replied. "Jimmy's never been fat. Jimmy can't get fat."

"Do you mean he's not allowed to?" I asked.

"Hm?" Mrs. Rosen was stirring marshmallows into the hot chocolate. "Oh, no, not that." And she laughed. "That's funny. I mean he just never does, never has. Of course, I would wish him to be heavier, but, as I said, I don't think he can. Some people are, you know, just, just...very slim."

I realized maybe for the first time neither she nor Mr. Rosen were, to use her word, slim people. They weren't fat, or anything, but they certainly didn't look underfed either. And if what we were learning in biology about genetics and inherited traits was true at all, you'd have thought that at least one of Jimmy's parents would have been a little on the skinny side.

Mr. Rosen came into the kitchen then. He walked over to the pot of hot chocolate and took a deep breath. "Mmm! That brings back the days." He turned to Kathryn and me. "When Mrs. Rosen and I first knew each other, before we were married — just about this time of year, a little earlier maybe, more the holiday season — we would go skating every day, and then Mrs. Rosen would bring me back to her momma's house and make me hot chocolate, just like this."

"When was that, Mr. Rosen?" Kathryn asked.

"That was...let me see, that was December, 1988. We were married March, 1990, the day before my forty-eighth birthday." He gestured at Mrs. Rosen. "What a birthday present, don't you think?"

Mrs. Rosen actually blushed. "Oh, Papa. Such *mishugas*." She looked at us. "Sorry. That means craziness."

Mr. Rosen was smiling as he went back to his story. "After that, we moved to, first, Washington, D.C., then for a short time to San Francisco, then to Ohio. Where we had Jimmy." While he was speaking, I saw Mrs. Rosen lift the corner of her apron to her eyes. Mr. Rosen saw, too. He leaned forward and gave her a kiss on the cheek. "A long time ago, isn't that right, Mamma. And now, here we are in Afton, and Jimmy is in high school, and his friends are here to eat your cookies."

Kathryn and I looked at each other and then at the plate of cookies. Somehow most of them had disappeared. "Oh, Mrs. Rosen, I'm so sorry. I won't have another crumb," Kathryn said.

"Please, please, eat all you like. I have more." Mrs. Rosen stepped across the kitchen, opened a cupboard, and brought out a large tin, the kind you buy from catalogues filled with nuts or fancy popcorn. She brought it over to us at the table and held the tin toward me. "Would you take the top off for me, Brian? Thank you. There, now Kathryn, you see? You shouldn't worry. Just put a few more on the plate. That's a good girl."

She turned to Mr. Rosen. "Poppa, if you pour the chocolate into the pitcher? Good. Now," and Mrs. Rosen picked up a tray with four giant size mugs set out on it, "we take the cookies and chocolate upstairs." Kathryn replaced the lid on the tin of cookies and gave it to me. I put it back in the cupboard. I offered to carry the tray of mugs upstairs for Mrs. Rosen; she accepted, and Kathryn carried the plate of cookies. Mrs. Rosen led the way upstairs. Kathryn followed, then Mr. Rosen, and I brought up the rear.

The stairway leading to the Rosens' second floor was very narrow and dim. Lit only by a small fixture on the ceiling, near the top of the stairs, and the carpet was dark, probably brown or blue or green. I think the tunnellike feeling of the stairway affected us because we moved up in silence. I had this fantasy that we were all servants working in the home of a very rich family, bringing a special treat up to the young master whom we all loved, and we all knew he was dying from consumption or one of those old-fashioned diseases weak people got in those days. I didn't really notice everyone else in front of me had slowed down until I almost stepped on Mr. Rosen's heels. Then I realized why we'd stopped. Jimmy was crying, and Harry was talking to him. You couldn't hear what he was saying, but you sort of knew by his tone he was trying to get Jimmy to stop, to feel better.

Mrs. Rosen stopped near the top of the stairs, leaving enough room for the rest of us. No one said anything out loud. The Rosens looked at each other. You could tell they were really sad and more, actually, kind of scared. Kathryn and I looked at each other. She raised her eyebrows, meaning something like, don't you think we should go in there? I nodded. "We'll go," Kathryn said, and we went.

We moved down the hallway — in its own way a lot like the stairway. Jimmy's room was straight down at the end. His door was partway open. I still had the tray which I was carrying in both hands. Kathryn had the plate of cookies in her right hand. We got to the end of the hallway and stood outside the door. Jimmy was still crying, Harry was still talking, but now we could mostly make out what they were saying.

"But Harry," Jimmy said through his tears, "you don't understand. You can't understand. What if it doesn't work? I'm afraid, Harry. I'm terrified."

And Harry said back, "I know, but baby it'll be all right. We'll make it all right."

"No it won't," Jimmy went on. "I'll be alone."

"No, Jimmy, no. Jimmy, come on. Baby you won't, if I can help it, anyway. I'll be right there, as close as I can, just as close as I can. You know I'll try. Take it easy. You don't know what's going to happen, but I'm so sure it will be fine!"

"Oh, yes, please be with me, please try, my own true Hal!"

Kathryn looked stunned. I felt my heart begin to pound. The door to Jimmy's room opened in, of course, from right to left. As open as it was, you could see between the door frame and the edge of the door. We both just sort of automatically looked to see what we could see. Jimmy's bed was on the left most wall of the room. You couldn't see the whole bed, but you could see from the foot to almost the head. Both Jimmy and Harry were on the bed. Jimmy was in the bed, under the covers. Harry was sitting next to him. Harry's left arm was holding Jimmy, like cradling him into Harry's shoulder. Kathryn pulled away, looked at me, and then stepped forward. She leaned her head around, stayed looking for a second, then pulled her head back. She whispered to me, "Come on," and then started back down the hall to where the Rosens were waiting.

The Rosens were standing very close together. Mr. Rosen was holding onto the pitcher with both hands, clutching it against his stomach. Mrs. Rosen was standing with her husband, holding onto to his arm. "Is Jimmy all right?" Mr. Rosen whispered.

"Yes, I think so," Kathryn answered, whispering too. "Why don't we just go ahead down the hall and make enough noise so they'll hear us coming?"

"A good idea!" Mrs. Rosen said. "Such a smart young lady, this one!" she announced to Mr. Rosen and me.

We all looked at each other. Kathryn and I gave the Rosens

our best imitation smiles. They did the same back at us. Then Mrs. Rosen said, louder than I expected, "I hope those boys are ready for my best hot chocolate."

"Well, I sure am," Kathryn put in.

And I added, feeling stupid, "I just want a chance at those cookies; they smell so great!"

With that we started down the hall. Mr. Rosen kept up the conversation, if you can call it that, by asking us about school that day. By the time Kathryn and I had said it was fine, we were at Jimmy's door. As Mrs. Rosen swung the door all the way open, she said, "Here we are, Jimmy. Poppa and I have brought chocolate, cookies, Kathryn and Brian."

Harry was sitting in front of a window on an oversized desk that took up maybe two-thirds of the wall space across the room from the door. One section, under the right window, was set up as a study area, with a desk chair in front, a work lamp, a mug holding sharpened pencils, and a few school books. To the left was a TV that was turned on although the volume was very low. I was pretty sure it hadn't been on before.

"It's a good thing you guys got here when you did," Harry said. "There's nothing but the most boring stuff on. We were about to be bored to...bored out of our minds."

"Not so much boring as terribly poignant,"[15] said Jimmy. His eyes were red and puffy. He was dabbing at them with a handkerchief. "Sometimes I find the old *M*A*S*H* episodes appallingly moving, as you can plainly see."

The Rosens looked slightly confused. They wanted to believe what Harry and Jimmy were presenting. I think actually they did. It didn't seem to occur to them that Harry couldn't see the television from where he was sitting or that Hawkeye and Trapper John sounded nothing like Harry and Jimmy.

Harry reached over and pushed the power button. I crossed the room and set the tray of mugs down at Jimmy's work area. I looked at Harry and said, "How's it going?" and sat next to him on the counter. Kathryn placed the plate of cookies on Jimmy's lap and then took a seat on the edge of the bed. Mr. Rosen brought the pitcher over to the mugs, poured hot chocolate into each one, then brought a mug each to Kathryn and Jimmy. I reached over, grabbed a mug, and handed it to Harry, then took one for myself. Mr. Rosen brought the pitcher back to the tray. "I'll leave the rest up here. There's enough for everybody to have more." He smiled at Jimmy.

"Well," said Mrs. Rosen, "you children have a nice visit." She looked over at Mr. Rosen. "Poppa?"

Mr. Rosen crossed back to the door where Mrs. Rosen had been all along. He smiled once again, at all of us. We thanked them for the hot chocolate and cookies. They said we were welcome. Mrs. Rosen said if we needed anything to come right down and help ourselves. She and Mr. Rosen would be in the living room, she said. Then they left.

I guess nobody wanted to be the first to say anything. Harry and Jimmy were waiting to see if Kathryn and I had bought their story about watching TV, and I guess we were waiting to see if they would tell us what had really been going on. The silence went on and on. Harry was finally the one to break it.

"I told Jimmy about school today. I told him it wasn't going to be any fun when he goes back. I told him Broom and his mutts and maybe some others were probably going to be giving him a hard time because he freaked out over the snake." It was pretty clear Harry was telling me and Kathryn what he didn't want to tell Jimmy, namely the part about people thinking or wanting to think maybe Jimmy was homosexual. That let me know how we were supposed to play out the rest of the visit.

Kathryn picked up where Harry had left off. "So, when *are* you coming back to school?" she asked.

"Perhaps not tomorrow, perhaps not the next day, but soon," Jimmy replied, in his own particular style.

"Could you maybe give us a hint as to what soon might mean?" Kathryn obviously was not ready to play games with any of us, and

Jimmy least of all. I don't think she appreciated the way Harry was protecting Jimmy from the truth of what was really waiting for him back at school. "I mean, I really think it would be good for all of us if we knew when to expect you."

Jimmy was about to answer, whether with the straight out truth or not I couldn't say, but Harry interrupted. "The doctor told Mr. and Mrs. Rosen to make sure Jimmy stayed out of school until he was one hundred percent rested. A concussion, you know, is not something to treat lightly. And when the concussion was as serious as the one Jimmy had, well..."

Kathryn looked across the room at me. Until then, she had been concentrating on just talking to Jimmy. She was obviously getting frustrated. I thought it was time for me to enter the conversation. "Wow, I didn't realize you'd hit so hard. Is that why you had the I.V. and oxygen and all that?"

Jimmy didn't answer right away. He looked over at Harry for help. This was really getting ridiculous. Almost every time anyone said anything to somebody else, some other person answered. I guess Harry didn't have a quick one ready, or at least he couldn't come up with one before Kathryn's frustrations boiled over.

"Could we please cut the bull? Look, Jimmy, believe me, I am so very sorry about what happened to you at school the other day. That was the meanest, stupidest, slimiest thing! Pretty much everyone knows who did it, and one way or another, he *will* pay for what happened. But that doesn't change what's going on now, and it certainly doesn't give you, or you either, Harry, a license to lie to your friends. I know you got knocked out when you fell down, but I do not believe you hit your head so hard your doctor had to stick tubes in your arm and in your nose, to say nothing about that monitor they had you hooked up to. And I'll tell you something else that neither I nor Brian believes: you were not crying just now because of what you were watching on *M*A*S*H* 'cause the TV wasn't even turned on until just before you heard us coming down the hall."

Both Jimmy and Harry started to protest. "Forget it," I said.

"That's the truth, and you know it. Your parents and Kathryn and I were all standing at the top of the stairs, and we could hear you crying, Jimmy. Your parents wanted us to come down here and see what was going on." Jimmy looked at Harry; Harry stared at me. I guess you could say he was surprised, but it was really more than that. I added, "So we did."

Now Jimmy and Harry didn't know what to say. I just knew they wanted to ask exactly what we had seen and heard. I guess I wasn't quite ready to let them off the hook, but Kathryn wanted things cleared up. She didn't want to make it any more complicated even if they did deserve it.

"Look, your parents were scared. They weren't ready for hearing you crying. Just before we came up here, Brian and I had been down with them in the kitchen. We were all talking and eating cookies and having a great time. They were happy you were home and all right, and, you know, they just weren't ready for that. So Brian and I came down to see what was going on. We peeked in and saw you weren't having, like, cardiac arrest or anything which is what your parents were probably scared about. And, so here we are, with notsohot anymore chocolate and exceptionally delicious cookies that nobody's eating. So what do you think? Shall we start this whole thing over?"

Sometimes I think Harry was like a knight or cavalier in another life. He slipped off the counter and walked over around the bed so he was standing next to Kathryn. Then he actually got down on one knee, took her right hand in both of his, and kissed it. "Thank you," he said, "sometimes I forget what a great friend you are."

Well, that made me feel pretty lame. I mean, I'm the one who was supposed to be Harry's best friend so I guess I thought it should have been up to me to save the day, as they say. In the long run, though, I guess that really didn't matter. Suddenly it felt like we were all close friends again, and no matter what Broom and his gang tried, we could probably figure out some way of dealing with it.

We started in on the room temperature chocolate and the plate of cookies, and Kathryn and I began to fill Jimmy in on the details of what had happened at school while he was gone. It felt funny telling Jimmy about things that had essentially happened to Harry. I wasn't really sure Jimmy hadn't heard most of it all before, but it was like we had to tell Jimmy all about what Broom and other kids had said, and especially about what had happened between Harry and Broom, not so much for Jimmy's sake as for ours. We needed to say everything, to put everything into words with Jimmy there to hear them, so what had happened would seem normal—or if not normal, at least true.

We'd told Jimmy the story of the last three days, all the gory details, from the time he was taken away in the ambulance until hearing him crying just a few minutes before. But there was still the part no one had brought up. Not surprisingly, Kathryn was the one with the courage to get that off our chests as well. "Jimmy, there's one more thing you need to know, or at least we need to tell you: a lot of kids are saying to anyone who'll listen that you're, well, that you're gay."

As soon as Kathryn started talking, I knew where she was heading, so I was watching Jimmy. When she got to that last part, he didn't react much, and certainly not the way I expected. He leaned a little farther back into his pillows, looked a little harder at Kathryn, and did something with his mouth that was maybe, almost, a smile. "Go on," he said.

"Okay. All the kids who were in the hall that day saw the way you grabbed on to Harry. I know that's not a good reason for them to be saying what they are, but you know what kind of jerks we go to school with. Anyway, before you come back to school, you need to know that at least some of the kids are going to give you a pretty hard time about that."

For the longest time the only thing you could hear in that room was the muted voices of the Rosens talking in the living room. Kathryn was still looking at Jimmy, but once she had begun that last part, I watched Harry. He was really good at not letting you know what he was feeling if he didn't want to, but I knew him too well.

When he's angry, Harry gets real tight in the mouth (that's the only way I can think to put it), and his mouth was very tight now. Then Jimmy sort of cleared his throat.

"Well, not that it matters what those kids say or think, and I assuredly wouldn't even consider giving them the satisfaction of dignifying their accusations with answers. But I'll share this with you because you are my friends, and please feel free to tell Melinda as well. If pressed for an answer, I would not classify myself as homosexual."

13
a Promise Is a Promise

I woke up in the middle of the night. I'd been dreaming though I don't remember even what the dream might have been about. As soon as I knew I was awake, I began to think about Harry and Jimmy.

We all had been kind of confused when Jimmy said what he had about being gay. I was practically positive Kathryn was going to ask him to explain what he meant by, "I would not classify myself as homosexual," but evidently she'd had enough heavy talk for the evening.

There's this word for how we all reacted when Jimmy said that: nonplussed. It means you don't have a clue what to do or say. Jimmy noticed — how could he miss it? — so he said, "Okay? Are we all friends still?"

We practically fell over each other saying sure, of course we're friends, we never stopped being friends. We didn't stay much longer after that, but for the rest of the time, we were mostly pretty relaxed and easy. Jimmy told some funny stories about how he kept having to explain to different nurses and aides that, yes, he was knocked down by a snake which took over his locker. Then Mr. Rosen came upstairs to say Mrs. Mullen was here. We said good-bye to Jimmy. All three of us left Mr. Rosen in Jimmy's room and went downstairs.

Mrs. Rosen was talking with Kathryn's mother. We thanked her for the chocolate and cookies. She thanked us for coming to visit. Then she thanked us for being such good friends to Jimmy. She hugged and kissed each of us, and said to give her very best wishes to Melinda. We said good-bye again, and Mrs. Mullen drove us home.

I got out of bed and went over to my desk. My room is on the street side of our house, and my desk is in between two windows that look out onto the street. I keep the right corner of my desk clear so I can sit on it and look out the window. There's a street lamp across the road almost exactly opposite the property line between our house and the Morrisons next door. The light is one of the old-fashioned kind, just a sort of shade with a bulb screwed into a socket in the middle. All the street lights in our section of town are like that. They were going to replace them with the modern kind that are supposed to be better for preventing crime, but some of the families on the street got up a petition to save the old lamps. They're prettier, and besides, we don't have that many crimes yet.

The summer after seventh grade, Harry and I used to meet under that lamp at three o'clock in the morning at least once a week. Just after school was over in June, my Uncle Bob gave me almost twenty books about a spy named Matt Helm. (Back in the sixties, I think it was, they made some Matt Helm movies. Harry and I rented one once; they're nothing like the books. The books are cool.) Harry and I went through them just about as fast as we could. We were always happy when a rainy day came along because then we could spend the day reading Matt Helm books instead of feeling guilty about not being outside, "in the fresh air." Somewhere along in that time, we decided what we were going to do when we grew up was join the CIA so, of course, we needed practice. Our practice sessions would last from three o'clock in the morning until just around five when the night began to change from being really dark to mostly smoky. We brought along notebooks to keep a record of "significant details." We'd go check out people's backyards to see what they left outside. We'd look inside cars on the driver's side to see if anyone had left keys in the ignition. You'd be amazed if you knew how many people do that. (Any car like that, we'd take the keys out and hide them under the floor mat. Not much better, I know, but at least that way you're making a car thief have to look around first.) And we'd always do surveillance on the all night gas station out on the main road through town. What we were really hoping was someone would try to hold it up so we could call the police and be heroes.

We did our spying almost the whole summer. We never told anybody about what we were doing — not friends, not siblings, and certainly not parents; one of the secrets to being a good spy is knowing how to keep things strictly between you and your partner. Who knows what would have happened if we hadn't gotten caught one night. That's a really long story I won't go into here. I'll just tell you we were conducting our surveillance of the gas station when we heard a voice behind us say, "Freeze right where you are!"

The police claimed they couldn't tell we were only kids. Harry insists to this day they were just trying to scare us, which they did. I don't need to tell you the rest. Whatever you think happened is close enough to being right. But I will tell you, in case you haven't already figured it out, that was the last night Harry and I played spy.

So here I was, sitting on my desk and looking out the window at the street lamp, and I started to wish that Harry and I were still friends the way we had been that summer after seventh grade. Being older, bigger, more grown-up — whatever you want to call it — is definitely cooler, but at the same time, it's so much more complicated. You can't be satisfied with pretending to be a spy anymore; you have to do things that are real even when there are things you just want to do instead of things you have to do. That was when I figured out what made me wake up: the idea of how complicated life had gotten these days, specifically Harry's and Jimmy's and Kathryn's and my life. I must have realized while I was sleeping that in reality, Jimmy actually hadn't answered Kathryn's questions about why he had been on oxygen and hooked up to that monitor in the hospital or about why he had been crying before we came in. When Harry did his knight in shining armor routine, those questions got lost.

I kept looking at that lamp, trying to figure out what was going on. A little more than six months ago, when I left to go to Canada for a canoe trip, pretty much everything was the way it had always been. When I came back, things had changed so much, but I didn't see it or didn't realize it. They ought to change that French saying, the one about "The more things change, the more they remain the same" (*plus ça change, plus c'est la même chose*) to "The more things change, the more they *look* the same."

I tried to line up what had happened to see if I could make sense of it. First, Jimmy had come to town while I was away. When I got back, I didn't notice anything different about Harry. He was Harry, my best friend, except that when it came to doing the kinds of things we had been doing together all our lives, he didn't automatically want to do them. Or do them with just me. He wanted to include Jimmy. And sometimes do stuff with only Jimmy. He, on the other hand, was apparently just as happy to be friends with both of us.

Harry and I used to say we were twins who had been separated at birth. To us, it helped explain how we were so much the same. Same ideas, same way of talking, liking the same things, not liking the same things. We wouldn't say that now because it obviously wasn't true. So maybe this whole thing wasn't only because of Jimmy. Maybe we were just changing.

The more I thought, the more awake I got. I began to feel I needed to do something, move around. There's a set of weights in the basement along with a rowing machine and a couple of exercise mats which belong to my sister. She is quite the athlete. I used to use the rowing machine sometimes, especially when I felt the way I did now, but it's pretty noisy, and I definitely didn't want to wake up my parents. I decided to go out and run. Running isn't something I do regularly either, but I'll go out and run once or twice a week. More than anything else, it's just fun, but now it seemed like a good way to change how I was feeling.

Even though it was January, it wasn't super cold, like zero or below the way it can be around here. The temperature was probably about 20 degrees so all I put on were some sweats, gloves, a hat, and of course, running shoes. Once you get moving, you warm up pretty quickly.

I left a note on my bed in case my parents happened to wake up and notice I was gone. One of the points they'd made when Harry and I were being spies was how upset they would have been if they'd noticed I wasn't in my bed. They explained how parents are always afraid something terrible is going to happen to their children no matter how grown up and responsible they might be. I decided not to run out on the main roads except to get from one residential street to another.

I went out the mud room door, jogged down the drive-way, and turned left. When I got to the end of my street, Dalton Lane, I went left onto Cramer Drive just far enough to get onto the next street down from ours, Edgerly Lane, where I turned left again. Then at the end of Edgerly, I turned right out onto Mellow Drive, far enough to go right onto Fillow Lane, back out onto Cranmer, and so on – you get the idea. I got as far as West Afton Road. Then I had to make a choice. I could either turn around and go back the way I had come, or I could go right, run up West Afton for about a quarter mile to Bremmerton Drive, then go right again and start the same pattern as before except in reverse. If I did that, I'd pass Harry's house before I had to cross Cramer again to get back to my neighborhood. Harry lives on Dillon Drive which is across Cranmer from Edgerly. That's what I decided to do.

Well, of course, you know that when I got to Harry's house, I stopped. I was feeling really good, physically. I'd stopped thinking so hard about Harry and Jimmy and all that had been going on. I hadn't really been thinking of much of anything, just noticing where I was going and how different everything looked in the middle of the night. But when I found myself getting closer to Harry's house, I began to want to talk to him about everything. Harry's room is in the back. You have to go through a gate to get into his back yard, and the trick is to do all that quietly because the Landises have a Labrador retriever, Wardell, that always sets up a huge racket whenever anyone comes to the door. Once the door is opened, all he wants to do is lick you to death, but before that, Wardell sounds like a hound from hell.

I was especially careful about not making any noise as I walked up the driveway, unlatched the gate, and stepped through. I left the gate unlatched just to avoid the extra noise. My idea was to toss pebbles up at Harry's window — not very original, I know, and not terribly smart given I was concerned about noise and all, but it was good enough for Tom Sawyer, and he had much more experience with that kind of thing than I did.

The problem with tossing pebbles at windows in January is getting pebbles in the first place; they tend to be frozen to the ground. Wearing gloves means you can't get a grip on a pebble at all, and taking your gloves off means your fingers get so cold trying to break a pebble loose from the frozen ground you wish very quickly you'd had a different idea in the first place. I had put my gloves back on, hoping I'd made the decision to scuff soon enough to avoid frost bite, and was getting ready to try to loosen some pebbles with the heel of my running shoe when someone right in back of me said in a very loud whisper, "What's up, dude?"

I screamed. Then Wardell began to bark. Harry rushed over to let him out so he could see he didn't have to alert the defenders of the castle; and I, since I was starting to hyperventilate, sat down on the walk. Once Wardell saw who the intruder was, he felt he had to apologize by licking me all over my face and stepping on my feet. Harry came and rescued me. "You okay?" he wanted to know.

"Yeah, I'm fine, just a little light headed."

"Put your head down between your knees for a minute," Harry advised, so I did. Wardell immediately came back over, stuck his head under one of my knees, and began licking again. I like Wardell a lot, but I'd rather faint than have him lick me, so I stood up, slowly.

Harry was standing back from me a little. You couldn't see much because the light from the street was mostly blocked by the house and the trees, but I knew Harry was smiling. He was dressed the same way I was.

"What're you doing?" I asked.

"That's a funny question coming from you. You're the one who's obviously been out running in the middle of the night in January. You do this often?"

"No. First time. How about you?"

"Me, too. Actually, I was just thinking about taking a little jog over to your house. To see if maybe you were up or something. To see if you wanted to talk or something," Harry said.

"Seems like a fine idea," I said, smiling back at him. "You have anything definite you wanted to talk about, or were you just looking for a way to use up the time till morning?" I was pretty sure we both knew what we wanted to talk about. The only question was who was going to bring it up first.

"Either way. I mean, I've had two hours of sleep. I'm ready to start classes, but I don't think anybody else is." He paused for just a second. "Except for you." Harry waited for me to continue the dialogue, but I didn't want to so he did it himself. "Jimmy was looking better, didn't you think?"

"Yeah, I guess so," I said. "But you know what – since you mentioned Jimmy – you know what I was just thinking a while ago?"

"You were thinking you wished Jimmy hadn't ever come to Afton." I hadn't been thinking about how much Harry and I did that, how often he and I just knew, more or less, what the other was doing or planning or worrying over. Since the beginning of this year, we really hadn't spent the kind of time together we used to so it hadn't happened much. His knowing just now, more than anything else, stunned me.

"Whoa! If you can do that seven times out of ten, we can take the act on the road. Actually, though, that's not exactly what I was thinking, but you're definitely in the right neighborhood," I said.

"Okay." Harry went on. "Did it have something to do with earlier tonight?"

"Yes." Now for some reason, maybe noticing something in Harry's voice that snuck in there for a second, I wasn't sure whether I really wanted to go on, but I'd sort of trapped myself into it. "What I was thinking was, you or Jimmy – or both of you – didn't answer Kathryn when she asked about the oxygen and stuff." Harry nodded so I went on. "And I was wondering: Did you do that on purpose or was it like just an oversight?"

When he answered me, I knew I'd heard right before; his voice was a little flat, but also sharp, so I guess whatever he'd had in mind to talk about wasn't exactly what I brought up. "Yes and no."

"Yes and no what?"

"Yes, it was on purpose, and no, it wasn't an oversight."

"Okay. That's kind of what I thought. So here goes: Harry, I want to know, I think I need to know. Why was Jimmy hooked up to all that stuff?"

"I can't tell you, but maybe..." He stopped to think about whatever he was about to say. I could see it when he changed his mind. "I just can't tell you."

I was totally surprised but in a disappointed way. There had never, ever been anything that either Harry or I had not been able to tell the other one.

I didn't say anything mostly because I couldn't imagine Harry wasn't going to go on somehow. I kept waiting and waiting, but Harry just stood there, looking at me. Maybe if there had been more light or something, I would have seen something in his face that I recognized, but there wasn't, and anyway I didn't. "Harry," I said finally, "why can't you tell me?" He didn't answer. "Can you not tell me because you know and aren't supposed to say or because you don't really know, either?"

This time he answered right away. "The first." Obviously he wasn't about to add anything else, so we were just left there more or less staring at each other. All I could think about was how Harry had always been the most comfortable part of my life. And now he wasn't.

And I was scared he never would be again.

Then Harry said, "Look, I'm really sorry, but I know."

I started to ask why when Harry held up his hand.

"I gave my word I wouldn't tell anyone else."

When Harry and I first started talking, right from when he sneaked up on me, I was feeling good. I was feeling as if we were going to get everything straightened out and from then on things would pretty much be the way they were before. Now I was feeling worse than when I decided to go out running. I wanted to say, "Come on, Harry, please tell me; I won't tell anybody else, I swear!" but I didn't. In my mind I could hear how the words would come out; they would have sounded whiny and almost as if I was going to cry. And I did almost want to cry. I felt mad, at Jimmy for moving to town and changing my life, for getting hurt the way he had, and for taking my best friend away from me. Also I felt mad at Harry for not liking me more than he liked Jimmy. I felt jealous and that made me mad, too. That really made me want to cry. And suddenly it seemed that how bad I felt was completely Harry's fault.

I took a step away from Harry. "I'm really glad we're such good friends, Har. It makes me feel really good knowing you trust me enough to share what's going on in your life."

"Wrong way to look at it, Brian. It's not a question of that," Harry said. "I trust you. I always have. This has nothing to do with whether or not I trust you or Kathryn or anybody. I can't even tell my *parents*. I was asked not to tell. I promised I wouldn't!"

"Sure, right. No problem. I understand a promise to someone you've known six months is more important than someone you've been friends with practically your whole life."

Harry didn't say anything for a while. That meant he was getting mad, too. What Harry did when he got mad – most of the time – was try to be calmer and more reasonable than before. "Brian, I have to tell you something for your own good. You are being a jerk and a little bit of a pain in the butt. As far as I'm concerned, you are my best friend and always have been. Making a promise to someone else doesn't change that even a little. Do you understand what I'm saying to you?"

That was a message. Whenever Harry would say that – "Do you understand what I'm saying to you?" – he was warning you he'd had enough of whatever dumb thing was going on. I don't remember the last time he had said it to *me* – possibly not ever before – but I'd heard him say it often enough. No one was exempt: not teachers, coaches, kids, parents, school psychologists, clerks in shoe stores, ticket takers at concerts, bottle and can redemption people. If you argued with Harry just for the sake of arguing, he'd eventually make his point one last, clear time and then say, "Do you understand what I'm saying to you?" You could say yes or no, but if you said no, that was always the end of the conversation. Harry would just say, "Too bad. I'm sorry." Then he'd either leave, or if that wasn't possible, he'd just stop talking. I wasn't quite ready to have Harry leave although I wasn't feeling any better.

"Yes," I said.

"Good," Harry said. "Anything else on your mind?" He was still mad.

"Yes," I said again.

"Okay Go ahead."

"What was Jimmy crying about tonight?" I should have stopped there. I could see Harry getting ready to answer me, but I don't think I ever really found out what he was going to say. Before I could think long enough to stop myself, I said, "And why were you calling him 'baby'?"

Quickly, Harry lifted his head. Then he leaned backward a bit. He looked at me as if I were something he'd never seen before or at least never ever expected to see. "What are you talking about, Brian?"

"Tonight, when Kathryn and I walked down the hall to see if Jimmy was okay?" Harry didn't say anything so I went on. "Kathryn and I and the Rosens were bringing the chocolate and cookies upstairs?" Harry nodded. "Remember, Kathryn told you we all heard Jimmy crying and you talking? And the Rosens didn't know what to do so Kathryn and I went to see what was happening." Harry just kept on nodding, letting me know he understood everything so far.

"So Kathryn and I got down to just outside Jimmy's door, and you were saying things like, 'Baby, don't worry, it'll be all right. Everything'll be fine, baby.'"

Harry stepped up so he was beside me. He rested his forearms on the gate and looked down at his feet. He didn't say anything for the longest time. I couldn't think what else to say. I just stood there, feeling dumb, and beginning to realize my feet were getting really cold.

Finally Harry turned to me. "Let's just say," he began. Then he started over. "Before *I* say anything, let me ask *you* a question. Is that all right?"

"Sure," I said, "ask anything you want to. I'm not the one..." but this time I stopped.

"I'm not the one what?" Harry wanted to know.

"Nothing," I said. "It was...it would've just been stupid. Never mind."

"Right," Harry went on. "Supposing I *was* calling Jimmy 'baby'. What would that mean to you? Why would you think I'd be doing that?"

This conversation wasn't helping at all. I was getting more and more frustrated. Rather than finding out anything to make me feel better, what I was hearing and what was happening was just making me feel madder and more like all I wanted to do was run away. "I don't know, Harry! That's why I'm asking. Wouldn't you want to know?"

"Maybe I hear things better than you do. Did that ever occur to you at all?"

"Harry, I don't even know what that means, and no, it didn't occur to me. Look, lots of kids at school are saying Jimmy's gay. Not just Broom, other kids, too. Kids we're friends with. And you're the one who had his arms around him. You're the one who took off from school to be with him. You're the one who was already over at his house by the time Kathryn and I arrived, and you're the one who was calling him 'baby'. If you were me, wouldn't you want to know what was going on?"

Harry was still looking at me in that funny way. "Maybe, Brian. Maybe I would. But *maybe* I'd figure that no matter what, you were still the best friend I'd known for all my life. And *maybe* that would be enough for me."

As much as I wanted to say, "Yeah, you're right. Let's just forget it," I couldn't. Instead I said, "But maybe not, too? Is that possible, Harry? Isn't it just a little bit possible the great Harry Landis might need to hear his friend was still his friend?"

He surprised me. "Yeah, that's possible."

"Thanks," I said, but it sounded totally sarcastic. "So, what's the answer? Why were you calling Jimmy 'baby'? You don't call anybody 'baby', not even Kathryn."

"Exactly." I had no idea what he meant by that, at least at the time, I didn't. I just wanted to hear him tell me something that would make things okay.

"So?" I said.

At first, Harry looked like he was going to say something, but then he didn't. "What's the answer, Harry?" The sound of my voice surprised me. I was almost crying.

Harry walked away from me toward the kitchen door. He stopped before he got all the way to it and turned around. "I'll tell you what, Bri. I'm going to give you two answers. You choose the one you like best. Only do me a favor?"

"What's that?"

"When you decide? Don't tell me 'cause I really don't want to know." He waited to see how I was going to take that. I think maybe he was hoping I'd sort of call this part off or something, but I didn't. "Is that all right with you, Brian?"

"Whatever you say, Har. However you want it." I replied.

"I don't think so." Harry sounded sad. "I think really it's the other way around. But anyway, here goes: Answer number one: what I really said was, 'Don't worry, *maybe* everything'll be all right; *maybe* everything will be fine.'" Harry waited to see how I was accepting that answer.

"So what's my second choice?" I asked.

"Come on, Brian, you know what you're second choice is. I don't have to tell you, do I?"

"Tell me anyway. Just for the record."

"Sure. Just for the record. Your second choice is I called Jimmy baby because he's my boyfriend."

I didn't make any reply, but it was obvious Harry thought I should. He continued. "Do you understand what I'm saying to you?"

"No, Harry, I don't understand anything at all. I don't understand what you're saying; I don't understand what you're doing; and I don't understand what's going on!"

Harry turned. He opened the storm door and held it open while he reached for the knob to the inside door. When he had the inside one open, he called Wardell and let him in. Then he turned back to me. I really thought he was going to come back out. In fact, I think Harry thought he was going to, too. But then he stopped. "That's too bad." Harry said. "I'm sorry. I'm really sorry."

He let the storm door go and it closed just as he stepped inside.

What I really wanted to do was follow him inside. What I did was let myself out the gate and start to jog home. I had gotten pretty stiff standing around talking with Harry. And then there's the fact that when tears freeze on your face, they sort of burn your skin. The run home wasn't any fun. By the time I got back in bed, it was just a few minutes before five. I had an hour and a half before I had to get ready for school. I spent the time in bed, but I didn't sleep.

14

Jimmy The Geek

"*What* is going on?" Melinda asked me. She found me at one of the tables in the cafeteria near the main entrance. Hardly anyone ever sits there because at least one of the teachers on lunch duty stands close by. Nothing against the teachers, but most kids don't feel comfortable talking when teachers are around.

"What do you mean?" I said even though I knew exactly what she meant, but I didn't feel like coming right out with an explanation.

"Come on, Brian. Give me a *little* credit. I get to the cafe late; when I get up to where the food is, there's no more pizza so I take a grinder even though I know it'll be practically uneatable. So when I get out to the table — you know, our table, the one we sit at — there's Steve Messer and his girlfriend, whateverhername is. So I go, 'Dude, what's up? Where's Harry?'

"And he's like, 'Who cares? Probably with his boyfriend.' So I go, '*Right!*' like really sarcastic, you know? And then I go, 'What about Kathryn?'

"And he's like, 'You walked right past her. Look behind you! She's over there with Miss Berry.'"

"So I look where he says, and he's right; she's there. And I say, 'Thanks a *LOT!*' Then I don't know whether to sit down there – I mean, it is our table – or just find someplace else to sit. So while I'm thinking, I see you over here."

Melinda put her tray down. "Brian, what is happening around here? Why's Kathryn with Miss Berry, and where is Harry?"

Along with everything else that was going on, keeping up with Melinda took a lot of effort. The truth was I really didn't have the energy, but at least her last two questions were easy ones. "I don't know and I don't know," I said.

"You have to know, at least about Harry. Brian, you're Harry's best friend!"

"Maybe not anymore." As soon as I said that, I wished I hadn't; especially with Melinda, you can't take words back.

Melinda almost climbed across the table. "You're kidding, right? When did that happen?"

I wanted to say something to calm Melinda down, but the problem was I didn't know what to say. Before I could come up with even a rough idea, she'd sort of filled in the gaps herself, more or less making it up as she went along.

"It's because of Jimmy, right? Harry's spending all his time with Jimmy and none of it with either you or Kathryn." Then Melinda apparently had a brain storm, which for anybody else would be like a quick sprinkle on a summer day. "*Oh my God*, Brian! Do you think Harry's gay, too?"

Now she had my full attention. "What do you mean, 'Too,' Melinda? Who says Jimmy's gay? Who's been saying that?"

"You know. I mean, you can always tell." She was stalling, but I wasn't sure about what. Then she fell back on one of her old tricks, namely, if you say something strongly enough, that makes it unquestionable. "Brian, everybody knows Jimmy's gay. That's how he got AIDS."

I knew I'd heard her, heard exactly the words she said, but I still couldn't believe she'd said it. This is a little hard to explain, but Melinda declaring Jimmy had AIDS was like going to Dr. Newberry for a cold, and he says I have cancer.

Some things, no matter what, you're just never ready to hear.

While I was more or less staring at Melinda, I guess with my mouth hanging open, I began to feel sort of creepy. Then I looked around me and knew why. Most of the kids near us were watching and listening as best they could. I really didn't want to keep having this conversation in the cafeteria. I stood up, stepped toward Melinda, and took her by the arm. "Melinda, I need to talk to you outside."

"Are you crazy? It's winter outside. Besides, I haven't finished my lunch."

"Come on, Melinda. This is important. You can bring your grinder. We'll go out the side door." By this time, I mostly had her on her feet and turned toward the door at the back of the room. She still wasn't happy; on the other hand, being hustled outside for a private conversation appealed to Melinda's sense of drama. She'd be able to talk about this for days. The only trouble was we had to walk past Broom's table. He and his group always sat next to the side door which led out to the parking lot. That way they could duck outside and have a cigarette or get stoned for class without much hassle. Most times, I don't think anybody noticed when they came or went. Hardly anyone cared anyway.

Sure enough, as we got closer to Broom's table, they were all watching us: Broom, Carl, Jerry and a couple of others, part-time Broomettes. We got right up to the door, and I was beginning to think we were going to get out of there without having to acknowledge their presence. No such luck, though. Just before I went to push open the door, Broom said, "Glad to see you're with a girl, Brian. I'd hate to think you were a fag like your buddy Harry." Then he looked at Melinda and smiled. That did not cheer me up. "Hey, Melinda. What's up?"

"Not much," she responded, with what seemed to me like a little uncalled for warmth. Then, sort of as an afterthought and perhaps to make up for not treating him with appropriate coolness, she added, "Besides, what do you care?" Broom didn't seem to need to touch that.

One of the big differences between me and Harry is that when I'm scared, I act it. Broom, as I've said before, is big and obviously strong. I know Harry is almost as scared of Broom as I am, but he won't let Broom see that. I, on the other hand, probably couldn't hide it if I tried. So rather than say anything, which always has the potential for making things worse, I decided not to answer Broom at all. Conversely, Melinda, either because she's naturally brave or naturally dumb, can't *help* saying something, and what she'd said already had clearly not satisfied her. I started to get the door open and hold it for Melinda when she settled on what else she wanted to say to Broom.

"Brian is not a fag, and probably either is Harry. They just happen to like Jimmy because he's very...likable. And besides, you can tell they're not 'cause neither one is even close to being sick, and when you have AIDS, you get all gross and skinny looking ... like Jimmy."

Melinda's forceful voice is metallic and penetrating. For sure, Broom and his pals were not the only ones who heard. Even so, what I should have done was just hustle Melinda outside without saying anything, but I didn't. "Broom," I said, my voice as steady as I could make it, "Melinda doesn't know what she's talking about. The only thing wrong with Jimmy is that he had a really bad concussion, as I'm sure you noticed. I saw him last night. He'll probably be back in school tomorrow or at least on Monday. All right?"

I really can't stand Broom. At first he didn't say anything. He just leaned back in his chair and put his feet up on the table. "Sure, Bri," he said finally, speaking louder than he needed to, much louder. "I'm sure you're right. I'm sure Jimmy doesn't have *AIDS*. Just because he looks like he's starving to death, and he has to run off to the hospital every time he gets a little scared, *and* he's a faggot if I've ever seen one. I mean, gee ... that's no reason to think *Jimmy the Geek ... has AIDS!*"

Broom folded his arms across his chest and smiled at me. I looked around the cafeteria. Nobody was saying anything. All the kids were looking over at us. The teachers on duty were talking to each other by the main doors, and I could see Miss Berry and Kathryn standing by the cash registers. Miss Berry had her annoyed look on; Kathryn looked more sad than anything else. I couldn't see how anyone could have missed much of what Broom said.

When I looked back at Broom, he and Melinda were staring at each other. I couldn't figure that out at all so I opened the side door and practically shoved Melinda out. I held onto her arm and walked her out into the seniors' parking lot. When we got in among the cars, I looked back toward the cafeteria. No one followed us out.

"Melinda, you are such a fool! I can't believe you! Why did you do that?"

"Thanks a LOT!" she said. "All's I was trying to do was help your precious friend Harry. Anyway, what's the big deal? Who cares if Jimmy has AIDS. You can't catch it unless you sleep with him. Everybody knows *that*. Right?" I didn't say anything. What was there to say? "Well, Brian, isn't that right?"

"Yes, Melinda," I said, "that is…" Then I changed my mind. "Listen, you twit, that's not the point! That has nothing to do with it."

Melinda digested that. Then her eyes got big. "Maybe he got it from needles?" She did a little gasp. "Oh my God! You think Jimmy does drugs, the kind you have to give yourself shots for?"

"I don't know, Melinda," I said. "I'm not the expert on Jimmy around here. Apparently you are."

She retreated to give thought. I was giving severe consideration to grabbing her and shaking her back into the present, when she returned. "I don't think you're right about the needles, Brian. I mean, you could pretty much tell if Jimmy was doing that kind of stuff, don't you think?"

I could feel myself getting angrier and angrier. The feeling was inside me and getting bigger and taking up space that belonged to things like my stomach and lungs and brain. It made me want to take hold of Melinda around her throat and squeeze as hard as

I could. I wanted to hit her. I wanted to kick in the side of some senior's cars. I wanted to scream.

So I did.

I stepped really close to Melinda and leaned toward her face. "How can you be so stupid? Why do you always have to say absolutely the *first* thing that pops into your so-called mind? Why can't you ever just keep your mouth shut? You drive me crazy, Melinda, you know that? If you thought about it for *fifteen* hours, you could not *possibly* have figured out something to say that was worse than you just did in there. You know what I can count on when you're around? Whenever there's a time that saying *precisely* the wrong thing would be the *worst* possible idea, I can count on *you* saying..."

At exactly that moment, Melinda put her arms around my neck, leaned against me, and started kissing me, doing the kind of kissing you see in the hot parts of movies. If someone gave me a million years to figure out what Melinda might have said or done to stop me from yelling and screaming at her, I never would have come up with that possibility. The other surprising part which I also don't think I would have thought of was that before I even got over being surprised at what she was doing, I started to kiss her back. And pretty much as soon as I did, she pulled away.

I might have started up again – talking, I mean, not kissing – at least to ask her what her kissing me had been all about, but the look on Melinda's face stopped me. It had no expression. Her eyes, her pupils really, were wide open and blank. Her head was pulled back as far away from me as she could get it. She didn't look scared, really; she reminded me of something or someone that just stopped functioning. All her systems were shut down. Somehow her capacity for processing was overloaded, and all she could manage successfully was breathing and standing up.

Together, our breathing slowed down. The tension dissipated, and we sort of slumped back away from each other, me leaning against one car, Melinda against another. Then, finally, we were just looking at each other.

The light came back on behind Melinda's eyes and she pushed herself forward away from the car behind her. "What's *wrong* with you?" she said. Her voice was perfectly back to normal.

I had no answer, no real answer, either for her or me. "I don't know," I said. "Look, I'm really sorry, okay?"

"Sure," she said. "No problem," but that wasn't the truth, and we both knew it. She never said a word about kissing me like that, and neither did I, ever, to anyone.

I took a couple of steps back, then walked away from Melinda and the cafeteria. The senior parking lot is bordered on two adjacent sides by the cafeteria and the gym. I walked away from the cafeteria along the gym until I got to the entrance to the parking lot. I turned right and headed for the main entrance to the school which was around on the other side of the gym.

Once inside the main doors, if you turn right, you just go back toward the cafe. I turned left. Going that way, you pass offices on both sides before you get to the classroom wing. The main school office is on the left. Across the hall are smaller ones for other administrators and people like Mr. Maslewski. I was just passing them, on that side of the hall, when someone grabbed my arm. As you could probably tell, I still wasn't in the greatest mood so when I felt my arm being tugged, I turned around quickly and jerked it away at the same time.

"Easy does it!" Miss Berry said.

"Miss Berry, I'm sorry. I didn't know who you were; I just thought..." I stopped because I had no idea what I thought.

"Don't worry about it. Can you come in here a minute?" She was standing in front of one of those smaller offices.

I didn't know what time it was, but I did know that class was about to start. Miss Berry knew what I was thinking. "If you're late, I'll give you a pass. Come on. This is important."

I stepped past her into the little office. Kathryn and Harry were already there. All these offices were the same. You didn't have much choice about how you were going to arrange things. There was enough room for a desk, a chair behind the desk, a filing cabinet in the corner to the left of the desk chair, and another chair facing the desk. You couldn't put two chairs there because then you wouldn't be able to open the door more than a crack. That was a dumb thing about these offices – the door opened in. Harry was sitting in the chair facing the desk; Kathryn was standing in front of the file cabinet. I hadn't said much of anything to Harry all that day so far, other than hello in homeroom. "Hey, dude," I said as I stepped in and stood to the right of the desk, mostly between Kathryn and Harry; I tried to give Kathryn a smile, but it didn't work out too well. Harry just nodded back at me; Kathryn said hi.

Miss Berry followed me in and closed the door. "Slide over and sit in my chair. I need to stand for a while. I've been sitting all morning," Miss Berry said.

I knew that wasn't true unless Miss Berry had suddenly changed the way she taught her classes. She was just being nice.

"Okay," Miss Berry began, "looks like we've got ourselves a problem here." She looked at Kathryn. Kathryn nodded. "I just wanted to check it out with you guys to see what's going on." Nobody said anything so Miss Berry went on. "I assume that stuff about Jimmy being homosexual and having AIDS is false. Is that correct?"

Kathryn and I couldn't say things fast enough. "Of course," we said. "It's all bull. Just a crock. Totally false." We were about ready to launch ourselves into a diatribe duet about the nature of the kids who would start – and/or believe – such garbage, but Miss Berry stopped us.

"Whoa, hold on, slow down, easy does it! Okay, I get the picture; you guys don't think those rumors are true. What about you, Harry? You didn't say anything."

She was right. Harry hadn't said a word. Kathryn and I looked at each other, then at Harry. He still didn't say anything.

"Hey, Harry! What's going on?" Kathryn asked him.

"Nothing worth paying attention to," he said.

"I don't agree," Miss Berry chimed in. "Look, a few kids have started these rumors. First, they are mean. And second, potentially dangerous. And," she paused a second, and when she went on, her voice sort of caught. "The rumors are about your friend.

"Okay so far?" I think we all nodded. "Good. Now a lot of the students here, maybe even most of them, are going *to believe* the rumors, at least for the time being. They're exciting and juicy and something different to talk about. Kids *like* that; you know that better than I do, right?"

Miss Berry looked down at Harry. He nodded. She looked at Kathryn and me. Kathryn nodded; I said, "Yeah."

"So, you don't see that as a problem worth paying attention to, Harry?" Miss Berry went on.

"Miss Berry, if you pay attention to rumors, don't you make them spread?" Harry asked.

"Yes," Miss Berry had to say since that was one of the things she'd taught us last year, "I guess that's so. On the other hand, if you hope to stop a lie from spreading, how can you do that without directly confronting the lie and the people telling it?"

"How do you know all that's a lie?" Harry asked. There was no doubt about it; Harry was acting strange. I didn't look directly at Kathryn, but I could sort of feel how she was responding — pretty much the same way I was. Harry went on. "Ask Brian if he believes Jimmy isn't a homosexual. Ask him if he believes, if he *knows*, Jimmy doesn't have AIDS. Ask Kathryn the same thing."

Miss Berry turned from Harry to me, then Kathryn.

Kathryn spoke first. "If you're asking me what I *believe* about Jimmy, I have to tell you that's different from what I *know*. I do not *believe* Jimmy has AIDS; I don't *know* he doesn't. I'm pretty sure Jimmy isn't gay; I don't know he isn't."

Miss Berry looked at me. "Brian?" she said.

"Same for me."

"You see?" Harry asked as though we had just proved something of major importance.

"See what?" Miss Berry said. She apparently didn't share Harry's point of view. Neither did I. Neither, I'm pretty sure, did Kathryn.

"What chance has Jimmy got if even the people who claim to be his friends are influenced so easily. Look, Miss Berry, the only thing Jimmy's done is be different from the rest of the kids he goes to school with. I got to know Jimmy pretty well over the summer and I *know*," — Harry spoke directly to me and Kathryn. Then he repeated that part — " I *know* he's a good person and worth knowing."

Miss Berry was about to say something but Harry went on before she could start. "And I'll tell you what else I know. What's been happening here in this school, as far as Jimmy is concerned, right from the very beginning of the year, is not fair! It sucks!"

"You got that one right, ace. No question," Miss Berry said, "but that isn't going to stop the same kinds of things from happening over and over again. Unfortunately, things that aren't fair happen all the time, probably more than the other way around. But here and now we've got something more definite and specific. I doubt there's one person at this school right now who hasn't heard someone say Jimmy has AIDS. And that he's gay. Harry, do you *know* whether that's true or not?"

Harry looked at Miss Berry as though he thought he hadn't heard correctly. "Are you seriously asking me that question?"

"I have to ask you that question seriously," Miss Berry said. "This is a serious situation."

"Yes," he finally said, "I do."

"So what's the answer?" Miss Berry pressed.

"I wouldn't tell you even if I could."

I think Miss Berry was beginning to understand how Kathryn and I had been feeling recently. Harry had the information, but he wouldn't share it. It didn't really matter much, at least to me, what the reasons were for his not telling. Ideas like trust and friendship and fairness, honesty, caring about someone, understanding someone else or even yourself were spinning and floating and darting around in our heads. The longer things went on and got more complicated, the more it seemed to me that Harry was the one who could change that. More than anything, I wanted everything to be simpler, to get back to normal, to the way it had been. I was even pretty sure Harry wanted that, too.

Miss Berry said, "Harry, if you won't answer that question, can you at least say why you won't?"

Harry didn't need to think that over at all. "I'll even tell you why I *can't*. That part's easy. I can't because, as Brian knows, I promised I wouldn't. *Why* I won't is more complicated. Let me put it this way: whatever there is to know about Jimmy doesn't matter. If he has AIDS, if he's gay, if he's from a different planet, he should still be treated the same as anyone else."

"Harry, we agree with you," I said, "but what *should be* and what *is* are different things. You *know* that." Then I thought of something that had happened a long time ago. "Look, Harry, remember when Jeff Boykin first came to school in sixth grade?"

Jeff was the first Black kid we'd ever gone to school with. So at first not many kids would play with him. Then a real jerk, Brad Lovetto, called him nigger. Next thing, he and Jeff started fighting. Harry and I and a couple of other kids tried pulling them off each other, and the whole time we were doing that, Brad was screaming about how his father said niggers didn't belong in Afton.

Harry sort of sighed. "Yes, Brian, I remember all that."

"Okay. So what happened?"

"All right I get it," Harry said.

"Say it anyway," I went on. "What happened?"

"I told Mrs. Mackay and Brad got in trouble."

"That's putting it mildly, don't you think?" I said. Mrs. Mackay, as we used to say, pitched a fit. She was so angry at Brad that we all got scared even though we hadn't done anything wrong.

"Right, Brian. Even for Mrs. Mackay, that was pretty major," Harry admitted.

"So, go ahead," I told Harry.

"Brian, we all know this story. Mrs. Mackay made Brad spend the rest of the day in the quiet corner. Then something happened with Mr. Lovetto and the school board. Next thing we know, the Lovettos move away. After that, no more problems. What your point?"

Kathryn took over for me. "The point is, Harry, the way Jeff was treated wasn't fair either, but you trusted somebody else to help. This time you won't. I don't know why, but I do know nothing's getting better; it's only getting worse."

Harry didn't respond. He just kept looking at us.

"Harry, what your friends are telling you is the truth. I think you need to loosen up a little. Whoever you made that promise to, I'd go back and ask to be let out of it."

Harry stood up. "Excuse me, Miss Berry. I need to get to class. May I have a pass please?"

Miss Berry leaned over and opened a drawer in front of where I was sitting. She took out a pad of hall passes. She leaned forward on the desk and began to write. Harry watched. He didn't look anywhere else. Miss Berry finished, handed Harry the pass, and stepped out of his way so he could open the door. He didn't say anything to me or Kathryn. He just left.

15
The Rock
♥ The Hard
Place

Afton is not that big a town. There are barely two thousand kids in all the schools including kindergarten so you'd think kids' bus rides wouldn't be that long, right?

Wrong. Afton is really spread out. Way back in the early fifties, I guess, before all the babies started booming into school, Afton was just a small town. Since then, though, it's become one of the "in" places to live for people who work in Hartford. Most of the houses in Afton are less than twenty years old, and you wouldn't believe how many more are being built right this minute. So the buses have to travel all over to pick kids up and deliver them.

Of course, the schools don't all begin their days at the same moment, but then again you can't have them starting at such different times that all the buses are being used for only one of the schools at a time. The first bus of the day arrives at the high school just a few minutes before seven. If you happen to live on that early route, that's just bad luck for you; and if your parents won't drive you to school on their way to work, that's even worse luck. That was the story for Kathryn that year. At quarter to seven the next day, I left my house to walk to school so that I'd be there when Kathryn's bus pulled in. She'd called me just before midnight the previous night and asked me to meet her. I was asleep, but I'd left my cell on. I woke up on the first ring. All Kathryn said was, "Brian, it's me. Can you meet me at the early bus at school tomorrow?"

I said, "Sure. What's up?"

"I'll tell you tomorrow. Thanks. Bye." And that was it.

We didn't go visit Jimmy the night before, but not because we weren't invited. As soon as I got home Mrs. Rosen called. "Brian? It's Mrs. Rosen, dear. I'm so hoping you'll be able to come by this evening for a visit. Seeing you all last night was so good for Jimmy, and Mr. Rosen and I enjoy seeing you, too." I said something about having to begin studying for exams; they actually were coming up in a little more than a week.

She said, "Oh, yes. Exams. Oh, I'm so sorry. Jimmy and Papa will miss you, but, don't you worry. You study hard. I'll give Jimmy your best." I said please for her to do that, and then I thanked her for the invitation. Then Mrs. Rosen added, "Jimmy certainly picked studious friends. Your Kathryn is studying tonight as well. I only just spoke with her, but Harry, he said he would bring his books over here. Are you sure you wouldn't like to come study here with Jimmy and Harry? You know, Brian, I just now took a pecan pie from the oven." I thanked her but insisted I really wasn't very good at studying unless I was alone. I said I'd try to come see Jimmy over the weekend. Then I asked when Jimmy might be coming back to school. "He will try on Monday," Mrs. Rosen said, "so he can take advantage of the review week? Yes? That's what Harry said you call it at your high school?"

"Yes, Mrs. Rosen," I said, "that's what they call it." Then she said good-bye, and so did I.

The only way onto or off of the high school campus is through the main gate. There's a fence about ten or eleven feet high that goes all the way around the school's property. Because of that I could see as soon as I got to school that something different was happening. From the gate, the drive leads directly to the main entrance. Six cars were lined up in front of the school where the buses pull up to let kids off. The way they had been parked left enough room for a single bus to get by, but only *just* enough. Six men and two women were standing around where kids would come out. I couldn't see who they were, but I could tell they were watching me pretty closely as I walked up to the entrance. They didn't look happy.

When I got closer, I saw I didn't recognize any of them except for one who I'm pretty sure was Derek Mistovich's mother. They looked at me really hard when I got closer. Then one of the men said something to Mrs. Mistovich, and she shook her head. When I was even with them, I looked over and sort of nodded. "What are you doing here so early?" one of the men asked. He was tall and big and well dressed.

I didn't say, it's none of your business, but I felt like it. Instead I said, "I'm meeting a friend on the early bus.

"Who's the friend?" Mrs. Mistovich said.

"Kathryn Mullen," I answered even though I didn't want to at all.

"Well, why don't you go wait for her inside?" one of the other men said.

"Yeah," another one who was dressed for working outdoors added, "you'll be a lot warmer."

"Sure," I said, "good idea." But then I just had to go on, "Is there anything I can help you with?"

"No thanks, sonny," the big, tall one said, "we've got everything under control."

I walked up to the set of double doors on the left and pushed through. I turned left as if I were going toward the classroom wing. On either side of the doors, the walls are mostly glass. I looked back outside as I passed. Most of the people were looking in my direction. I moved beyond the glass then turned and walked to the other side of the entry way which is fairly wide. I sort of sidled back the way I had come until I could see outside again. Their attention had turned back to the gate out by the road. I waited.

Within five minutes, the early bus, the one Kathryn would be on, pulled up. This one isn't usually full. By January, many of the kids have figured out ways to get to school that lets them sleep later.

As soon as the bus came to a complete stop, the doors opened. I could see the kids getting up from their seats to get off. Before anybody got to the door, though, the tall man climbed on the bus. I couldn't hear anything, of course, but I could see what happened. First he leaned over toward the bus driver and then the door closed. After that, he turned toward the kids, put his arms out in front of him, his palms facing down, and then he casually flapped his hands. He was telling them to sit down I guess because that's what they did. Then he did some talking. After about a minute more, the bus door opened again, the tall man got off, then the kids started getting off. Kathryn was last.

When she came through the double door, I raised my hand to get her attention. I didn't need to though; she saw me right away. "What was that all about?" I asked as she came up to me.

"I'll tell you in a minute. Let's go down to the cafe," she replied.

The cafeteria is open every morning from seven o'clock on. You can get a pretty decent breakfast there until 8:15. After that they sell stuff like doughnuts and Danish pastry and cold cereal until 9:30 which is when they have to start getting ready for lunch. Kathryn didn't say anything at all until we got into the cafeteria and in the line for food. Then she asked if I was hungry at all.

Actually, I was. I told Kathryn I could go for a bagel, which they also sell, and reached for my wallet. She said, "Never mind, Brian. It's my treat. I mean, I'm the one who got you here so early." I started to say no, that's okay, and reach again for my wallet. She put her hand on my arm to stop me. "I mean it, Brian," she said. So I thanked her and let it drop.

When Kathryn paid for our food, she took the tray and led us to a table over by the windows looking out on the student parking lot. We sat down. Kathryn passed me my bagel and the glass of juice I'd also ordered. She put milk and sugar in her coffee and started to butter her toast. She still hadn't said a word about what had happened on the bus.

"Come on, Kathryn, tell me. What did that guy want?"

"He wanted to know if Jimmy Rosen was on the bus."

"Why?" I asked.

"He didn't say, but can't you guess?" I shook my head no, but I was beginning to think I did know and that gave me a creepy feeling. She went on, "Do you remember last year, I think it was in Florida somewhere, when they stopped those kids who had AIDS from going to school? Remember, on the news? Those obnoxious parents blocking the way? And they had to get the police? I think the family's house burned down or something, and they moved away."

"Yes."

"Well, that's basically what I think is going on here."

"Was that Kenny Mistovich's mother out there?" I asked.

"I think so. And the tall one is...are you ready for this? The tall man, the one who came on the bus and talked to us? I'm pretty sure that's John Battistoni's father." John is the president of the Student Council.

I said, "You think John knows what he's doing?"

"Who knows?"

"If my father did that, I'd move," I said.

John Battistoni is a good person. My guess was he didn't know, but even if he did, what could he do about it?

"Are they planning to stop every bus, you think? They're going to be kind of disappointed, aren't they?" I was remembering Mrs. Rosen said Jimmy wasn't coming back till Monday.

"Why?" Kathryn said.

I'd assumed Mrs. Rosen told Kathryn the same things she'd told me, but I was wrong. As I was filling Kathryn in, I watched one of the freshmen run into the cafeteria and run over to a group of his classmates. He said something I couldn't catch, but whatever it was, the whole group pretty much leaped to their feet and ran out into the hall headed down toward the main entrance.

We'd finished eating. I drank the rest of my juice, and Kathryn decided to take her coffee with her. We dropped off our trays and headed out. Rather than go all the way down past the offices to that entrance, we took the doors by the gym.

Outside, five buses were lined up waiting to unload. Two more were just pulling in through the gate. Each of the five buses had one of the so-called adults on it. Mr. Battistonii was standing outside the first bus in line. Mrs. Mistovich and the other lady were with him. He was facing Dr. Frank and Mrs. Gerardi, the vice principal. They were arguing. Kathryn and I walked slowly toward them. There were a few other kids standing between the entrance and Dr. Frank and Mrs. Gerardi, and we could see a whole bunch of kids inside the doors of the main entrance. We got to within twenty feet or so, close enough to hear but, we hoped, not close enough to draw anyone's attention.

"What you are doing," Dr. Frank was saying, "is illegal."

"As far as the health and well-being of my kid is concerned, I don't give a damn what's legal and what's not. Clear enough Dr. Frank?"

"And that goes just the same for the rest of us as well," Mrs. Mistovich put in.

Dr. Frank looked at Mrs. Mistovich. Then he said, "I'm certain it does." He turned back to Mr. Battistoni. "Very clear. But, if you don't stop interfering with the buses, I'll call the police. Clear, Mr. Battistoni?"

Dr. Frank and Mrs. Gerardi had gone out without coats or jackets. They were both blowing on their hands. They started to head back inside when the lady standing next to Mrs. Mistovich lunged to get in front of them.

"Isn't your first job making sure these kids are not exposed to fatal, life threatening diseases."

Mrs. Gerardi answered her. "Mrs. Barney, I spoke late last night with Dr. Persiccio after he visited Mr. and Mrs. Rosen. He said they talked about the rumor. They told him there was no possibility – none – that Jimmy could have AIDS. He's never even been exposed to HIV. If it's good enough for Dr. Persiccio, it's good enough for me."

Mr. Battistoni took over again. "Come on, Mrs. Gerardi. Of course they said that! What would you say?"

I turned around for a second to see what the situation was on the buses. The kids had all lowered the windows trying to hear what was being said. When I turned back, I saw Kathryn had walked up to Dr. Frank and Mr. Battistoni. I would have joined her, but it was too late. She took a sip of her coffee and waited for them to acknowledge her presence.

"Excuse me, " she said when they looked at her, "this won't really resolve the issue, but it might solve the immediate problem. Dr. Frank, Jimmy isn't planning to come to school today. Brian," she turned toward me, "spoke to Mrs. Rosen last night, and that's what she told him."

"Is that true?" Mr. Battistoni and Dr. Frank said together, looking at me.

"Yeah. Yes sir," I said, only looking at Dr. Frank.

He turned to the three parents in front of him. "Mr. Battistoni? Shall I call the police?" At that moment, two more buses pulled up behind the others.

Mr. Battistoni looked at Mrs. Mistovich and Mrs. Barney. "Tell the men on the buses they can let the kids off." The two ladies started toward the buses, and Mr. Battistoni turned back. "Dr. Frank, if the Rosen boy shows up at school today, I'll sue you personally. And Dr. Persiccio, and the district. Unless we're satisfied with the way this matter gets handled, we'll be back here Monday morning. Count on it!"

Dr. Frank's voice is never loud, and he's the kind of man who smiles most of the time, not because he thinks it's a good idea so much, but more because he likes people, kids especially. When he answered Mr. Battistoni, his voice was still not loud, but it did remind me of really cold metal. Plus, he did not smile.

"Mr. Battistoni, if you do, the police will be here to greet you. And you may count on that."

Nobody said anything for way too long. Dr. Frank finally said, "Jimmy Rosen will be permitted to attend this school, no matter what. That is the law of this state as well as the policy of the Afton Board of Education."

He waited for anyone who wanted to say something. No one did. "Have a nice day," he said to Mr. Battistoni.

Dr. Frank turned to Kathryn. "Thank you," he said, and then he and Mrs. Gerardi turned and walked up to the main entrance. Dr. Frank opened the door for Mrs. Gerardi, and she stepped through.

The adults were off the buses. The kids were getting off and telling each other what had happened. Mr. Battistoni and his group were moving toward their cars. Kathryn and I turned and headed for the doors. Dr. Frank turned back around, too, and as he stepped through the doors he said to Mrs. Gerardi, "I think we need to hold a school meeting before too much of the day goes by."

16
Except for Mr. Huggar

I know why schools have to have homeroom. First of all, for attendance. Second, when there's an announcement that a lot of kids need to hear. And third, homeroom is a place to go before the day really begins where you can change over from being a son or daughter to being whatever version of a student you are. So for at least those three reasons, homeroom is good. There's also the part about homeroom that's not so good.

Here's what happens: When the bell rings, one or two kids race in at the last minute, and then more or less, everybody gets quiet. Then Mrs. Gerardi usually gets on the public address system, says good morning, and reads the daily bulletin and maybe a special announcement or so. At the end of the announcements, Mrs. Gerardi says, "Moment of silence, please." What happens then depends on your homeroom teacher.

Ours, Miss Berry, takes the moment of silence seriously. She doesn't make it last long, only a few seconds really, but she gets really upset when anyone even whispers. Last year, our teacher didn't care about it, in the beginning. At the end of the first week, Harry went to him and said he didn't think it was fair for everyone to talk during the moment of silence if there was someone who wanted to use it seriously. The teacher said he didn't think there was anyone like that in the room. Harry said, "Well, excuse me, Mr. N., but you're wrong about that. I know of at least two people." Mr. N. said he supposed that one of them was Harry. Harry said, "That might be true, Mr. N., but it doesn't make any difference. If there's only one person, it wouldn't be fair to wreck it for him." Mr. N. made a big public production about how from now on *everybody* in the room had to be quiet because Mr. Landis wanted to use the moment of silence. He was probably thinking most of the kids there would give Harry a hard time about it so Harry would change his mind. He was wrong about that, too.

When the official announcements and moment of silence are over, that's it, but everything so far hasn't taken up more than two or three minutes, so you just sit there for another four or five minutes, waiting for the first period bell to ring.

That morning's homeroom was different. First of all, the feeling of the conversations kids were having, what English teachers call *tone* or maybe it's *atmosphere*, was quiet. Nobody was talking in whispers exactly; we just felt as if we were talking about some terrible accident or how somebody had died unexpectedly. When guys you know have done something dumb or stupid and gotten caught, you just talk about it in a normal way. But, when adults act like that, that makes you talk quietly. I don't know why that is. All I know is I felt weird; I was a little angry, a little embarrassed, too, I guess; and somewhere I even felt a little sorry for them. From what I could tell, just about everyone else thought the parents had been total jerks.

After following Dr. Frank and Mrs. Gerardi back inside the building, I went with Kathryn to her homeroom. I still didn't know why she'd wanted me to come meet her, but I did know I wasn't looking forward to seeing Harry. Only Beverly Niles was in the classroom when we walked in. She looked up and said hi, but then went back to whatever she was working on. Different homerooms are, well, different, and Kathryn's was one where mostly kids worked on assignments.

Kathryn and I walked to the back of the room to be as far away from Beverly as we could. "Okay," Kathryn started, "forget about the buses for a minute. What are we going to do about Harry? Oh, and remind me to fill you in about Melinda."

To tell the truth, I didn't want to do anything about Harry. Plus, I certainly hadn't wasted any time thinking about Melinda. I had pretty much come to the conclusion that Harry was acting like a jerk, too. I was mad at him, and while I hadn't really given it much thought, I guess I was intending to stay mad for the time being. If there was anybody we ought to be doing something about, I was thinking, it was Jimmy. I was trying to figure a nice way to say all that when the loudspeaker in the classroom came to life.

"Excuse the interruption. Will the SAT, please report to the conference room in the main office. All SAT members, to the conference room at this time." SAT stands for Student Assistance Team. Most of what they do centers around kids who drink or do other drugs. They aren't like a discipline committee; they just try to identify kids who are in that kind of trouble, or who have other problems, and get them some help. The SAT also is in charge of dealing with any crisis that might happen to anybody at school such as if somebody might commit suicide or if there was a really bad accident where kids got hurt or even died, things like that.

"That's got to be about this morning, don't you think?" Kathryn asked me.

"What else?" I said. "Listen, I'm going to go hang out down around the office for a few minutes to see what's up. I'll see you in Math, okay?"

There really wasn't much to find out. I saw Miss Berry going into the office as I came down the hall. I leaned up against the opposite wall, but I really couldn't tell much. I didn't see anyone else I knew was part of SAT go into the office, but that didn't mean they weren't already there.

I did see Broom. He walked by with a contingent of Broomettes. At first, I thought he wasn't going to notice me, but then just as he was one step beyond where I was, he turned around. He made a face like he was really surprised to see me. "Why, hello, Bri-ANN. I almost didn't see you. And how are you today, Bri-ANN? Jeez, Bri-ANN, you look like you lost your best girl! Sorry 'bout that!" And with that, he and his crew started laughing in this loud, forced way. Then the bell for homeroom rang.

I waited for them to get through the doors leading to the academic wing before I started to follow. I had no idea what Broom wanted me to think with that little skit, but I did know that if I'd followed behind them right away, they would have carried their routine on for a lot longer.

When I got to Miss Berry's room, Harry wasn't there. Right away the second bell rang. As usual, there were still kids out in the halls, but today Mrs. Gerardi and Mr. Bolls, the head of the guidance office, were in the hall shooing kids into their rooms. Less than a minute later, the loud speakers clicked on and Dr. Frank's voice followed. "Homeroom will be cut short this morning. We will *not* be making any of the usual announcements so I urge you to check the daily bulletin yourselves. A bell will ring in four minutes. At that time, homeroom teachers will escort their students to the auditorium. All other faculty are expected to attend."

When the kids from my homeroom got to the auditorium, Mrs. Gerardi was standing on the center of the stage in front of a microphone. All the lights were on in the audience, and one or two of the stage lights had been turned on as well. Rather than letting us see Mrs. Gerardi better, though, the lights cast a shadow on her face because they were more or less aimed at the top of her head.

Once all the homerooms were in the audience, she spoke into the microphone asking everyone to please take a seat. Just about all of us did what she asked, probably because we really were wanting to know what was going on and what the deal with the buses that morning had been. Then she said, "I'm sorry to have to ask you to wait, but we're not going to begin this meeting until all the seniors have arrived." As I said before, seniors who didn't have a first period class didn't have to come to school until later, but no later than 8:45.

Once they got to school, they were supposed to sign in at the office. For the next fifteen or so minutes, seniors kept arriving, at first one or two at a time, but as it got closer to 8:45, they began coming in to the auditorium in larger groups. Then, a couple minutes after 8:45, about twenty came in together. The auditorium was really quiet; the underclassmen were sitting in all different places, so the late seniors had to sit wherever they could, and usually they couldn't find enough seats to sit together. Meanwhile, each time a group came in, Mrs. Gerardi would ask them, "Please quietly find yourselves a seat." That actually turned out to be pretty funny. Seniors always act like they know everything that's going on, but these guys were completely clueless. It was probably the only time they wished they'd come to school early.

Finally, at almost nine o'clock, Dr. Frank got up on the stage and Mrs. Gerardi stepped back away from the microphone. The next day, Saturday, all Afton High School families received a letter from Dr. Frank. I'm going to quote the whole thing right here because the letter was essentially the same as what he had to say to us in the auditorium that morning except I don't think he'd had time to write much of anything down before the meeting.

Dear Afton High School Family,

We have had a regrettable situation develop here over the last few days. One of our students was the victim of a prank. I use the word victim advisedly, for the prank, if indeed we can continue to call it that in these circumstances, was calculatedly vicious. It was intended to terrorize and as such was in no way acceptable. As an aside, let me state that at such time as we have proof as to the culpability of the perpetrator, the student or students involved will be subject to the most serious disciplinary measures our Code of Conduct prescribes.

This is the situation as it has developed so far: The victim of the prank had to be hospitalized. He has not yet returned to the High School. During this student's absence, two rumors concerning him have surfaced. The first has to do with the young man in a personal way. I will not dignify the rumor by restating it here. If it has not already reached you, I or any other member of the Student Assistance Team will be happy to discuss the matter with you on an individual basis. (The names of the team members are listed below.)

The second rumor I would prefer to treat in the same fashion as the first, for I feel its creation was motivated by the same misanthropic[16] attitude as the first; however, that is not possible. It has already become a community wide issue.

This morning, several members of the Afton community, all parents of Afton High School students, met the school buses on their arrival here at the high school. Individual parents boarded buses. Their purpose was to prevent the young man, the victim of the prank, from leaving the bus to attend classes. They did this because they believe the young man has AIDS.

(At this point, when Dr. Frank was talking to us, he paused, and he didn't say anything for a long time. He was quiet for so long that kids were starting to wonder if he had lost it. But nobody said much of anything. Again Dr. Frank was not smiling.)

First: No one who is currently attending Afton High School has Acquired Immune Deficiency Syndrome.

Second: If anyone did, or if anyone ever does, develop HIV or AIDS, he or she will certainly be welcome to attend all Afton High School functions to the extent that he or she is able to do so. As I said to the

parents this morning, that is both the law of the state
and the policy of the Afton Public Schools.

Beginning first thing on Monday (at the meeting
he actually said, *"For the remainder of this day),* *I*
expect that neither of these rumors will be further
repeated. I expect that no one – neither student nor
teacher nor administrator nor anyone else fulfilling any
of the other functions so necessary to maintaining the
successful day to day functioning of this high school –
will allow him or herself to be used by the person or
persons who are responsible for the creation and spread
of these most despicable rumors. I know beyond any
doubt that I am speaking for the majority who spend
their days here. This kind of personal terrorism, which
is precisely what these rumors constitute, is neither
acceptable nor tolerable.

Sincerely yours,
Michael B. Frank, PhD
Principal, Afton High School

At that point Dr. Frank said, "Now I'd like you all to go quietly
to your first period class or study hall. Except for Mr. Huggar."

Of course just about everybody in the whole place looked
around to see how Broom would react. This was one of the times
when Broom's predictability hung him up. Broom and his crowd
and others like him always sit in the back row, no matter where they
are — classroom, auditorium, driver's ed. class — so when Dr. Frank
said that, pretty much the whole student body whipped around in
their seats to look toward the back of the auditorium.

Broom had stood up as soon as he heard his name, probably
thinking about making a quick exit, but Coach McClaren, one of
the P.E. teachers and the varsity football coach – and he looks it,
too – was blocking his way out of the row on one side; and when

Broom looked down to the other end of the row, Miss Berry was down there. Then he made a big show of not caring that for the first time anyone could recall Dr. Frank had singled out someone in front of other people, and Broom was that someone. Broom sat back down, draped his legs over the back of the seat, and waved with both hands at Dr. Frank.

The rest of the school did as we had been asked.

17

Broom &
Melinda Sittin'
In a Tree

I didn't catch up with Kathryn again until lunch. She was waiting for me outside the cafeteria, and we went through the lines together. I didn't think I was very hungry until I started smelling the food; then I changed my mind. I ordered a couple of hamburgers and some French fries. I knew I'd regret my choice. Not all the food that comes out of the cafeteria kitchen is bad, but the hamburgers almost always are, it's just that sometimes things smell so good, you make yourself believe they're going to taste that way, too. Kathryn was having the salad bar so she didn't take anything but skim milk while we were in the line. She put together her salad, then we went to find ourselves a table.

The table we usually sat at was full. I saw one with only a couple of freshmen sitting at it and nudged Kathryn with my elbow. She looked at me and smiled, and I didn't know why. I nodded toward the table, and we headed in that direction. Before we sat, I asked the kids there if anyone else was coming to join them. They shook their heads no. We put our trays down next to each other.

As I started to sit, Kathryn grabbed my arm. "Look over there at that table in the far corner, the one just the other side of the main entrance."

I did. All I could really see was Broom standing with his back to the rest of the room. I could tell he was talking to a girl for obvious reasons because I could see she had a skirt on, but I couldn't tell who it was. Or maybe I could but wasn't letting myself recognize her for some reason.

"Who's he got there?" I asked.

"You know who he's got there, you just don't want to believe it."

About then, Broom sort of scooched a little to his left, and I could see clearly he was talking to Melinda. "What's she doing, Kathryn?"

"That's why I wanted you to meet me this morning. You know, Melinda didn't go over to visit Jimmy last night either. Want to know what she did instead?"

"She went out with Broom?" I said that mostly because I didn't want to believe Melinda could do something as dumb as that.

"Not exactly, but you're very close. Around 8:00 last night she called to tell me Geoff Brabeck was having a party, and she wanted me to go with her. I told her I'd already said I couldn't go over to visit Jimmy. That's when she said Mrs. Rosen had called her, too. You want to know what she said? The is a quote: 'It's going to suck enough to watch out for him when he's back at school. Who wants to spend time at his house?'"

"She said that to Mrs. Rosen?" I couldn't believe even Melinda could be so insensitive.

Kathryn looked stunned for a moment, I guess by the possibility. Then she relaxed. "No. She couldn't have. She was just telling me that. But that's bad enough, don't you think?"

I didn't answer her about Melinda, mostly because, really, I wasn't completely sure Melinda wouldn't have said that to Mrs. Rosen if it had popped into her mind. Kathryn was about to go on, but what she'd said about a party just then penetrated my mind. "Wait a minute. What party? Who has parties in the middle of the week? Who *goes* to parties in the middle of the week?"

"I know, but Melinda said it was going to be a real party, a Major

Party. I mean, I asked her basically the same thing. She said, 'Come, on Kathryn. Get a life! What good is it being a sophomore if you can only go to parties on weekends?'"

I'm going to take a break here and explain what a Major Party is. If you already know, just go ahead a little till you find the next big space.

In Afton, pretty much every weekend somebody's got parents who go away. That's how a Major Party starts. When a kid's parents are going to be gone, he or she decides to have a party. At first, he tries to tell only his friends, but it doesn't take very long for one friend to mention the party to someone else who really isn't a friend. By the end of the day, practically everybody knows a Major Party is planned for the weekend. On top of that, once the party is going, there are always other kids who just cruise around until they find a house with a lot of cars parked outside. When the fighting starts – and sooner or later at Major Parties, there is almost always a fight – it's usually between two different groups like jocks and burn outs or even something stupider, football players and soccer players. You almost get the idea from listening to the stories on Monday mornings that if no fight breaks out, kids don't think it was a good party.

Harry and I had been hearing about Major Parties since middle school. Here's what you always heard about them. There were always at least two kegs of beer and "whatever else you could want, man!" I know that sounds like an exaggeration, but it isn't. Of course, we always wanted to go to one to see what it was like. The closest we got before high school was one night when we resurrected our spy techniques.

Word about a Major Party makes its way down to middle school because there are usually one or two or more eighth grade girls who are sort of overly socially mature, and they get invited. Naturally, they have to tell their friends all about what they're going to do. (It's always a big deal for an eighth grader to be "going out" mostly because it involves sneaking out or some other kind of complicated plan so your parents don't know what you're doing.) Once one friend has been told, about a half hour later, all the kids in the middle school know who's having the party and which girls are going to try to go.

The house where the party was being held that Harry and I decided to spy on was way up on Afton Mountain. It had been built right down the slope from this rock ledge, like on a cliff. We rode our bikes up the mountain, which was maybe the hardest bike riding I've ever done in my life, not so much because it's steep and long which it is, but more because the cars on that road just really zip along, and there's not that much extra room for bikes. We stayed with our bikes until we got close to the driveway leading to the house then we stashed them out in the bushes and climbed up the back side of the hill. The ledge turned out to be the perfect spot. You could lie down and crawl right up to the edge. The house was sideways to the ledge, with a swimming pool out back, and a screened in porch on the back side that led into the living room. Pretty much we could see whatever was going on in the kitchen and living room, and everything that was happening around the pool and on the porch. And what was going on was ridiculous.

There were at least two kegs of beer that we could see, and about an endless supply of beer in cans. Everybody was drinking. Empty cans were all over. And people were obviously smoking pot because we could smell it even if we couldn't see it. While we watched, more and more kids showed up until we began to realize that more and more of the kids we were looking at weren't from Afton at all. After maybe an hour, we heard shouting from inside. We looked around until we could sort of tell that some guys were yelling at each other in the kitchen. Then I guess they started shoving and maybe fighting for real. One guy must have hit or pushed another pretty hard because all of sudden a body sort of flew across the kitchen and banged into something. Maybe there were pots and pans hanging on the wall he hit because a really loud clanging noise happened when the one who had been pushed dropped out of sight. About two minutes later, two big guys Harry and I thought we recognized from the high school football team dragged a kid outside. They left him just about a foot away from the pool. We thought he was unconscious, but in less than a minute he started groaning. Then he dragged himself over toward the pool, leaned over the side, and started puking.

That was when Harry asked me if I'd seen enough. I nodded. We slid back from the edge and into the bushes. We were almost back to our bikes when cars started peeling out of the driveway and away from the sides of the road. When we'd left our bikes, only about five or so cars were parked on the road. The rest had been lined up in the driveway going to the house which was pretty long because it had to go all the way around behind that cliff. Anyway, by now, cars were lined up on both sides of the road for maybe half-a-mile and at least half of the people who had come in those cars were trying to leave all at the same minute. They weren't being too careful about the way they were doing it, either. They were just jumping in their cars and starting them up and trying to leave as fast as they could. More often than not, doing that would make their car fish-tail like crazy and come really close to hitting another car or a tree. Harry and I were still fairly far from the road, so mostly we couldn't see clearly. We could just hear tires squealing and sliding, music cranked up so loud the bass would sort of reverberate in your stomach, kids yelling and cursing at each other to get out of the way, and all like that.

The air around the road was almost right away totally filled with dust clouds which we could see because of the car's headlights stabbing through them. We couldn't tell what was going on, why everybody was in such a panic about leaving, but it didn't stay a mystery for long.

A few seconds later two Afton Town Police cars came up the road. The second one turned sideways to keep anyone else from leaving, and the other just kept coming slowly up toward the driveway where it stopped. Two cops got out and started walking toward the house. Harry and I sneaked up to our bikes, and made our way through the bushes down past the cruiser.

From what I've heard that is still pretty much what a Major Party is like. I still haven't been to one. Guys have a hard time getting to parties before they get their licenses. I suppose when I do get my license, I'll probably go to see what one's like from the inside, but to tell the truth, I'm not really in a hurry.

Kathryn saw that I had sort of fogged out. She said, "Brian, come back."

"I don't know," I said. I thought Kathryn had asked me a question.

"Don't know what? What are you talking about?"

"What?" I was feeling really dumb. "Sorry, I was having like a day dream or something."

"No kidding. Are you back? Ready for the rest?"

"Yes," I said.

"You're with me? Major party? Melinda. Yes?

I nodded.

"Okay. So anyway, I told Melinda I couldn't go to Geoff's party. 'Well, O.K.,' she said, 'but I hear it's really going to be really cool.' So she went, and evidently Broom was there."

I couldn't believe Kathryn was so calm. I really didn't understand that. I was listening to her, but I was also thinking how I'd act if I ever saw Harry doing something I wouldn't have ever believed he could do. "Late last night, just before midnight, I'm downstairs fixing myself some tea. Just when the water comes to a boil, I hear the back door open.

"I practically jumped out of my bathrobe. Guess who it was?"

Melinda, I was about to say when Kathryn went right on. "You don't need to guess 'cause you already know it was Melinda.

"At first she just stands there with this goofy smile all over her face. Then she leans back through the doorway and says in this really loud, almost shouting whisper, 'Thanks a lot. See ya' later, dude!'

"'Who was that?' I ask her. And she goes, 'Geoff, he gave me a ride over. I told my mom I was spending the night at your house. That's cool, right?'"

"You're kidding?" I said. "What about if you weren't still up?"

"That's what I said. And she goes, 'No problem, I would've just let myself in and slept on your floor.' She knows we never lock the back door."

I just shook my head.

Kathryn went on. "She comes in and more or less drags me to the kitchen table. 'Kathryn,' she goes, 'you'll never guess who I ended up with at the party!'

"So I'm like, 'Broom,' but I wasn't being serious, you know? Well, she freaked. 'Oh, my Ga-od! How did you know?'"

"Now you are kidding, right?" I said.

"Nope. And believe me, I was as surprised as she was. She finally calms down enough to tell me the rest.

"She's at the party a while and having a pretty good time until somebody shoves somebody else who bumps into her and spills a plate of chili or whatever all over her. Next thing, a guy is helping her wipe it off, and the guy turns out to be Broom. Then she says, 'Kathryn, you aren't going to believe this! Broom is really this totally radical dude!'"

Kathryn had my full attention. I was not looking at Broom and Melinda. I was not thinking about Harry. I just wanted to know what happened next. "Did you tell her she was right?" I wanted to know.

"What? About Broom?"

"No," I said, "about not believing it."

"Yeah. Pretty much that's <u>exactly</u> what I said."

My head felt like it was getting pumped up with air. "I cannot believe this."

Kathryn leaned forward toward me, her eyes really bright. "Wait, there's more. Melinda could not stop telling me how cool Broom is." Then Kathryn does this amazing imitation of Melinda. 'I mean, Kathryn, you'll see. He's like nice and funny at the same time, you know? I mean, I was totally amazed.'

"She was wrong about that. I was the one totally amazed, not to mention speechless. Her thing now is that what Broom is like at school is all just an act. 'Really, Kath, you just have to get to know him. I mean, he didn't say one mean thing.'

I started to say something, just to fill the silence. She put up her hand to stop me.

"No, wait. Here's the part that's really going to blow you away. Ready?"

"As I'll ever be."

"Melinda said that Broom said that he and Melinda and Harry and I should go on a double date." She leaned back in her chair to let that image ferment a few seconds. "Can you see that, Brian?"

I said, "Oh, yes, absolutely. Harry would be extra excited about that. Probably give up baseball for a chance of that."

I looked over at the freshmen. They had obviously been listening avidly to all we'd been saying. "Pretty interesting, hunh?" I said to them. They just smiled and nodded and turned away.

"What do you think, Brian? Think we're going to be able to count on Melinda to help with Jimmy much when he comes back?"

"I'm thinking not," I said.

Kathryn stopped, but now she didn't seem so calm. She turned to look over at Melinda and Broom, but they had left. "Do you want to tell Harry about it or do you want me to?"

More than being upset about probably having lost her friend, I think Kathryn was sort of dreading having to tell Harry. The way she saw it, what Melinda had done was more like a betrayal than anything else. The whole idea didn't make me feel too good either.

"First one to see him gets to tell him, all right?" I said. "Or wait. How about I just call him now?" I reached for my cell.

"No, in person's better," Kathryn said. "First one to see him tells him."

That was a big mistake because neither of us saw Harry till the next day. And that was such a weird day, we didn't remember to say anything about Melinda.

18
The Birth of KOSFOD

Whatever happened to Broom after Dr. Frank's speech, it didn't make him happy. At the end of the next period, I was in the cafeteria. It's where you're supposed to go if you don't have a class. About five minutes before the bell, Broom and his Broomettes came bombing into the cafeteria, the Broomettes hustling to keep up. He stramped through the tables. If a chair was in his way, he grabbed it and tumbled it to the side. And he definitely went out of his way to find chairs in his way. His two stooges followed, kicking the fallen chairs, to show their loyalty I guess. Our school is kind of lenient as far as behavior goes, but Broom pushed beyond even our limits.

Mr. Skelley, a science teacher, was on duty. He's a pretty nice guy; he's quiet and basically tries not to get into hassles with kids if he can possibly avoid it. This time he figured he couldn't avoid it. He got to his feet in a rush and maneuvered his way quickly through the tables to meet Broom in the middle of the cafeteria. Mr. Skelley and Broom ended up practically nose to nose. Broom said, "What's your problem, Skeleton Man?"

I wish I could give Broom a little credit for being a little clever, but Mr. Skelley isn't even a particularly thin man so all Broom was doing was playing with his name for the sake of being Broom-rude.

As you would expect, his buddies loyally appreciated his wit by giggling

Mr. Skelley said in the Broomettes direction, "Excuse us a moment, won't you please?" He led Broom a few steps away. Whatever he said didn't make Broom any happier. Broom said, "I don't think so, Skelley. I'm really upset, man, so get the fuck out of my face!"

Mr. Skelley said something else, and Broom said, "Call whoever you damn well please. I fucking really don't fucking care!" (As my mother would say, when Broom gets excited, he demonstrates the depth and breadth of his vocabulary.)

Broom tried to brush by Mr. Skelley. He didn't judge his distance very well - probably didn't want to – and he bumped Mr. Skelley hard enough so he would have fallen except a table was in the way. Broom kept moving through the cafeteria to a table in the back corner. He took the seat right in the corner, put his hands on the table and glared at the room. Carl and Jerry caught up and sat one on each side.

I looked back at where Mr. Skelley was still standing. His face was real red. He looked at Broom, started toward him, but then changed his mind. Instead he went into the faculty dining room to use the phone. You could hear his voice – loud, angry-sounding – but not make out the words much. He hung up, then went back to stand in the middle of the double doors to the cafeteria. I'd bet it wasn't more than thirty seconds before Mrs. Gerardi came marching in.

Mrs. Gerardi is one of the most ordinary looking ladies you could ever imagine. She's a normal height for a woman. She has brown hair and a regular, pretty face. She's maybe a few pounds overweight, but that seems common for most teachers when they start to get older, after forty or so. If you ever saw her, you really wouldn't give her a second thought unless one of two things happened. The first one might be if, say, you saw her drop something and you went to pick it up. Then when she gave you a smile while she said thank you, you would feel yourself get a little brighter, and the feeling would stay with you for quite a while. The second might be if you did or said something rude or mean whether to Mrs. Gerardi or someone else. In that case, whatever she would say to you, there would be something going on in her eyes that turned your intestines very cold.

It tells you something about Mrs. Gerardi that when Broom saw her walking in, he stood up, but didn't move at all. He didn't say anything, he didn't look at anyone but her. Mrs. Gerardi walked up and stood right in front of him. She spoke to the Broom boys but never took her eyes off their leader. "Carl. Jerry. Time to leave." They left.

Broom's not exceptionally tall, but he's at least six feet so he's taller than Mrs. Gerardi. Somehow you'd expect that would put her at a disadvantage; it didn't. Mrs. Gerardi appeared to poke him in the chest. "*You* will follow me!". Broom's color changed until he began to look more gray than anything else.

Mrs. Gerardi turned to leave. Broom followed her. She walked down the hall toward the offices but turned down a corridor on the right. Down that way eventually you get to the library. On the way, though, are the art rooms and the woodworking shop. In a corner of the shop is a small room. Maybe it was once the shop teacher's office. Now they use it for in-school suspension.

Mr. Field was waiting for them there. Broom walked in and sat down. Mr. Field nodded to Mrs. Gerardi, shut the door, and took a seat at the teacher's desk.

Considering what happened to Broom and it being Friday, I was thinking the weekend might be pretty good. It wasn't. It sucked; and sorry, but there's just no other way to put it. Beginning with dinner Friday night, the weekend definitely was an uphill climb the whole way.

To begin with, when I got home and opened the refrigerator to take out some peanut butter for a sandwich, I found the peanut butter jar was empty except for about a half a teaspoon. That's not such a terrible thing if there's at least another jar of peanut butter in the cupboard which that day there wasn't. I know that not being able to have exactly the kind of sandwich you want for a snack when you get home from school isn't the end of the world, but sometimes it can be pretty hard to take. While I was deciding whether or not I was hungry enough to settle for something else, Mom came home. She'd already heard about what happened with the buses that morning — don't ask me how — so, of course, she wanted to know the details.

When I finished filling her in, she wanted to call Dr. Frank right away for an update. I told her I was pretty sure, first of all, Dr. Frank was really busy, and second, she was more than likely going to be getting a letter about it all the next morning anyway. Well, that stopped her from calling the school but not from calling Mrs. Landis. The two of them were on the phone for at least an hour. I went up to my room and decided to poke at some of my assignments until dinner. I ended up reading on my bed. At some point or other, I fell asleep.

I slept for a long time. When I woke up. I knew it was late, later than dinner time. I got up on one elbow, dug out my phone, and flipped it open. It was almost a quarter to eight. I switched on the light and sat up and got off my bed.

At the top of the stairs I could hear my parents talking in the dining room. When I walked in, they were sitting at their normal places with empty plates in front of them. They looked up and smiled when I walked in and sat at my place, in front of which there was nothing at all. My mother kept smiling at me.

"Hi, honey. Are you hungry?" I nodded and made a noise that meant yes. "Good, " she said. "There's soup on the stove. It's probably not very hot any more, but it will warm up quickly, and I made you a tuna fish sandwich. That's in the fridge."

Taking a nap you didn't expect to take, waking up too late for dinner, then even thinking about eating lukewarm soup and a cold tuna sandwich! What a perfect Friday night! "How come you didn't wake me up?" I asked.

"I went up to do just that, Bri," my father said, "but your mother said to leave you alone if you were asleep. I gave you a couple of shakes, but you were out cold."

"But Dad, it's practically eight o'clock! Weren't you ever going to wake me up? If I'd slept all night, I'd be just about starving!"

"We meant to," Mom answered, "but we just got so involved planning the demonstration."

I interrupted her, not her favorite thing. "What demonstration?" She didn't seem to mind.

"Sunday's demonstration," she went right on, "and I'm afraid we didn't notice how late it was getting."

And now you know exactly why the weekend sucked. In less than twenty-four hours, my parents, Harry's parents, Kathryn's mother, a bunch of other parents, Dr. Newberry, and some "concerned" citizens, organized a demonstration in support of kids' rights to education whether they have AIDS or not. Which in this case no one did.

Speaking for just the ones I know well – my parents, Harry's, Kathryn's, and Dr. Newberry – I can tell you that they are not dumb people. They may not be geniuses or anything, but they are reasonably bright people so you're probably wondering what they thought they were doing. I explained to my parents how Jimmy did not have AIDS, so they were demonstrating about nothing. They said they understood, but the principle was the same. "A small group of unthinking, insensitive, boors,"[17] my mother said, "are trying to bully a larger group of people into behaving in a distinctly inhumane and un-American way. And...that is wrong!"

So on Saturday, Kathryn and Harry and I — Harry not speaking to me at all, you need to understand, and only being polite to Kathryn — had the dubious pleasure of making signs. A few of the catchiest were:

Keep Our Schools
Discrimination Free

Kids Rights
For Kids

KEEP AFTON
BIGOT FREE

1, 2, 3, 4!
Freedom's What
We're Fighting For!

PARENT
AID FOR
STUDENTS!

Then we went to the mall and handed out flyers (homemade and run off on our church's copy machine) and put them on parked cars in exactly every plaza parking lot in Afton, of which Afton has more than its fair share.

The rest of the time we were gophers for the "organizers". (In case you don't know, gophers are people who "go for" things, such as more coffee, a blue marker, poster board, etc. Don't think we – me, Kathryn, and Harry – were the only kids involved. Most of the other adults who spent any time at Demonstration Headquarters – that's what Mom called the church basement where the "organizing" went on – dragged one or more of their kids with them, but all those guys managed to escape after an hour or so. Because we were the children of The President (my mother, of course), VicePresident (Mrs. Landis), Secretary (Mr. Landis), Treasurer (Mrs. Mullen), Special Advisor (my father,) and Medical Consultant (guess who) to the Committee to Keep Our Schools Free of Discrimination (KOSFOD), they kept us there the whole day.

Toward the end of the afternoon, while Kathryn and I and a girl named Jen Tompkins were each making one more sign, and Harry was helping the KOSFOD officers straighten up the church basement, a policeman wandered in. He acted like he wasn't sure he was in the right place. He looked around, saw what we were doing over at the table with the posters and signs, and took a few steps over in our direction. "Good work you've done there. Very neat. Nice lettering," he said.

"Thank you," Kathryn answered.

At that point, the others in the basement noticed the policeman. Mr. Landis walked over in our direction. The policeman smiled at him. "Excuse me, sir, are you in charge here?" he asked.

Before Mr. Landis could answer, my mother walked up and joined them. "Chief Rossi, what a nice surprise! Did you hear about our plans for a demonstration?" My mother knew the names of just about everyone who worked in any capacity for the Town of Afton.

Chief Rossi looked carefully at my mother. "I'm sorry, ma'am. Have we met?"

"I think not, but I've heard you speak before. Just last month at the PTO as a matter of fact. I'm Maureen Lister, the president of KOSFOD." The chief looked blank so Mom explained in more detail. "The Afton Committee to Keep Our Schools Free of Discrimination." She heavily emphasized the words that made the acronym.[18]

"Pleasure to meet you," the chief said, taking off his hat and offering my mother his hand to shake, which she did. "I hope I didn't put you to sleep that evening. Public speaking isn't really my forte."

"Not at all. I was actually quite interested in all you had to say." Then, figuring Chief Rossi hadn't just happened by to chat, my mother changed the topic. "Now, how may I help *you?*"

The chief put his hat back on. "Well, Mrs. Lister, I'm not sure. Do I understand you intend to hold a demonstration tomorrow afternoon?"

"That is correct, Chief Rossi." Then my mother got this sort of bright look on her face, as though she'd just figured something out. "Oh!" she said. "But I'm sure we won't require police protection, Chief. We're going to be quite peaceful and orderly. We've no intention of being disruptive."

The chief actually looked a little worried. "I'm not so sure about that. In any case, that's not really what I came here for. Mrs. Lister, you can't demonstrate within the town of Afton without a permit to do so. And I know you don't have a permit."

That was a stunner. They were all pretty sure they'd thought of everything, but nobody ever thought of a permit. After a pause, my dad said, "I'm Ben Lister, Chief. I assume you know most if not all of the particulars, both as chief of police and as John's father." John Rossi was a junior at the high school. I knew who he was. He wasn't a bad guy really, just sort of harmless.

"Yes, Mr. Lister, I do."

"You know about the commandeering of the buses yesterday, Chief?"

"I do. That will not happen again."

"And you know why those odious bigots, boors, and yahoos were there," my mother said, getting back into the conversation. The Chief nodded. "Well then, don't you agree that some response is called for?"

"Mrs. Lister, as I suggested, if an attempt of any kind is made to disrupt the high school on Monday, there will be an appropriate response. Now, I am correct, am I not, that you have *not* obtained a permit for this demonstration?"

Mom's face was blank. She turned to the Special Advisor who was beginning to flush a little pink around his ears and cheeks. As the only one with past experience in this kind of thing, he had evidently messed up. Dad looked over at Mr. & Mrs. Landis and Harry. They apparently had nothing to say either. I caught Harry's eye. He gave me the look that meant, "This is pretty interesting, huh?" I nodded.

The President of KOSFOD regained her composure. "I'm sure that won't be necessary, chief. This is not our nation's or even our state's capitol. We are not planning to interfere with the workings of Afton's town government. We merely intend to draw attention to a situation that has the potential for visiting grave injustice and creating a dangerous divisiveness among the people of our town. I'm certain, as the chief law enforcement officer, you have a vested interest in seeing neither of those possibilities come to pass."

"Yes, ma'am, that's certainly true, but I also have a responsibility to uphold the law, and the law states that you may not hold a public demonstration unless you have previously obtained a permit to do so."

Mr. Rossi was being reasonable. He hadn't leaned on his position as Chief of Police. The only problem was, Mom was not in a reasonable mood. She'd spent a long time preparing for her demonstration, and she was not about to let it go graciously. I knew just by looking she was keeping her face from smiling or frowning or doing anything. It was her "This is as exciting as buying milk" look.

"Chief Rossi, I will certainly not dispute with you as to the laws governing public demonstrations," my mother said in a voice to match her look. "However, I must point out that, first of all, the First Amendment to our Constitution protects our rights to free speech; secondly, as I have already stated, we have no intention of causing any sort of disruption or disturbance. We are not, after all, protesting our country's involvement in a foreign war. We merely mean to make our position clear vis-à-vis discrimination, small mindedness, and mean spirited intimidation."

The Chief's tone of voice matched the KOSFOD president's one hundred percent. "Mrs. Lister, I didn't come here to threaten you. I want you to know that I'm personally sympathetic to what you're trying to do. But that has no official bearing on our situation here. If you or any member of your group persist tomorrow in attempting to carry out an illegal demonstration, I will have no choice but to place you under arrest. Please, don't make me have to do that."

My mother and father looked at each other. Then they turned to the Landises and Mrs. Mullen and the Tompkins all of whom had drifted over to hear what was going on. She looked at Dr. Newberry and moved a bit closer to him. "If the medical consultant feels the need, we are confident that proceeding without his further affiliation will not compromise our efforts."

Dr. Newberry said, "The medical consultant feels his participation will endanger neither his practice nor reputation."

Mom nodded, smiled, and turned back to the chief. "Thank you so much for your time and concern, Chief Rossi. I can assure you that we will take your words to heart."

The chief didn't look too assured, but my mother didn't leave him much maneuvering room. He'd given us his message. Either KOSFOD would heed his warning or they wouldn't. "Good day, Mrs. Lister. I wish you all a pleasant evening." Then, as though he wasn't sure he really wanted to say it, he added, "And a quiet and peaceful day of rest tomorrow."

After Chief Rossi left, we got back to straightening up. Kathryn and I joined Harry gathering up everything we'd been using to make the signs. Harry kept repeating to himself, "Oh, boy. Oh, boy. Oh, boy. Yeah, Obboys. Good. Fits them well."

"What are you talking about?" Kathryn asked.

"What?" Harry looked blank. Then he got it. "Oh, you mean Obboy?"

She nodded. "Brian's mom just called the guys trying to keep

Jimmy out of school, 'Odious bigots, boors, and yahoos.' So, OBBOY! It's a good name for them."

"Good as any other, I guess," I said. I was hoping that exchange was Harry's way of getting us all back together again. It wasn't. He went right back to what he'd been doing without another word.

At about six-thirty as we were all getting set to walk out, Mrs. Mullen and Kathryn came over to where Harry and I were putting our jackets on. "Would you boys care to join Kathryn and me for pizza and a movie?" she asked.

"That's sounds perfect!"

After I'd blurted that out, I thought to check out Harry. I'd answered maybe a little too quickly. I didn't mean to take the lead away from him like that, and I probably should have waited for him to say first since Kathryn was his girlfriend; but I was really needing to get away from the President and Special Advisor for a while. He was already looking at me when I turned to him. He said to Mrs. Mullen, but mostly looking at me, "No, thanks, Mrs. Mullen. I promised I'd help Jimmy review some more for his exams. But thanks anyway; maybe another time." And then he looked at Kathryn the same way he'd been looking at me – a little bit just blank, a little bit unhappy, a little bit angry.

What Harry said and the way he looked at us while he said it had kind of a gloomy effect on the rest of the evening. The pizza wasn't as good as it usually is or else the way we were feeling made it taste funny. One good thing though, Mrs. Mullen didn't mention the next day's demonstration or even ask us about school the day before. Instead she got us talking about different things, like how we thought we'd do on the PSATs that you can take when you're a sophomore and even what colleges we might be thinking about, especially state colleges as opposed to out of state schools. And believe it or not, we – mostly Mrs. Mullen and I – had a fun time talking football. It turned out she had been a New York *Giants* fan, too, when she was younger, which was the coolest part of the whole evening, and practically blew Kathryn away because she'd been totally convinced her mother didn't know the difference between football and pole vaulting.

On the way to the movie, Mrs. Mullen talked about how the film we were going to see was supposed to be really good, which I had heard, too. So of course, the movie turned out to be not good at all; in fact, it was dumb. Here's the theme: adults are lame and don't know anything, but kids are smart. If adults just leave them alone, everything is so much better. The basic problem was the movie adults weren't realistic at all. I mean, if every single adult was as stupid as the ones in those movies, you might believe in the movie. But *every* adult isn't.

After the movie was over, and we were all back in the car, Mrs. Mullen turned to me in the back seat and said, "Could either of you two manage some ice cream or maybe something else by way of a snack?"

I was pretty much used up by then so I had to say no thanks, which wasn't actually so easy since I was really liking being out with Kathryn. Mrs. Mullen turned to look at Kathryn, but she just shook her head no. Kathryn was wiped out, too. "That's just as well. Tomorrow's a big day," Mrs. Mullen said, reminding me of exactly the thing I didn't want to remember.

Mrs. Mullen dropped me off at a quarter to ten. I thanked her and Kathryn both, and we all said we'd see each other tomorrow at the demonstration – Mrs. Mullen definitely being the most enthusiastic – then I went in.

As I figured, my parents were huddled over the dining room table with Mrs. Landis and some other man I didn't know. They introduced me and asked if I'd like to join them. I said no thanks, that I was really beat and needed to get some rest for the big day tomorrow. They smiled at that, said goodnight, and went back to their plans.

19
Something's Happening Here

Believe it or not, the most complicated part of planning the demonstration was where to hold it. The high school seemed like the logical place, but no one would notice. It's three miles outside the main part of Afton on a road that doesn't go anywhere that people would be going on a Sunday afternoon. Somebody suggested one of the churches, but the organizers worried about people passing by and not understanding what was going on. They might think something bad was happening at the church.

What the KOSFOD officers settled on was a march. That was Mr. Landis's idea. Back in the seventies, he was involved in demonstrations and marches protesting the Vietnam War. He talked everyone into marching because, he said, you had a better chance of getting noticed, especially if the march inconvenienced traffic or anything like that. (Mom pretended not to hear that part.) The plan was for everybody to meet in front of Walmart, the biggest of those shopping plazas I mentioned before, and then we would make our way to the high school so we would end up in the appropriate place.

So at one o'clock on Sunday afternoon, I drove with the president and special advisor of the Afton Committee to Keep Our Schools Free of Discrimination to the Walmart shopping plaza. The flyers we'd put out said the demonstration would begin at two o'clock, but my mother thought that as the President she really had to be the first one to arrive. She needn't have worried. We got there even before the police did.

The Landises joined us about fifteen minutes later. They have a Jeep Cherokee so they brought all the signs from the day before. We were just unloading and stacking them when the fist police car pulled into the parking lot and stopped about fifty yards away. One of the regular patrol officers was driving, but riding shotgun was Chief Rossi. The driver stayed in the cruiser, but the chief got out, leaving his door open. Then he just leaned forward, both hands resting on the car roof and watched us.

For a while none of us did anything, just watched Chief Rossi watching us. Then my mother said, "All right now, let's get those signs stacked and ready to hand out."

"Will he really arrest us?" Mrs. Landis wanted to know.

Mr. Landis shrugged. Mrs. Mullen laughed in a way that would make you know she was Kathryn's mother. Mom didn't answer.

"Brent, did you call the *Afton News*?" she asked my father. He nodded that he had. "Did you tell them to send a photographer as well?"

"No, not in so many words. But I'm certain they wouldn't miss a photo-op like this one." My father said that a little sarcastically. He didn't much like trendy ways of saying things.

"All right. We'll keep ourselves busy until the people from the *News* arrive, but until then, let's not do any..." she looked over at the chief, "*Demonstrating!* When they do get here, I propose we distribute our paraphernalia to whoever has come to join us and begin our march. Chief Rossi will just have to do whatever he feels is necessary." She looked at the adults first and then at us. She smiled, and both my father and I knew she was sort of hoping the Chief would try to arrest her. "Anybody not willing?"

No one answered, one way or the other. We stayed huddled for the next ten or fifteen minutes. A few more people arrived in the parking lot and made their way over to our group. When they got close enough, my mother or some other member of KOSFOD would explain what was going on. A couple of them left right away, but most didn't.

Shortly before two o'clock I noticed another group of people had gathered at the far end of the parking lot. They were pretty far away, but I recognized John Battistoni's father. I pulled Kathryn back out from the crowd around the KOSFOD officers. "Look over there at those people. Way over at the far end. You recognize anyone?"

"OBBOYs," she said, using Harry's name.

I left Kathryn and sort of squirmed my way toward my parents. "Dad," I said when I had gotten up beside him, "those people who were stopping the buses Friday morning? Look over there. The tall man is Mr. Battistoni, the boss of the OBBOYs."

"The what?"

I explained. He looked over at them. "OBBOYs. Interesting," he said. "Well, we shall see what we shall see." My father said that a lot. Basically it meant he understood what you said to him but not exactly what to do about it.

The last person to arrive was a lady dressed pretty much all in black. She had two cameras hanging around her neck and a small note pad in her hand. She must have known Mr. Landis because she walked right up to him. "I'm from the *Afton News*," she said. "Is this the demonstration we were called about?"

"It will be shortly," Mr. Landis told her.

My mother noted the arrival of the *Afton News* by raising her voice. By this point, I'd say there were maybe thirty or forty people standing around her. "May I have your attention please. Please, may I have your attention!" Everyone quieted down fairly quickly. "Thank you, and thank you all for coming. I really have very little to say. As I told Chief Rossi late yesterday afternoon, we have no intention of causing disruption or making a disturbance. We have a very simple message to deliver: we want to keep our schools free of discrimination. We will march from here to the high school where we will stand vigil for one hour. Those of you who would care to carry one of these signs here, help yourselves. If not, that's quite all right. Any questions?"

One of the men at the back of the crowd called out, "What happens if Rossi tries to arrest us?"

"Why, then," Mom told him, "I suppose we'll be taken to jail."

"Then what?" the same man wanted to know.

"I couldn't say," my mother replied. "I've never been arrested before. Have you?" That got a little bit of laughter, but no answer from the man. "Any other questions?" There were none. "Well, then, let's be on our way."

All the officers of KOSFOD as well as a half-dozen or so others picked up signs. I did not; neither did Harry or Kathryn. Then the whole group fell in behind the KOSFOD leaders and headed for the entrance to the plaza.

Chief Rossi meanwhile had of course been watching everybody preparing to move. I can't say he looked very happy. He closed the door to the cruiser, motioned to his driver, and the car took off, at a high rate of speed, as the police like to put it, with its lights flashing. It came to a sudden stop in front of the plaza entrance, effectively blocking any cars from being able to go either out or in. The Chief and his driver got out of the car. The Chief, now equipped with a megaphone, was already facing us, the marchers; his driver came around the front and stood next to him.

"You are in violation of Statute 5208, of the Town of Afton, which prohibits unlicensed, organized marches for purposes of demonstration. I order you to desist and disband, or face arrest."

We kept marching. Chief Rossi repeated his warning word for word. We kept marching, although maybe a little less energetically. Chief Rossi turned and took a step toward the cruiser in back of him. He reached in through the open door on the passenger side, picked up the microphone to his radio, and spoke into it. Then he turned back toward us and repeated his warning except that when he got to the end, he said, "For the final time, I order you to desist and disband, or face arrest." The main body of marchers slowed down perceptibly. The KOSFOD officers did not. As a result, a gap opened up between most of the marchers and our parents.

Then two things happened: First, a state police bus pulled into the entrance to the plaza and stopped behind the chief's car. Then from behind the actual Walmart store, three more Town of Afton police cruisers came speeding up, their lights flashing. The cruisers rushed to a halt in perfect formation next to the chief's car.

Second, OBBOY started chanting and walking towards us. "Hey, hey, ho, ho! Jimmy Rosen's gotta go! Hey, hey, ho, ho. Jimmy Rosen's gotta go!" Their voices were somehow louder than anything else going on around us. And they sounded mean or angry, or maybe mean *and* angry is closer.

Chief Rossi's life was abruptly more complicated. He figured the KOSFOD leaders were not for the moment about to march onto the main road, so he sent his driver off after OBBOY. Then he advanced on KOSFOD. The other Afton officers hustled to join their chief. As the police got closer to our parents, the rest of us moved backward, all except for Harry. He stayed where he was, essentially by himself now.

The OBBOYs scattered like cats as the Chief's driver approached them, so in a way, they turned into a bunch of little obboys. At first, they stopped chanting, but when they realized they only had to worry about one policeman, they started up again. The officer would take a few steps toward one group; they'd separate and back away from him just as kids do when they're playing tag — not really running away, just staying slightly out of reach. He'd give up on them, turn toward another, and that one would do the same thing. If there hadn't been so much tension because of KOSFOD, the police, and OBBOY, the whole scene might have been pretty funny.

I guess Chief Rossi didn't exactly know what to do. I don't think he really wanted to arrest the demonstrators, but he didn't appear to have a choice. On the other hand, he couldn't exactly ignore the OBBOYs. After all, they were doing more demonstrating than

KOSFOD at that point. Even so, he raised his megaphone and began to speak into it. "You are under arrest for conducting an unlicensed demonstration. Put down your signs down and come forward one at a time."

Mrs. Landis answered him. "Chief Rossi, what about those OBBOYs?" Obviously Dad had told her. Just as obviously, Chief Rossi had no clue.

Mrs. Landis continued. "They're demonstrating more than we are. How about arresting them first?"

Understand, Mrs. Landis had to shout all this pretty much as loud as she could because by this time I would say that practically anyone who'd been in any of the plaza stores was now outside watching, and beginning to shout and yell as well. It didn't take long for the onlookers to take sides one way or another. The ones who were on our side, who saw the KOSFOD signs and agreed with them, were just yelling at the police about why didn't they go catch burglars and drug dealers. The idiots who supported OBBOY took up their chant which by now was "Two, four, six, eight; fag free schools are really great."

While all this was going on, the *Afton News* lady was going berserk, running around, trying to take statements, snapping pictures with both cameras, taking notes.

Chief Rossi finally decided he was going to have to act. He spoke to his men, and they moved to advance toward OBBOY. That turned out to be a mistake, but one I don't see how he could have avoided. Including himself, Chief Rossi now had a total of nine men. OBBOY outnumbered them about four to one. The police had to split up. For a short time, none of the chanters reacted. They just continued moving and shifting around away from whatever policeman was headed in their direction. The only hint something bad was about to happen was that the OBBOYs were looking nasty, not to mention greatly teed off.

The policemen changed strategy. They more or less spread out in a line and headed toward the OBBOYs to herd them away from

KOSFOD and toward the entrance to Walmart. At first it looked like that was going to work, but then about a dozen or so of the men began to sprint toward the demonstrators.

Essentially, they came running from all sides. When they got close, they didn't really slow up. The Rioters waded into the Demonstrators, cursing them, pushing, shoving, and trying to rip the signs out of their hands. KOSFOD was not inclined to give up its signs. In the melee, Demonstrators were pretty quickly on the losing end and not just because they wouldn't let go of their signs. As I said, the Rioters were all men and all mad, the Demonstrators about half and half, and more surprised than anything else. In only a minute or so, more than a few found themselves on the ground.

Then Mrs. Landis got bumped from behind. She went darting forward, tripped over somebody else's leg, and then fell hard. That was when Harry came flying into the picture, and I do mean flying. I first saw him as a streak. He tackled the guy who knocked his mother down. He had him from behind around the neck and was not about to let go.

The Chief and his men caught up to the action.

Understand, all of that last part probably wasn't more than three minutes from beginning to end, so apart from Harry who'd been by himself and closer to what was going on than the rest of us, no one had thought to do anything to help out the demonstrators. By the time the group I'd been with started to move forward, the police were there. The attackers were too smart to want to keep up the struggle. They split, some carrying captured signs, but most not. They ran in all different directions out of the parking lot — some behind the stores, some across the main road, some I don't know where. They'd obviously parked their cars in different locations just in case. The only one who didn't get away was the one Harry tackled. They were both down in a heap, Harry still on his back, still with his arms wrapped around the guy's neck. Two of the policemen pulled Harry off and a third grabbed the man, who was by then having more than a little trouble getting enough air.

The rest of what happened was just sad. Chief Rossi was completely out of patience and not about to listen to excuses or explanations. He arrested all of the Demonstrators who had been attacked, the man Harry tackled, and Harry as well, probably because he didn't let go of the man's neck when they asked him to. Once the chief had all those evil doers on the bus, he used his megaphone to read them their rights.

The police wouldn't let Kathryn and me come with our parents so we had to get rides on our own which didn't turn out to be a problem. The Shortlidges, an older couple who live on our street, happened to have been shopping when all this mess took place. They saw it all, including Kathryn and me being left behind. Mr. Shortlidge came up and offered both of us a ride. We asked him to take us to the police station, but he insisted that wouldn't be a good idea. No matter what, we couldn't change his mind.

Mr. Shortlidge motioned toward where he had his car parked, and we all walked over to it. After he had unlocked the doors, Kathryn and I got in the back. Before he started the car, Mr. Shortlidge put his arm across the back of the front seat and leaned around to face us. "You'll need to give me directions to your house, young lady."

"Oh, no thanks, Mr. Shortlidge. That's very kind of you, but I'll just wait for my parents at Brian's house."

"It's no trouble, my dear, no trouble at all," Mrs. Shortlidge said. "We really don't mind one little bit."

"I appreciate it, Mrs. Shortlidge, I really do, but I really think I'd rather not be at home alone just now."

"We quite understand." Mr. Shortlidge started the car, backed out of the parking space, and headed for the entrance to the plaza. Just as we got there, the light changed from green to yellow. Mr. Shortlidge stopped even though I'm pretty sure he could have made it, but if he had, I probably would have missed seeing Broom and Melinda.

Mrs. Shortlidge definitely lives up to the first part of her name so I had no trouble seeing over her head and out the front window. I wasn't really looking at anything in particular, just sort of gazing around. Without knowing why, I found myself doing this really abrupt double-take. Then I looked back, and I knew why.

I took a hold of Kathryn's elbow. At first I was just going to lean over and whisper, but I didn't want the Shortlidges to think I was saying something about them. They were pretty much talking to each other about the afternoon's events. I said to Kathryn in a low voice, "Look who's standing in front of Iggy's Pizza."

Kathryn leaned up and over toward me so she could see between the Shortlidges, then her mouth dropped open. "I cannot believe it! You think they've been here the whole time?"

"That's a pretty good guess," I said.

Twenty minutes later, Kathryn and I were back at my house, sitting in front of the TV, looking at but not watching some basketball or football game or something. Neither one of us was up for talking much. Kathryn fell asleep. I just stayed looking at the TV. Three hours later, just before six o'clock, the officers of KOSFOD, their special advisor, and Harry pulled into our driveway. Dad's lawyer, Mr. Baird, who turned out to be the man I didn't know when I got home the night before, had gotten everyone released "on their own recognizance," except for Harry. He had to wait for his parents, then he was released into their custody. Mr. Baird then drove the miscreants back to Walmart so they could pick up their cars. There they all decided they needed a drink so they came back to our house.

Kathryn and I met them in the kitchen. While Dad and Mom were getting ice and glasses and soda and whatever, they gave us the final piece of good news. "Just in case," Mr. Landis said to us, "you were perhaps under the impression that this day might have a silver lining? The man whose head Harry tried to twist off was Mr. Huggar, Broom's father."

Harry blushed and smiled a little. I smiled back. No matter what Mr. Landis thought, as far as Harry and I were concerned, that part definitely was a silver lining.

20
Hey, Hey.
Ho, Ho.

To tell about Monday – I mean the part I *need* to tell about – I have to tell about everything that happened earlier that day. My freshman English teacher, Mr. Luke, was completely strict about "the five paragraph essay." As far as he was concerned, if you couldn't write a good five paragraph essay, you probably wouldn't get into any college, never mind a college of your choice. And if your first paragraph didn't have "direction steps," your paper was doomed. So here are the direction steps about Monday: Jimmy came back to school, Melinda completely sold out, Broom finally learned that Harry doesn't lie.

The details are easy enough, and I'll get to those, but I need to say something to get you ready to hear about that day. You see, when Monday was finally over, we all knew something important, something big had happened to make us different. We had changed or been changed, and maybe those changes were going to last forever. Looking back, of course, I can see how everything had been in the works, so to speak, all along; I know it didn't all just suddenly happen on Monday, but Monday definitely nailed everything down.

Ever since I can remember I've wanted to be bigger, which I guess really means older. One of the reasons my sister turned out to be such a good athlete is that my father played games with her since she could first walk. I can remember seeing them hitting a field hockey ball back and forth, shooting baskets, or even just working outside with hedge clippers and things like that. I always wanted to join in or help, and, of course, they both would say I was too little, that I'd have to be bigger to use these tools or play field hockey or basketball or to shoot a rifle or to go trout fishing (yes, Beth *does* do all that stuff, and really well, too). Even shoveling snow and raking leaves were activities I would have to be bigger to do. Mom remembered the phrase I invented to explain all the things I would accomplish later in life. If I was riding in the car with her, I'd say, "When I'm biggerto, *I* could drive." Or as she prepared dinner, "I could cut the bread when I'm biggerto."

Dad's parents used to insist that their children come home for long visits twice a year, on the Fourth of July, then again at Thanksgiving. They still lived where my father and his five brothers and one sister grew up. Needless to say, the house was big. I enjoyed those visits a lot because there were all these places for my cousins and me to play. The Gramps (our name for our grandparents) had a pool, a big, old fashioned one with a deep end that was really deep so you could dive off the board and not even come close to hitting the bottom. And there was a bathing cabin for changing your clothes, with a side for girls and another for boys. Of course, the pool was empty in November, and we weren't allowed to go into it even though it looked like it would be fun, and once or twice we actually did climb down a ladder into the deep end just to see how it felt to do that; but the bathing cabin was always open even in the winter. There was also the garage that was a separate building and was big enough to hold five cars. The garage had a full attic that the Gramps turned into a playroom for all of us cousins. It was full of things like tables and chairs and games — board games, a Ping-Pong table, cards, and stuff like that — but the best part was just that we could go up there and be alone. There was a phone that only worked between the Gramps' house and the garage attic. Whenever we went in there, we had to call up and say we were there, and also we called when we left.

Out in back of their house were acres and acres of woods. The summer when I was five, my father and my Uncle Reid built us all a fort out of trees they cut down themselves. It wasn't a tree fort; it was a real fort like in the old Western movies with John Wayne. It had a gate and a little sort of cabin inside. Before we got too old, we'd play games of being mountain men or African explorers or spies. (You can probably guess what summer that was. Most often, Harry would come with us on July Fourth.)

As much fun as we would almost always have playing during the day, I also liked the end of those days, before and after the grownup dinner. We kids all ate early, around six o'clock. At that time we were supposed to stay away from the grownups until after they had their meal. Somehow or other I mostly managed to end up in the living room with my grandparents, parents, and uncles and aunts while they had cocktails. I sat on one of those wooden chairs that are mostly for decoration and listened to them talk; and all the while I would think that if I could have a wish, I'd wish to be like them, right away. They were always having such a good time. They were always so interested in what each other was talking about. They were so relaxed and sure of themselves. They were so grownup.

Anyway, that's my long way of getting around to saying that after Monday was over, I felt different but I couldn't describe it, even to myself. That night, the second time I woke up and had trouble getting back to sleep, I figured it out. I was feeling grownup, except that now I didn't much like it. Grown-up certainly didn't feel the way I wanted it to back when I was little. I wasn't having a good time; I didn't want to talk about anything; I didn't even want to think about anything, and I had no idea why anything was the way it was.

As I mentioned before, Dr. Frank sent that letter home to every family of every student at Afton High School. Unfortunately, it didn't seem to do much good. Even before I got close to school at 7:30 Monday morning, I could tell something was happening. Traffic was backed up all the way to the stop light at the intersection of Cranmer Drive and West Afton Road, about a half mile from the high school. That just doesn't happen on West Afton Road.

As soon as I could get across the intersection — not too hard to do with all that traffic going nowhere — I started jogging. I would have run, but I was wearing my backpack with most of my books which I usually take home over weekends. I was close enough to the school in about five minutes to see what was going on. Essentially, the "bad guys" from the day before — the OBBOYS — were the ones causing the problem. Everyone I had seen on Friday was there on Monday, plus some others. This time they had their own signs which mostly they had painted over the ones they bagged from KOSFOD the other day.

Chief Rossi was back with his megaphone and eight of his officers, but this time he'd been joined by an equal number of state police. The combined force was keeping the demonstrators across the road away from the entrance to the high school. I don't know why they were allowed to be holding their demonstration while we had gotten in trouble for ours. Maybe they were on private property and could do what they wanted, or had even gotten a permit somehow. All I can tell you is they were there, and nobody was trying to make them go away.

Every passing car slowed way down to see what was happening. What was holding up the traffic, though, was the police were stopping each car trying to turn in to the school. It was checked to make sure whoever was in it really belonged at Afton High. People like me who walked to school were also being checked. One Afton policeman was checking the occupants of the cars against a master list he had on a clip board. The list covered three pages. The state trooper checking pedestrians, who happened to be a woman, had her own copy of the list. That's the way she put it: "All pedestrians please line up along the fence over here." I got into the pedestrian line, but I kept moving backward so I could stay out there and watch what was going on. Every now and then the officers checking cars would call another one over, and then they'd have to hold up traffic even more so the car that had pulled up to the gate could back up. That was quite the trick since only one lane of cars was able to move by the school in the first place. Whenever Officer Penney — I managed to get a clear look at his nameplate — found a car that didn't have anyone with a legitimate reason for wanting to enter the high school grounds, he was highly annoyed.

Once I saw what was going on, I more or less expected to see Broom and Carl and Jeff over on the other side of the road with their parents – Mr. Huggar, complete with neck brace, was carrying the ROSEN GO HOME sign – but they weren't there.

Then while I watched, I saw Broom's car, packed with Broomettes, move up in the line of cars blinking to turn into the high school. That really confused me. I figured Broom was going to use all this as an excuse for having an extralong weekend. More than that, if I were one of those parents, and I really believed someone with AIDS might somehow infect my children, I wouldn't let my kids go to school.

When Broom got up to Officer Penney, everyone in the car gave his name. Officer Penney checked them off his list, and Broom was waved through the gate. That's when I decided to stop watching and go on through myself. Trooper Childs found my name without any trouble, and she gave me a smile when I thanked her for letting me through.

Afton High School was not a relaxed place to be that morning. For one thing, every single teacher, or so it seemed, was already at school. That was pretty unusual since school didn't officially start until 7:45, and you could always see at least one or two teachers driving in either just before or just after that time. Not only were they already there, they were all outside their class rooms, standing around in the halls. Every once in a while, Dr. Frank would walk by, saying hello and smiling when he did, but otherwise looking pretty serious. Mrs. Gerardi was also moving around, but she mostly always did that anyway. Other adults you didn't usually see around first thing in the morning – the guidance counselors, Mr. Maslewski, and three P.E teachers – were circulating in the halls also.

Pretty obviously what everyone was waiting for and what a lot of people were worried about was Jimmy's coming back to school. Miss Berry's room was already open. Harry wasn't there. I actually hadn't really expected he would be. (I didn't know whether we'd have anything to say to each other, but I was going to give it a try. Maybe the demonstration and his being arrested would give us something to talk about that wasn't Jimmy.) I left my backpack on the seat of my desk and went out to find Kathryn. That wasn't so easy to do. She wasn't in her homeroom, and she wasn't in the halls — at least I didn't see her. A girl I asked said she was in the cafeteria, but she wasn't.

On my way back from the cafeteria, while I was passing the offices, I heard my name. I looked over to my right and saw Kathryn sitting in the same office Miss Berry had taken me and Harry and Kathryn in that day the week before. I crossed the hall and stepped in. Melinda was sitting in the chair behind the desk. She was looking fed up.

Kathryn didn't say hello or anything like that. She just said, "Melinda thinks the people who want to keep Jimmy out of school are right."

Melinda didn't say anything. Kathryn went on. "Tell Brian what you told me a few minutes ago, Melinda."

"When?" Melinda said in a voice half-whiny and half-annoyed."

"Don't, Mel!" Kathryn snapped at her. "A few minutes ago in Mr. Krupa's room."

Melinda didn't say anything so Kathryn went on. "A few minutes ago in front of at least a dozen other kids, Melinda told me if I was ever around Jimmy again, I should be very careful because you can 'catch' AIDS just by touching someone who has it, especially around the fingernails. I'll bet you didn't know that, did you, Brian?" Kathryn never once took her eyes off Melinda.

"Actually no," I said.

"Actually, I'll bet even Miss Berry didn't know." That Kathryn said right to me, then she turned back to Melinda. "Should I tell Brian precisely how you 'catch' AIDS from someone, Melinda, or would you like to?"

Melinda was clearly angry. "All right!" she spit out. She faced me. "It comes out on your fingernails!"

I couldn't catch up to that statement no matter how hard I tried. "Say again?" I said.

I almost didn't recognize Melinda from the way she was looking at me. She narrowed her eyes and made a tight, nasty little smile that you'd expect to see on somebody's face who just heard about her worst enemy drowning in a storm gutter. "Look at your hands," she said like she was finally proving a point we'd been arguing about for hours. I did what she said, but she could tell I didn't see what I was supposed to. "See how your fingernails grow like from inside your skin. That's where the AIDS germs are. If you have it, the germs are all over your fingers, and anything you touch or anybody is going to totally have the germs all over them, too." She leaned back. She looked like she was going to add, "See, smarty pants!" but she said nothing more.

"Tell him the rest," Kathryn said. I had a hard time imagining what more there could be.

"That's all," Melinda said. I don't think Kathryn had ever been really angry at Melinda before. I don't think Melinda even knew Kathryn could be angry the way she was. For sure, I didn't.

"That's not what you said in homeroom," Kathryn said. Then she turned to me. She exaggerated every word the way people do when they talk to very little children, except she was not being nice. "Brian, do you know why you or I or Miss Berry never knew how easy it is to catch AIDS before now?"

She was not in a good mood. I answered her very straight. "No, Kathryn, I don't," I said.

"Do you want to know why you didn't know that, Brian?"

"Yes, Kathryn, I do."

"Well, Brian, you may find this hard to believe, but Melinda swears it's the truth: The reason almost no one knows how easy it is to catch AIDS is that it's a plot, a conspiracy, a cover up, between our government and – are you ready? – *Africa*. And do you know how it started? Africa has too little food, but lots of uranium. We have too much food, but not nearly enough uranium."

She turned to Melinda abruptly. "You just jump in here any place at all if I get anything wrong."

She turned back to me. "So Africa set up this deal with our government. *Our* country has too many people, right? So Africa sent some AIDS virus here to kill off a few million people. In exchange, *we* send them the extra food we won't be needing anymore, and then they send us their extra uranium. Neat, hunh?"

As Huck Finn used to say, that was too many for me. "You're not serious?" I said to Melinda.

"It's *true*. Why won't anybody *believe* that? Haven't you ever heard of coverups before? What about when they covered up about the Twin Towers? The government cover-ups things all the time. *Everybody* knows that."

"Who told you about *this* cover-up?" I asked.

"Never mind. What *difference* does it make?"

Kathryn stood up and moved to the door. She looked out in the hall, leaned back in the office and shut the door. She twisted the little button in the door handle to lock it.

"What are you *doing*?" Melinda didn't like the looks of what was happening, whatever that was. I wasn't sure I knew what Kathryn was up to either. "It's almost homeroom," Melinda whined.

"Melinda," Kathryn said, "you are not leaving here – none of us are leaving here – until you tell me where you got this story. And don't tell me your parents, 'cause I won't believe it."

Melinda thought that over for about nine seconds. She had been friends with Kathryn for a long time. She knew Kathryn never said anything she didn't mean. "Broom," Melinda said. Both Kathryn and I reacted with groans and grimaces. "He's not as dumb as you think, you know. He read it in a newspaper."

Kathryn said, "Nobody ever accused Broom of being dumb. In fact, I'm sure he's pretty clever. But he is also pond scum, and you ought to know that, Melinda." Kathryn reached for the door knob, twisted it and started to pull open. Melinda stood up and moved toward me. Although she didn't smoke herself, she reeked of cigarettes.

"That *was* you with Broom yesterday, over at Walmart," I said. She didn't say anything at all. Her face was a total blank. "Are you and Broom going out?" Melinda didn't answer. "What are you doing with Broom?"

"I like him," Melinda said, her face still empty.

"Why?" I asked. Kathryn opened the door and moved out of the way. I was pressed up against the wall so Melinda could slide by. She stopped right in front of me. "When I found out how much we had in common," she said.

"Like what?" Kathryn wanted to know.

"Like I hate fags as much as Broom does."

"How many gay people have you ever known?" Kathryn asked.

Melinda was still right in front of me, but she had turned toward Kathryn. "Maybe none."

She turned to look at me. "Maybe one or two. Or three."

Then she left.

Kathryn was very quiet for a minute or so. Her eyes were red and full of tears, but she wouldn't cry. She snatched a tissue from the box on the desk and blotted her eyes. She said, "I think I'm going to go find Mrs. Gerardi. Maybe you better see if you can find out whether Harry and Jimmy are here yet."

I said I'd do that. We walked down to the academic wing together. Then Kathryn went upstairs to the second floor while I continued straight on. Our homeroom was on the first floor.

Almost all of the kids who belonged in our homeroom were there as well as the usual three or four others who hung out with their friends before the first bell rang, but not Harry. I asked if anyone had seen him, and, of course, no one had. I was about to head out into the hall again when the bell rang and Miss Berry rushed through the door. "Okay, gang, you need to grab a seat. We have to get started." So that was that. I hoped Kathryn's search was more successful than mine.

Miss Berry took attendance. She told us about a couple of items we might be interested in that were on the morning bulletin. Then Dr. Frank came on the public address system.

"Good morning. I'd like to say a couple of things to you this morning. I would have preferred meeting with you all together in the auditorium, but the faculty and I also feel that we don't want to disrupt this day anymore than can be helped.

"First, as we are all aware, a demonstration is taking place on the other side of West Afton Road, directly across from our high school. Those demonstrators have the right to express their opinions, but they do not have the right to disrupt the process of education that goes on here. Consequently, I am asking you to pay as little attention to them as you possibly can for as long as they remain. I know that among the group of demonstrators are some of your parents and other relatives. I appreciate the awkward position that puts you in, but I believe your first responsibility while you are here needs to be to your own education and the education of your school mates. I ask that you keep first things first in your minds, especially today.

"Second, I'd like to welcome Jimmy Rosen back to school. As you know, Jimmy was out last week as the result of receiving a severe concussion here at school. While Jimmy is not entirely recovered, he has decided to return specifically to benefit from this week of review for first semester final exams.

I expect you will all welcome Jimmy back as the opportunity presents itself to you and offer whatever assistance might be appropriate.

"Thank you, and have a good morning."

21
Bat Boy In The Boys' Room

Jimmy and Harry got to school together without anyone knowing about it or seeing them because Mr. Peters, the drama teacher, gave them a ride in his van which isn't really designed for passengers. It used to be a delivery van and belonged to an older guy Mr. Peters had breakfast with every day who owned a dry cleaning store but then had a heart attack. At first he tried to sell his business, but nobody wanted to buy it, not even his son. So he had to sell all his equipment, and Mr. Peters bought the van for practically nothing. He renovated it into this really cool camper.

Toward the rear along the right side he'd put in a bed, and, believe it or not, at the foot of the bed a small wood stove for heating and cooking. Just behind the driver's and passenger's seats was a small table with two chairs; across from the bed was a chest of drawers which I think Mr. Peters said he'd built himself. There was a battery powered lamp on the wall by the bed, another on the table, and a third on the chest. Above the table on a special shelf, Mr. Peters had a dock for his iPod and in the corner behind the driver's seat a small refrigerator. The whole inside was lined with cork and the floor was covered with carpet remnants. The important part as far as Jimmy and Harry were concerned was that the van had no windows on the sides so no one saw they were riding with Mr. Peters.

When the bell rang to end homeroom, which is the same thing as the warning bell for first period, Jimmy and Harry were already standing by the lockers outside Jimmy's first period class. Nobody was really aware of them. When that bell rings, you tend to leave homeroom pretty quickly, not so much from not being able to wait to get to class as from wanting to be able to spend more time out in the hall before class starts.

As soon as the homeroom kids were gone, Jimmy and Harry entered. Jimmy sat right up in front but away from the door, and Harry stayed with him until the bell to begin the period, then Harry went to his own class. All of this maneuvering had been worked out beforehand with Jimmy, Harry, Harry's parents, the Rosens, Dr. Frank, and Mrs. Gerardi. Mrs. Gerardi made out a pass for Harry that excused him from being late to every class that day and got him out of class two minutes early.

The system worked well. With his full day, good for any occasion pass, Harry was ready, right outside Jimmy's classroom, when the bell rang. They'd wait behind to let the main rush die down a little, then Harry would go with Jimmy to his next class. That's usually not very far since most classes are held in the academic wing. Even art wasn't much of a problem since the art rooms are down toward the offices. But the P.E classes are in the gym, close to the cafeteria. Probably the system would have worked completely if it hadn't been for the P.E. classes. And, of course, Melinda.

Jimmy had P.E. fourth period while Harry had science. At the start, everything worked the way it was supposed to. Harry came down to the gym with Jimmy, waited around for Mr. Francis, and then went on back to the academic wing.

In case you thought different, Jimmy did not participate in P.E. even before the whole snake thing. When the classes were like a lecture about STDs or Drugs & Alcohol, he did participate in that, but most of the time P.E. is one sport or another. Jimmy didn't do sports. On those days, he sat in the bleachers and studied. So in theory, he was going to be as safe at P.E. as he would have been in Geometry. But you know the problem with theories, right? There are pretty much always situations theories don't cover.

Evidently, about ten minutes before the end of the period, Melinda came into the gym and walked over to Mr. Francis. In the winter, P.E. is mostly either basketball or volleyball. That day it was volleyball. Mr. Francis was acting as referee. That meant he was standing up on a ladder by the net, calling balls in or out, keeping the score, and keeping track of which team was supposed to be serving. Melinda asked him something, and he nodded yes and sort of gestured toward Jimmy sitting behind him in the bleachers. The kids playing volleyball thought he was indicating a change in serve so some of them started screaming he'd made a mistake while the others cheered because they thought he'd given them a break. Mr. Francis had to strain to get that all straightened out. The next time he looked, Jimmy was gone. That didn't concern him because Melinda had said she had a message for Jimmy, so naturally Mr. Francis thought he'd gone with Melinda. Which turned out to be true, but not in the way Mr. Francis thought.

Fifth period, as I'm sure I mentioned before, is when kids begin to eat lunch. Kathryn and I were some of the first ones in the cafeteria. We'd decided to go to our usual table and save places for Jimmy and Harry, just in case. We weren't sure they'd want to be eating with us or even if they'd be eating in the cafeteria at all, but we figured that was at least something we could do. We'd only just sat down when Harry appeared in front of us. "Okay," he said, "so what happened?"

I looked at Kathryn to see if she knew what Harry was talking about. She didn't. "What happened about what?" I said and then, "Where's Jimmy?"

"That's what you're supposed to know. Melinda was waiting for me when I came out of class. She said Jimmy'd gone home, and you guys knew all about it."

Harry knew right away something was wrong. "What's the matter?" he wanted to know. "Why are you looking so scared?"

We looked at each other. "You never saw him, right? Me, either," I said.

"What's going on?"

Kathryn was actually pale. "Harry, I forgot to tell you something about Melinda. She's convinced Jimmy has AIDS, and that anyone can catch AIDS just by touching him."

"No way!" Harry said, but then he realized. "Broom, right?"

We nodded. Harry stared at the table in front of him, then his head snapped up. "Shit!" he said. He turned away and headed for the door. A second later Kathryn and I figured out what he meant. We left and hurried to catch up with him.

Harry was standing outside the cafeteria, looking down toward the offices and the academic wing, then turning and looking to his left toward the stairway to the locker rooms, then down the other way where the music rooms and side door to the auditorium were. He heard us come up to him. "Brian, go down to the classroom wing and check around there. I'll start up at this end. Kathryn, go find Mrs. Gerardi or someone."

We took off at a run. I left Kathryn when she turned into the offices. I went to the upstairs corridor first to check the bathroom. There were still classes going on up there – those kids eat during the second lunch period – and a teacher was on hall duty. I tried just walking past him as if I was supposed to be there, but he asked me if I had a pass. "No, sir, I don't, but this is sort of an emergency situation," I said.

"Just what is the nature of the emergency, Mr. Lister?" he said. I thought of Harry's not liking it when teachers called you by your last name.

"I need to find Jimmy Rosen," I explained, thinking that just about everybody must know about Harry being Jimmy's escort for the day.

"What class is Mr. Rosen in this period?"

"He doesn't have class now," I said, "he eats first lunch."

"Then I suggest you look for him in the cafeteria," the teacher said.

"I was just in the cafeteria. That's why I'm looking down here. He's not in the cafeteria. He's disappeared."

"Why don't you try to find Harry Landis? He's supposed to be baby-sitting Mr. Rosen today, isn't he?"

"Harry sent me down here." I was beginning to feel very frustrated. "Listen, please. Jimmy's disappeared, and we think he's in trouble. Can I please look in the bathroom? Or could you?"

He thought that over for a second or three. His eyes got sort of droopy and he said, "Well, if Mr. Landis sent you down here, then perhaps Mr. Landis can give you a good-for-whatever-ails-you pass as well. Why don't you return to Mr. Landis and see if he can arrange that?" Which just goes to prove that kids don't have a monopoly on being the only jerks in the world.

I gave up and went down to the first floor. Since there were no classes going on, nobody much cared whether kids went in that corridor or not. As soon as I got within a few feet of the bathroom, I knew they were in there. I should have thought of checking downstairs first. Obviously they wouldn't be anywhere within hearing of a teacher, no matter what sort of fool that teacher was. I was about to turn around to go get Harry when I heard a funny sound. It wasn't exactly a scream; it was too low and in a way too quiet, but for sure the sound meant someone was in trouble, more than likely Jimmy. And before you think it: no, I don't know why I didn't think to use my cell, but, yes, I definitely should have.

I had no idea what I was going to do. I just pushed open the door being as noisy as I could. I was aware of some guys down at the end of the bathroom where I was, but it was only Broom I really saw. He was standing in the entrance of the last stall farthest. What I could see at first was his back, but even in that first moment, there was something about the way he was holding himself, sort of hunched over, that made me not pay attention to anyone else. Right away, my stomach started knotting. The door banging open startled him, and he half turned toward me. Then I could see more.

Jimmy was down on his knees. Broom was holding on to his ears, holding his head up, and Jimmy was hanging on to Broom's wrists. Broom was wearing rubber gloves, and a surgical mask, but that wasn't the worst part. What Broom was trying to do to Jimmy was the worst. It was the kind of thing a guy would be afraid of having happen to him if he was ever sent to prison. You can imagine it, I'm sure.

When Broom saw who was at the door, he smiled behind the mask. "Hi, BriANN. I'll be with you shortly. You can stay and watch, though." I was so stunned by what I was seeing I didn't move fast enough. When I finally went to turn around, Carl and Jeff grabbed me, one by each arm. They yanked me farther into the bathroom. A third guy – I didn't' know him – stepped up behind me and hooked me around the neck with his right arm. Then he shoved his left fist into the small of my back, in a way forcing me in two directions at once, forwards and backwards.

That's when I got my best look at Jimmy. Except for some red and puffy patches on his cheeks where I guess Broom or someone had slapped him, he was actually less than white. His skin looked as though you could see through it down into the veins and muscles and bones. His eyes were darting all around the room, looking for something safe or hopeful, I guess. Then he looked at me. From then until the moment his eyes closed, he never looked away. Jimmy was making that sound again, louder and thinner than a moan, but not loud or strong enough to be a scream – maybe mewling is the right word.

Once Broom saw I wasn't going to cause him any trouble, he turned back to Jimmy. "Come on, sweetheart," he said, "be a good little girlyboy. You're going to like me much better than Harry, I just know you will. You don't mind the rubber, do you? Anyway, you shouldn't. Safe sex, you know. Come on, now, or Daddy Broom will have to get rough again." All this time Broom was trying to maneuver Jimmy's head so that he could get at him. Obviously Jimmy was keeping his mouth shut as tightly as he could.

Broom started to get red in the face. Suddenly he let go of Jimmy's left ear and slapped him across the face. He hit Jimmy very hard and would have knocked his head into the side of the stall except that he was still holding him up with his left hand. Jimmy's mouth slackened open for a second and Broom thrust at him, but Jimmy closed up again too quickly.

"You're not being very nice, Jimmy-wimmy," Broom said, kind of through his teeth. Then this sort of sick-happy look spread around his face. "Ooh. I have an idea! Let's see how long you can hold your breath?" With that, Broom reached around behind Jimmy with his right hand and cupped the back of his head. Then he moved his left hand to hold Jimmy's nose closed. Almost immediately Jimmy tried to pull his head away, but he just couldn't. He wouldn't have had the strength anyway, even if nothing else had happened at all. The panic in Jimmy's eyes got bigger and bigger and crazier. He was still looking directly at me; his eyes started to bulge out. He was trying as hard as he could not to breathe. I made a try at jerking away from the guys holding me, but the one at my neck just squeezed and pushed harder. Jimmy only managed to hold his breath a second or two more anyway. When his mouth opened and he sucked in, the noise was like when you let air out of a balloon really slowly — a high squeaky squeal. Before Jimmy could get even a part of the air he needed, Broom got to do what he'd been trying to do all along.

Right away Jimmy's body began to jerk. I thought he was trying to pull himself away, but it wasn't that. He wasn't making his body jerk; it was doing it all by itself. Then there were gagging noises, and about three seconds later, Jimmy was throwing up. The vomit erupted from his mouth and spewed all over Broom's crotch – into his pants I'm fairly sure, and all down the front and over his boots.

"You slimy little faggot!" Broom yelled. "Look what you've done to me, you scum bag." Holding Jimmy up with his left hand, Broom drew back his right, made a fist, and then hit Jimmy exactly in the middle of his forehead. That's when Jimmy closed his eyes. That's also when the bathroom door slammed open.

I knew Harry was there. He didn't say anything, but he didn't need to. Something just changed suddenly, and I knew what had changed it. About a nano-second later, the guy who'd been holding me around the neck said, "Ooomph!" and let me go. He faded down onto the bathroom floor making that terrible sound people do when they have no breath and can't make their bodies breathe.

I jerked my arms backwards, and Carl and Jeff let me go. All three of us turned toward Harry. He was standing beside the crumpled up kid, holding his baseball bat. He hadn't brought it along just to look tough. Harry was mad. He'd already used the bat once, and it was pretty clear to me, anyway, that he was looking forward to using it some more. I stepped to my left. The other two moved away toward Broom who was not looking happy.

"Excellent. Couldn't be better. Couldn't have hoped for more. I'm gonna remember this, Broom," Harry said. "Rubber gloves, mask, slimy crotch, and a limp rubber sticking out your fly." Broom started to say something, but Harry took about a half step toward him and went right on. "And you're going to remember, too, Broom, because you are in some deep shit now."

Broom attempted a recovery. He worked at putting himself back in his pants, but the rubber gloves made that operation a little too hard to manage. Nevertheless, he tried to sound like he was still in charge. "And just what do you think you're going to do with your little toy bat, Har?"

Harry didn't miss a beat. If he was worried about Broom at all, nobody would ever have known it. He said, "Make you cry, Broom, if you're lucky." Harry stepped toward him. As he did, he swung the bat against the first stall door he could reach. You could hear the bat moving though the air in the bathroom. When it hit the door the noise was dull and somehow worse than if it had been very loud. The door slammed back against the side of the stall, then rebounded forward again with just about as much force. It flapped back and forth a couple of more times before swinging to a stop. The door was dented and one of the hinges had pulled away from the frame. "What do you think of that, Broom? You're next."

Despite himself, Broom had winced. He looked over at Carl and Jeff. "Let's take this asshole," Broom said to them.

"Let's not!" Harry said. He took another step forward, reversed his hands on the bat and this time swung it against the mirrors above the sinks just in front of where the other two were standing. This time the noise was kind of tinny, but the effect was just as stunning. Shards of shattered mirror sprayed the room, flying mostly away from Harry and me. Broom's friends cowered backwards, into the farthest corner away from Harry. Broom covered his eyes and tried to move toward them, but Harry cut him off with another swing of the bat at another stall door only one removed from where Broom had been assaulting Jimmy. Now Harry was within easy reach of Broom.

Broom was suddenly a different person. He was frightened. I don't think he'd ever been made to feel that way before, at least not like this, not because of another kid. He was looking at someone he thought he knew all about, but, surprise!

This Harry wasn't one Broom had seen before. In fact, I'd never seen this Harry before, and even though I was on his side, rooting for him to win, I knew I didn't want to know him well. At that moment, Harry didn't care about anybody: not himself, me, or Jimmy lying crumpled next to the toilet in back of Broom. All this guy wanted was to hurt Broom as badly as he could.

Harry turned his shoulders to his right and lifted the bat up as though he were facing a pitcher. He shifted his feet, squaring them to give himself the best angle on Broom. Broom tried to move left and then right so as to weaken Harry's position, but each time he did, Harry would just close in a couple of inches more until Broom's angles of possible retreat were entirely eliminated. For a second or two, all movement stopped, then Harry dipped the bat down toward his hips, stepped forward with his left leg, and swung at Broom from the waist.

As soon as Harry started his swing, Broom dropped to the floor. I don't think the bat hit him, but Broom's head and shoulder and the bat were passing through the same space at just about the same time so I don't absolutely know. Broom hit the floor just as the bat hit the frame of the stall in back of him.

Now Broom was lying on the floor in front of the stall. He had his hands over his head, pulling his chin down toward his chest. He was clearly expecting Harry to keep swinging the bat at him, but that's not what happened. Harry had pulled the bat back so he could swing it, but he didn't. Nobody moved; nobody said anything, but you could hear Harry breathing, long, slow, and very loud.

Broom must have decided it was finally safe for him to try to move. His hands slipped away from his head and down to the floor. Pressing his palms down, Broom started to raise himself up. "Not a good idea," Harry said, and he swung the bat again, right at where Broom's head would have been if he'd kept on raising it.

Broom dropped down as flat as he could get, but his body angle had changed. This time he went down on his back. The bat swung just inches above his nose and crashed once again into the stall frame. Harry pulled the bat back again right away. He leaned over and shoved the bat forward so it was right in front of Broom's eyes. There were two deep v-shaped dents in it. "If I'd hit you, Broom, my bat wouldn't be dented now. Who's going to get me a new bat, Broom? You? Are you going to take responsibility for the damage to this bat?"

Broom was convinced Harry had gone crazy; he might have been right. Broom stared at the bat, and Harry held it still for him so he could get a good look. Just about then, Carl and Jeff started to slide along the edges of the sinks toward the door. I know Harry didn't see them, but he sure must have heard them. Without looking in their direction, he stepped to his left and swung the bat across his body. Smash! Right in front of Jeff's nose! Another mirror shattered and flew across the bathroom.

Broom thought Harry was distracted. As soon as Harry looked away, Broom started to push himself with his feet away from Harry and toward me and the door. He kept his eyes fastened on Harry's bat.

Harry heard him and turned back. He stepped over him, straddling Broom as he moved backwards. "What do you think you're doing, Broom? Where do you think you're going? I'm not done with you yet. Stop!"

And Broom didn't stop. In fact, he didn't even pause. He just kept slowly sliding himself over the tile floor, not moving fast at all, but moving steadily nevertheless.

"Broom," Harry said, raising the bat up in the air as you would an axe if you were going to split wood, "I'm not going to tell you again."

But Broom didn't stop.

So Harry swung the bat.

I was so sure Broom was about to die. It looked to me as though Harry's blow would bring the bat right down in the middle of Broom's forehead, but instead it hit the floor to the left of his head. He hit the tiles so hard they shattered. Some of the fragments sprayed Broom's face; a couple thin lines of blood trickled down his cheek. Whether it was seeing the blood or something else I don't know, but Harry went berserk. He started chopping with the bat up and down and up and down, all around Broom's body, not ever actually hitting him, but not missing him by much either.

He had the bat in a choked up grip. He'd make a short swing up, then down, just missing Broom's elbow. Short swing up, then down toward his head again. Short swing up, then down between his legs. Short swing up, then down by a knee. Harry kept shifting his position so he could swing at another part of Broom's body. The smartest thing Broom did was try not to move. If he had, I'm sure Harry would have hit him, and Harry was swinging so hard, Broom would have been badly, badly hurt. I don't know when Broom closed his eyes, but it must have been almost right away. What else could he do but close his eyes and wait?

Then abruptly Harry stopped and I could see why.

Broom was crying. No, not crying. He was sobbing like a little kid out of control.

Harry stepped away from him and Broom just curled up in a ball. He looked down at him, then raised the bat once more, high over his head. He just stood there looking at Broom. Broom realized the blows had stopped. He uncurled enough to raise his head. He looked up at Harry's face and the bat.

"No," Broom cried. "No more, no more, please no more. Please, pleasepleaseplease no more!"

Harry looked down at Broom. His mouth was tight and his upper lip was shaking. A noise started to come out of him, not because he wanted it too but because he couldn't help it. His hands tightened on the bat. When Broom saw that he must have thought he was dead. He turned his face to his left and lowered his hands so they were on each side of his head, palms facing up. He just blubbered. Harry lifted the bat even higher, then slowly brought it down by his side. He leaned over, way down so his face was just inches away from Broom's right ear.

"I never break a promise, Broom. Never!"

Harry didn't move. He stared at Broom, didn't make a sound, seemed not to breathe. Then Harry straightened up and stepped away. "You all right?" he said to me. I nodded yes. He handed me the bat and went to see how Jimmy was.

Broom was curled up again. I looked at his two friends. They were standing very still, making no noise, trying to breathe as little as possible. "Why don't you guys get out of here?" I said, but not in a voice I recognized as being very close to my own, "and take him with you." I pointed the bat at the kid on the floor. They helped him to his feet and left.

I stepped around Broom and walked over to the stall where Harry was pulling Jimmy out. His color was mostly blue, and he was still unconscious. I remember thinking that was too bad in a way because Jimmy had missed seeing Broom pay for what he'd done.

Harry got him out and straightened his legs. Then he looked sharply down at Jimmy. "Jesus, Brian, I don't think Jimmy's breathing!" He put his ear down to Jimmy's mouth and evidently couldn't hear anything. "Brian, get the nurse. Quick! Get the nurse!"

I didn't feel too happy about leaving Harry alone in the bathroom with Broom especially when Harry started giving Jimmy mouth-to-mouth. It didn't seem possible for Harry to do that and keep an eye on Broom, too. "Harry, what about?" and I pointed at Broom.

Harry looked up. "Never mind! Go!"

I put Harry's bat down next to him, on the side away from Broom who was still curled up and still basically crying. Then I headed out to find the nurse.

As soon as I got out in the corridor, I saw Kathryn and Miss Berry coming the other way. I ran up to them and told them Jimmy needed the nurse. Miss Berry asked me where Jimmy was. When I told her, she said she'd help Harry. "One of you two go get the nurse; the other go to the office and tell them I said to call an ambulance."

So we did. Kathryn went to the office, and I brought Mrs. Coffman to the bathroom. She told me to stay outside and not let any kids in. Moments later Kathryn returned with Dr. Frank. He nodded to me and went in. Kathryn waited outside with me.

A few minutes later, Officer Penney and Trooper Childs came down the hall. By that time quite a few kids were standing around asking me and Kathryn what had happened. The boys wanted to know why they couldn't go in the bathroom. Trooper Childs went inside and Officer Penney started clearing the hallway. He was pretty nice about it, but he was also obviously not going to let anyone stay around. He just said that an ambulance was on its way and they needed the hall clear to be able to do their job. He asked that we all go on to our next classes or down to the cafeteria.

All the kids did what he asked, except for Kathryn and me. We just stepped over to the classroom across the hall. The door was locked. I don't think there was a scheduled class there that period, but we stood more or less facing the door as though we were waiting for our teacher to arrive. When the hall was cleared, Officer Penney went into the bathroom, too.

The ambulance arrived almost immediately. We could hear the siren first. Then Mrs. Gerardi led the two EMTs through the doors at the end of the hall, the one you're only supposed to use in case of fire. They were wheeling a stretcher which they rolled right into the bathroom. It didn't take more than a minute to do whatever they had to do. Then they were on their way out with Jimmy on the stretcher. He had a mask over his mouth and nose. Harry came out right behind them, then Mrs. Gerardi, Miss Berry, and finally Dr. Frank. Miss Berry saw me and Kathryn and came over to us. The rest followed the EMT guys and Jimmy back out the same set of doors. Broom was with Trooper Childs.

"How's Jimmy?" Kathryn asked.

"Not so good," she said.

"How's Harry?" I said.

"He's not so good either."

*

22
Little, Less, Nothing.

This time Harry got to go in the ambulance. He told the paramedics he was Jimmy's brother, and none of the adults there apparently said anything. Anyway, nobody tried to stop him. After the EMTs wheeled Jimmy out, Harry caught up and walked right beside the stretcher. He looked up at me as they passed, and I knew Miss Berry had been telling the truth. Of course, Jimmy was still unconscious so he didn't know whether Harry was there or not, but Harry definitely needed to be with Jimmy. Then they were all down the hall and through the doors and gone.

After all that, Kathryn and I couldn't even think about staying at school. We asked Miss Berry if she'd give us a pass to go use the phone. Instead, she took us with her down to the offices, found us an unoccupied phone, and hung around while we made our calls home.

My mother was at work, but Mrs. Mullen was home. After I told my mother a really short version of what happened, I asked her if she'd give me permission to leave school. I said I'd probably go over to Kathryn's house, if it was all right with Mrs. Mullen, until dinner time. My mother said that would be okay so I let her tell that to Miss Berry. That made it official. Then Kathryn called her mother. Mrs. Mullen said Kathryn certainly could come home, and I was welcome to come, too. When I got my mother, Miss Berry took the phone again, and fifteen minutes later Kathryn and I were in Mrs. Mullen's car.

We didn't do much of anything for the rest of the day. We studied a little for our exams the next week. We played three games of Parcheesi with Mrs. Mullen who won all three, and then we watched *Cheers* re-runs. Once in the middle of the afternoon we tried to call the hospital to find out how Jimmy was, but except for saying Jimmy was in Intensive Care, they couldn't tell us anything because we weren't family. We called the Rosens, but of course they were at the hospital, and we didn't know their cell number, or even if they had one, come to think of it. We just thought we'd try anyway.

After the second *Cheers*, I got up from the couch I'd been sitting on with Kathryn. I said, "Well, thanks a lot, Mrs. Mullen for letting me spend the afternoon, but I'd better be going."

"Brian," Mrs. Mullen said as she got up from her chair, "wouldn't you like me to drive you? It's really no trouble." I was about to say no, I don't mind the walk, when Mrs. Mullen went on. "Why don't you stay and have dinner with Kathryn and me. Afterwards we can all drive to the hospital to find out about Jimmy. Then I'll drop you off on the way home."

I looked at Kathryn to see what she thought of the idea. "Yeah, do that," she said. "I think that's a good idea."

I called home to see if it was okay. Mom said it would be, but Mrs. Mullen didn't have to drive me home because she and Dad were planning to go to the hospital, too. They said they'd meet us there. They wanted to see how Jimmy was doing.

When that was settled, Mrs. Mullen said to Kathryn, "Would you and Brian mind frozen pizza and salad for dinner. It's just that I forgot to take anything out of the freezer this morning, and if you two don't mind, I really don't much feel like going out again. The market's so crowded at this time of day."

"Fine by me, Mom. Brian?"

"Frozen pizza and salad is my second favorite thing to eat whenever I'm a last minute dinner guest," I said.

"And a gracious one to boot!" Mrs. Mullen smiled. "You, sir, are welcome at the last minute any time."

I would have bet she actually did have something ready to make but only enough for just Kathryn and her. Kathryn volunteered us to make the salad which was fine with me. In spite of everything, or maybe even a little because of it, being with Kathryn was making me feel good.

In a way, I didn't want to be feeling like that because of what had happened at school. I couldn't get scenes from the bathroom out of my head. All afternoon I kept flashing on Jimmy's eyes looking at me while Broom held his ears or had his hand clamped over Jimmy's mouth, and the look on Jimmy's face just before Broom hit him that last time. When I'd do that, my heart would start to beat, I'd feel my teeth clench, and the only thing I could imagine doing that would make me feel better at all was grabbing Broom and hurting him, hurting him as badly as I could. Then that would make me think I should have done something daring or heroic like knocking my head backwards into the guy holding my neck or stomping down on his feet or biting his arm and screaming for help, or really anything at all except what I did.

And each time that happened, Kathryn noticed, and she'd tell me to take it easy or calm down or just not worry; or she'd just touch my arm and say, "It's okay, Brian." I liked the sound of my name when she said it, and I liked how warm I felt when she touched me. Then I'd remember she was actually still Harry's girlfriend, and in a way I'd feel bad at the same time.

I really wanted to say something about the way I was feeling, but I wasn't sure how to start. If I had asked Harry, he'd have said, "Just start. Whatever you say will be good enough for openers." Actually, that might not have been true since I would've been asking him how to open up a more-than-just-friendly conversation with his girlfriend, but I followed the advice anyway.

We were in the kitchen. Kathryn was taking lettuce and cucumbers and carrots and things out of the refrigerator and handing them to me to put on the counter. I took a deep breath and asked, "Are you and Harry still going out?"

I thought the question was going to get a fairly big reaction, but all she did was straighten up, a green pepper in one hand and three radishes in the other. She looked at me while she thought about what I'd asked. She handed me the pepper, then the radishes.

"I don't really know," she said. She turned back toward the refrigerator, looked inside the vegetable drawer for a second, then slid it closed, and swung the refrigerator door shut. She turned back to me and leaned back against the refrigerator, crossing her arms in front of her as she did. "We haven't been anywhere together, just the two of us, or even spent any time alone at all since way before Christmas. And we haven't really even talked since the other day with Miss Berry. So I don't know. But, you know, I don't really think so." That thought obviously made her sad. "I guess we're not, really," she concluded.

I thought she was going to ask me why I had asked, but she didn't, and that was good. I was pretty sure she knew why anyway. She motioned toward the vegetables I'd put on the counter. She pointed toward a magnetized knife rack that was fastened on a cupboard door just above the counter. "You start cutting up the vegetables, and I'll wash the lettuce." She picked up a head of lettuce, took their salad crisper out from a cupboard under the counter, started tearing leaves off and dropping them into the crisper. Without looking at me, she said, "I'm glad you're here, Brian. I feel better with you here. This afternoon would have been a lot harder alone."

"I know," I said. "Me, too."

****

At the hospital after dinner, the man at the desk said Jimmy was still in the ICU. He told us we couldn't visit him there unless we were part of his immediate family, but there was a waiting room on the ICU floor. He gave us special visitors' passes, and we took the elevator up to the eighth floor. The doors opened just in front of the nurses' station. A sign on the wall behind said WAITING ROOM with an arrow pointing to the left. "Yes?" the nurse behind the desk said.

Mrs. Mullen said, "We're here about Jimmy Rosen." She gathered our passes and handed them to the nurse. "Can you tell us how he is?"

"Are you family?" the nurse wanted to know. She was putting the passes in a cubby or someplace just in front of her but out of sight.

"No," Mrs. Mullen said. "Just friends."

"The Rosens are in the waiting room," the nurse said without answering Mrs. Mullen's question. "You may join them."

Each one of us thanked the nurse. She hadn't really done anything, but it was just the kind of situation where you thank people no matter what.

The waiting room was much bigger and nicer looking than I had expected. It was two shades of blue. A dark blue carpet on the floor, and the bottom half of the walls were painted the same color. About three feet up, the blue changed from dark to very light. The chairs and sofas were part wooden and part upholstered, and the upholstered parts were, naturally, blue. The whole waiting room was divided into almost two rooms. In the first, in addition to the chairs and a couple of tables with magazines, there was a television in one corner. Three people we didn't know were sitting over by the TV looking at it, but I don't think really watching.

The people waiting to find out about Jimmy were in the second room. It was marked off by a kind of half-wall with a half-doorway through the middle of it. It was pretty much the same as the outer room except for not having a television. Harry and Mr. and Mrs. Landis and Miss Berry were already there. And, of course, so were the Rosens. They were sitting together in the far left corner. Harry was sitting across from the Rosens. His mother and father and Miss Berry were standing more or less in the middle of the room. Harry looked up as we came in. He gave me a smile, and I smiled back.

Mrs. Mullen and Kathryn went right over to the Rosens. I didn't know whether to go over to Harry or to the Rosens, so I stayed with the others in the middle. Miss Berry reached out and kind of slugged me on the shoulder. "How ya' doing, Bri?"

"Okay, I guess," I said. "What's up?"

"I don't know," she said. "I just don't know."

I thought I'd better go over to the Rosens, so after I said hello to Mr. and Mrs. Landis, I moved over to where Mrs. Mullen and Kathryn were talking to them. As I moved into the group, Mrs. Rosen sort of pulled Kathryn down into the seat next to her. "You're a good girl, my Katty. Good to Jimmy!" and she squeezed both of Kathryn's hands in hers. I had never heard Kathryn called anything else before, not by anyone. I liked the sound of Katty, the way Mrs. Rosen said it.

I stepped forward a little. I wasn't going to say anything. I didn't really know what to do or what to say or how to say it; I just waited until either of the Rosens noticed me. Mr. Rosen looked up at me first. "Brian," he said. "How good you are to come here! Jimmy will be so proud to have so many friends to come help him recover."

"It's good to be here," I said, and immediately thought that if I'd tried, I couldn't have said anything dumber.

"Look, Sarah, Brian is here, too," Mr. Rosen said to his wife.

Mrs. Rosen looked up and smiled at me, and that made me want to cry. She reached out and took my left hand in both of hers. "Yes. Of course Brian's here too! Jimmy has such good friends." She held onto me with her right hand and took Kathryn's hand with her left. "Such good friends," she repeated, squeezing both our hands twice, then letting them go.

My parents walked in just then. I stood up and kissed my mother when she came over to where we were. I started to reach for my father's hand, but he put both his arms around me and gave me a hug. That was just the right thing. My dad had a way of doing that. I hugged him back.

While my parents greeted the Rosens, I looked over at Harry.

He was still all by himself, sitting down, looking up at the rest of the people there, but, like the people in the other part of the waiting room with the TV, not really watching them. I stepped out of the group and walked over. He didn't look at me or say anything so I just sat down in the chair next to him. "What's up?" I asked.

"Too much, man," Harry said. "Too damn much."

"I know what you mean." I didn't know what else to say, so I didn't try. I just sat there doing what Harry was doing, looking at the rest of the people. My parents had drawn chairs over so they could sit facing the Rosens. The Landises and Miss Berry were having their own conversation, still in the middle of the room, and even though the television from the next room wasn't turned up very loud, it added just enough extra so you had trouble understanding what anyone in those other groups was saying. They were talking about something other than Jimmy; I could tell that for sure. My parents are really good when bad things happen. They can get people to think and talk about other things even if they don't want to. My mom can say something funny even about whatever bad thing has happened. She helps you not take the situation so seriously. I knew that was what she was doing now because every now and then I could see the Rosens smile and even give a little laugh.

"Your mom's really great at this stuff," Harry said. "I wish I was."

"Yeah," I said. "She really is," and I turned toward Harry. He didn't look terrific. His eyes were pretty red and looked as though they were sort of trying to disappear into their sockets. His hair looked stringy and pressed down the way hair looks when you first wake up in the morning before you get a chance to brush it or take a shower.

"Are you all right?" I asked. "I mean, about what happened in the bathroom?"

"I don't know. Dr. Frank didn't say anything when he came in. I mean, there wasn't really any time; but he noticed. Anyway, I don't care. I'd do it again only next time Broom wouldn't get off so easy."

That made me remember my last sight of Broom. "Speaking of Broom — do you know what happened to him?"

"No, I don't," Harry said. "Still in there on the floor, blubbering?"

"No, man, he's not. You missed that part. It would have done your heart good." If anything was going to brighten Harry up, I thought this bit of news had the best chance. "Broom is in custody, dude. Those two cops who came into the bathroom took him away just after the EMTs and you guys left."

"No kidding," Harry said, not even close to being pleased. Then he dismissed that part and said, "I wonder how he's going to try to get me back?"

"Harry, I don't think you even need to think about that. You turned Broom into a jellyfish, man. You're like his personal nightmare now." Then I had to laugh. "You've taken care of the whole family. First you clothesline his father and all his friends see him taken down by a kid, then you just about waste Broom. If you want to worry about something, worry about how much it's going to cost you to fix up that bathroom."

Harry laughed a little. He said, "Did you know Broom's old man tried to press charges?"

"No way! For what? Attempted decapitation?"

"No, but probably only because he didn't think of it. For assault and battery or some such thing. He didn't get far, though. Chief Rossi told him, 'Under the circumstances, Mr. Huggar, there really isn't enough evidence to support your claim. And the Afton Police Department is not inclined to view your complaint in a friendly light."

"Let's hear it for the chief!" I said, using a phrase that Harry and I always used to say to each other about things people would do that we approved of.

"Wait! That's not the end of it. Since he can't get me on criminal charges, he's going to sue me. Dad's lawyer says he doesn't have a chance, but he's going to do it anyway."

I started to respond when I saw a doctor dressed in those green suits they wear while they operate coming into the waiting room. She had her mask down around her neck and one of those operating room caps in her left hand. I nudged Harry who was looking at me so didn't know the doctor had come in. She paused in the middle of that half-door way. By that time, everyone had noticed her and all talking stopped. The Rosens and my parents and Kathryn stood. The Landises and Miss Berry turned around. Harry and I stayed where we were. Although the doctor's face was blank, I didn't have a good feeling about what she was going to say.

"Mr. and Mrs. Rosen, " the doctor said, "I'd like..." Then she changed her mind. "Excuse me, may I speak with you a moment. We can use the staff lounge just down the hall."

First Mr. Rosen's face got very flat and gray and old. Mrs. Rosen took a deep breath and seemed to hold it. She looked at Mr. Rosen, took a step or two toward the doctor, but then must have changed her mind. "No," she said. "Here is fine," she said. "All these good people love Jimmy, too."

The doctor didn't feel that was such a great idea, but I think at the same time she understood. She moved across the room to stand directly in front of Jimmy's parents. I guess somehow or other we all must have known what she was going to tell us, but, at least as far as I was concerned, I held on to my hope as long as I could. I couldn't see the doctor's face anymore, but I could hear her much too well. "I'm sorry," she said. "Jimmy's heart was too weak. There was too much damage. We couldn't keep him going any longer."

And there it was. Everyone had nothing to say – or too much to say and no way to say it. The Rosens slumped toward each other. The doctor and my parents seemed to think they were going to faint or something because they all reached out toward them. But Mr. Rosen straightened up, and Mrs. Rosen leaned toward him. He put his arm around her shoulder. "We'll say good-bye to Jimmy now," he said.

The doctor said, "Of course," and she led them from the waiting room down the hall.

Although I didn't remember standing up, I had. With no

warning, everything had gotten very intense, very concentrated, and the thing I found myself paying attention to was my breathing. I was taking very shallow, very quick breaths. I looked around the room. Everybody's face was empty, numb, and everybody was breathing just the same as I was, like there was something poisonous in the air, and we didn't want to get too much of it in our lungs. With each breath, I shifted my glance to another person: my mother, my father, Miss Berry, Mrs. Mullen, Mr. Landis, Mrs. Landis. I turned to look at Harry. That's when I noticed he wasn't standing next to me anymore.

I turned farther around. Harry had moved away from the door, to the corner of the room. He was holding himself up very straight. From behind, he looked angry. I moved over so I was standing next to him. His teeth were clenched and his eyes were glassy. He was standing so still. Then his chest began to shake. He tried to keep his mouth shut and let the air out through his nose. The sound was ragged and jerky. When tears began to spill, he made fists and jammed them into his cheeks.

I reached over for his hands. I took hold of his wrists and tried to pull his hands away from his face. He was pressing them against himself as hard as he could. When he felt my hands on his, he tried to jerk away, but I was holding him very tightly. He tried again, more for the sake of doing something than really trying, but there wasn't any force left in him. If he hadn't already stepped away from the door, I think he might have tried to leave, but as it was he was pretty much boxed in. So he stopped trying. Like Mrs. Rosen, he just sagged. He leaned toward me, dropped his hands, and stopped trying not to cry. I let go of his wrists. He dropped his head forward, and let his hands fall. Harry began crying so hard, his whole body shook. Then I was crying too, for Jimmy, of course, but for more than that. I was crying for Harry and me as well.

I shuffled around so I was standing more next to Harry than in front of him. I put my arm around his shoulder. I just meant to give him a sort of semi-hug, but as I did, Harry turned toward me. He put his arms around me, and I did the same. Then we were just holding each other, holding on to each other, while we cried.

I have no idea how long it took for anything from then on to happen. I only remember clearly that later on, when I was in bed and couldn't seem to stop crying, Mom came in, sat on the edge of my bed, and brushed my hair with her hand the way she used to when I was little. She did that until I fell asleep.

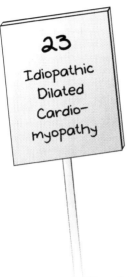

23

Idiopathic
Dilated
Cardio-
myopathy

Every other time I ever went over to Harry's house, I walked in the back door. If I knew his parents were out, I'd just go looking for him which wouldn't normally take very long. When Harry's at home, he's usually in his room. I understand why he likes it so much; it's a good room to spend time in, but if I describe the room, that won't explain why it's so good. I mean, Harry's room has just about everything anybody would want to have, anything anybody might need, but so does mine; so do the rooms of most of the guys I know. I take that back; Harry's room has one more window than mine.

Harry's room faces the back of his house. Three windows look out over his backyard. Beyond the lawn are so many trees that except for on a bright day in the winter, you can't really see the back of the house on the next street over. Another two windows face the side, looking out toward the garage.

Harry's desk is under those two side windows; his bed, a bunk bed left over from when he and his brother shared a room, is in the corner next to the desk. Under the three windows is a long table he made out of a piece of plywood which he set on stacked up milk crates. I helped him sand down the plywood until it was as smooth as a playground slide. Then we stained it light brown, and spent you wouldn't believe how long – it was more than days – rubbing it down with furniture wax. It looks really good. Harry says it's the best piece of plywood in all of New England if not the entire Eastern seaboard, and he's probably right. Once when we were kidding around, I asked him if he'd leave me the table in his will. He said only if I promised to wax it once a month. He keeps his computer and music system on that table.

In the corners to the left and right of the three windows are bookcases mostly filled with books except for where Harry shoved other things into empty spaces. His baseball glove lives on one of the shelves, and he stores his stone collection there – one from anywhere he has ever been – camp, Jersey shore, every stream he's ever been fishing in with his Dad, "secret" places (we used to call them *hideouts*) he and I discovered since from before I can really remember. I can't tell one stone from the next, but I know for a fact he knows exactly the Where and When of every single one.

On the top shelf to the right of the windows, overlooking his desk, is an empty Wild Turkey decanter (that's a special kind of bourbon) his Uncle Howe gave him. It was made in 1976, the Bicentennial year, and is supposed to keep getting more valuable every year because there was only a limited number of them made; his uncle said Harry's supposed to use it to help pay for college. There are a bunch of photographs, mostly of Harry and his family taken on vacations or at Christmas, and other times like that; but also some of them are of Harry and me, and there's one of Kathryn. The pictures are "randomly placed" here and there on the shelves. And then, of course, he keeps his CDs on a shelf to the left of the table that is even with the table itself.

Finally comes the supply shelf which Harry keeps stocked with gum (sugarfree), Pepperidge Farm goldfish, those small cardboard cartons of apple juice – he swears he prefers it warm – a tin of chocolate chip cookies – his mother makes a fresh batch every Sunday night – blank paper for math, lined paper for written homework, extra pencils, extra pens, a small wooden box with a lid for paper clips and thumb tacks, and a stapler. The thumb tacks are for the bulletin board on the back of the door to the closet that's on the opposite side of the room from his desk. The door to his room is in the center of the wall opposite his plywood table. If you open it too far, you'll bang it into the foot of the bunk beds.

Harry's room is wallpapered. The background color is a kind of light rust and the paper has pictures of old-fashioned toys on it: toy soldiers, drums, wooden trains, circus wagons, hoops. The floor is mostly covered by a rug that is dark blue, and the windows have curtains the same color. The curtains are closable, but up until the day of Jimmy's funeral, I never saw them that way.

Now that I've taken the time to describe it, I still can't tell what made Harry's room so special. Take my word for it: that room was a good place to spend time. I miss it.

Anyway, when I got to Harry's house from the Rosens', I didn't go to the back door; I walked up the front walk and rang the doorbell. I don't think I did that because of everything that had happened between us before Jimmy died; it was just that I felt like I had a different reason for coming to Harry's house that day.

Mrs. Landis answered the door. They had left the Rosen's some time before. She said hello and was I all right and what a good job I had done speaking at Jimmy's funeral. I said hello and yes I was and thank you. Then she said, "Just go on up. Harry's expecting you." That was a little bit of a surprise.

You probably noticed that I haven't said anything about Kathryn, about whether she went to the funeral or not. She didn't, and again, Harry was the reason. It wasn't that she didn't want go or felt she couldn't go; Harry asked her to stay with him while it was going on. If you think that made me feel a little bad, it did.

Harry's door was closed. I knocked, and he said right away, "Come on in, Brian."

Kathryn was sitting in Harry's desk chair. She'd pulled it out and turned it so it faced the bunk beds. Harry was sitting on the bottom bunk, cross-legged. Kathryn was as dressed up as I was, but I had no idea why. I have to admit I was hoping she'd left already so I could talk to Harry alone.

I walked in and over to the table. That was when I noticed the curtains were closed. I pushed one of the curtains out of the way and looked out at his backyard. There really wasn't much there to look at. I turned around, pulled out the stool Harry used at his table, and sat on it. It's about as high as a bar stool because the table is pretty much that high.

Kathryn said, "Hi, Brian. How are you?" And that's exactly what she meant.

I didn't have to think about the answer. I'd already been thinking a lot about how I was. "I'm okay," I said.

"Good."

"Yeah."

I looked at Harry. He didn't say anything. Instead he pressed his lips together and kind of gave me a quick nod. I knew what he meant. "That wasn't the most fun thing I've ever done," I said, "and I really wish you both had been there." Then because there was no way I could think of quickly to tell Harry what I needed to tell him, I filled them in on what the service had been like, who had said what. I was right about how Harry reacted to Joe Sider, and he said pretty much what I'd been thinking at the time.

"See?" he said, "See what a good thing it was I didn't go?" I wasn't ready to admit that by a long way. Harry pressed his point. "If I'd been there, Brian, you and I would have gotten some major dirty looks. There's no way I could have listened to that without cracking up, funeral or not. Then *you* would have started and that would've only made it worse. No, I'm thinking you were better off without me."

I had to say what I thought. "I don't think so, Harry. You were Jimmy's closest friend. At least here in Afton you were; there's no question about that. And I've got to tell you, I sure as hell didn't notice anyone our age who might have come from Oakhurst wherever-the-hell-that-is Ohio!"

I was really surprised at how mad-sounding my voice was, but at the same time, I didn't care because it felt good. "You should have been there. You should have been the one to say something, not me." I looked over at Kathryn, I think because she was expecting me to. "And so should you, Katty." I used the name Mrs. Rosen had for her partly because I liked the sound, but mostly because I thought it would help me make my point. Kathryn hadn't been looking right at me when I started speaking to her, but when I called her Katty, her eyes flattened up into mine. They sort of flashed brighter for a second, but then they settled back to normal.

"I know. You're right, Brian, but then I knew that all along. I didn't go because Harry asked me to be with him. I thought it over. I decided it was more important for me to be here. I had Mom drive me over to the Rosen's last night. I explained to them. I'm pretty sure they understood why I couldn't be there."

I guess I could have figured that out on my own if I'd tried at all. Other than my mom, if there's anyone I know in the world who wouldn't do anything to hurt someone else if she could help it, that would be Kathryn. I turned to Harry. "How about you? Did you tell the Rosens you wouldn't be there? Did you tell them *why* you wouldn't be there?" Harry said nothing. "Could you tell *me* why you couldn't be there?" I felt myself getting close to crying, and the worst part was how much by surprise that feeling was taking me.

"I sent a note with Kathryn. I said how sorry I was about everything; I said I was especially sorry I couldn't be at the funeral."

I felt like saying something mean about how I'll bet the note really made them feel better, but I didn't. It wouldn't have been fair.

No other words were in my head that I wanted to say just then. I turned my head to look at Kathryn. She was watching the blue rug, concentrating on it pretty hard. Out of nowhere, Harry said, "Did you hear how I found out where you and Jimmy were?"

Only at that exact moment did I realize I had no idea how Harry had figured that out. I guess I'd assumed he looked in whatever places he could think of until he found the right one. Evidently, that wasn't the case.

"No, now you mention it. I didn't."

"You want to?" he asked. "It was almost funny."

I said, "Why not?"

"I'm going to use the lavatory." Kathryn stood up from the desk chair. An expression appeared on Harry's face as though he was suddenly afraid he was going to be cheating her out of something. "Go ahead," Kathryn said as she stepped toward the door, "I've already heard it, remember, Harry?"

"Oh, yeah," Harry said. "Right."

Kathryn left and I said, "So, how <u>did</u> you know where we were?"

That was exactly the line Harry had been waiting for. He smiled the way he did when he felt especially good about having done something really clever. "Melinda told me."

"No way!" I said. "Never." Harry just nodded. "How did you manage that?" I asked.

Harry was still smiling. "I found her in the girls' locker room down by the gym."

"Come again?"

"You heard me: In the girls' locker room, in their bathroom," Harry said, looking smug. "See, when I first started to look for Jimmy, I thought I'd check out the cafe, just to be sure, you know?" I nodded. "Then I went to the boy's locker room. Nobody was in there, but I thought I could hear Melinda's voice. I stepped into the bathroom there, and sure enough, I can hear Melinda talking. The sound was coming through the vent. I guess their bathroom is back-to-back with ours. Anyway, she was telling someone that when Broom got through with Jimmy, he'd never show up at school again."

"So you heard her say where they had Jimmy?"

"No. I went in there. She totally freaked. They all freaked, come to think of it. Except for why I was there in the first place, it was probably pretty funny."

"What did you do?"

"Not much really," Harry said. "I just grabbed her and started dragging her over to the first stall. I told her I'd drown her if she didn't tell me where Broom had Jimmy."

At first I was having a little trouble imagining Harry doing all this, but then I got this really vivid picture in my head of Harry standing over Broom, that bat up over his head, looking as though he were about to commit murder. "Melinda believed you'd do that?"

The door to Harry's room opened and Kathryn came back in saying, "She had to. He would have."

"Yeah," Harry said. "I think I might have done that. Now I think about it, I was angrier at Melinda than I was at Broom."

"How come?" I asked.

"'Cause at least Broom was honest. I mean, in a way, he played fair. He hated Jimmy from the first day he saw him, and he never pretended anything else. But Melinda cheated. Whether she'll ever admit it or not, she was lying all along."

Kathryn touched my shoulder as she slipped by and sat back down in the desk chair. Harry uncrossed his legs and slid to the side of his bunk. He looked at her first, then at me. He said, "Do you know why Jimmy died?"

That question took me completely by surprise. "Sure. What the doctor said that night. His heart couldn't take it. He had a weak heart." Harry didn't say anything. I looked at Kathryn. "Isn't that right? Isn't that pretty much what the doctor said?"

Kathryn said, "I guess so. That's what I remember, at least." She turned to face Harry. "Are you saying that's not true? Jimmy died of something else?"

"In a way yes, and in a way no," Harry said. "Yes, Jimmy had a weak heart; he had idiopathic dilated cardiomyopathy."

I had no clue what any of that meant and I guess I looked it.

"His heart was weakened and enlarged and couldn't pump blood efficiently, and that affected pretty much everything else."

I didn't know what to say. I mean, what was there to say? So now we knew why Jimmy never did anything the rest of us did, and I guessed that explained Jimmy's appearance. Pretty much it explained everything about the way Jimmy was, except two things.

"Harry, why didn't Jimmy let people know?"

He was ready for that one probably because he'd been expecting it. He did what he used to do all the time when he and I would find ourselves on some side of an argument that wasn't the most popular side to be on. He answered my question with one of his own. He said when you did that, you were redirecting the point of the argument so you could control the way it would come out. He must have forgotten he'd taught me about that. "How would you have treated Jimmy if you'd known that any, *any* kind of exertion at all might have killed him?" Harry said. "Be honest. Would that have changed anything about the way you treated him?"

"You're damn right!" I said. "I would have made sure I helped him any way I could have!"

"Like how?" Harry went on.

"I don't know. Like, you know, carry his books, or, get his lunch for him – stuff like that I guess."

"How about you, Kathryn? Would you have treated Jimmy differently?" Harry said.

"I'm not sure, but I guess so." She thought about that for second. "Yes, of course. I don't know what I could have done, but I would have tried. Anybody would. Almost everybody would."

Harry waited a second or two. "That's it. Jimmy didn't want to be taken care of. Back in Ohio, back in Oakhurst, Jimmy was always singled out. In front of his classes, in front of his whole school sometimes, they'd make announcements:" Harry scrunched up his face and used this nasal sounding, elementary school teacher's voice. *'Jimmy Rosen is very sick and could easily have to go to the hospital if all his friends and schoolmates aren't very, very careful.'*

"He and his family moved to Afton, because Jimmy was in line for a heart transplant at Hartford Hospital. Usually they can give you drugs if you have what Jimmy did, but maybe because they couldn't figure out why Jimmy had it in the first place, the only thing they could do was give him a new heart.

"Jimmy agreed to the move on one condition. He made his parents promise he'd be allowed to go to school without the whole world knowing he might not make it through a day if everyone didn't treat him as if he were made of glass. I don't know for sure how he forced them into that, but I can guess."

Harry looked at me in an odd way, as if he was asking permission to go on. "And?" I said.

"You may not have been able to see it, but in a way Jimmy was tough. He'd made up his mind that coming to Afton was at least going to be a chance for him to be as close to the same as everybody else as he could be. There wasn't going to be any compromise about that."

Kathryn got up from the chair and came over to where I was still on that stool. She leaned back against the table. "All right. That explains a lot about Jimmy, and I can see how what happened to him in the bathroom was more than his heart could take – come to think about it, I'm amazed he survived the snake. But now you've started letting us know stuff, how about telling us why you couldn't go to Jimmy's funeral?"

Harry nodded his head. "Okay, but I'm not sure you'll get it.

"One day last summer, after Jimmy had told me about his heart, but before you," Harry looked at me, "came back from camp, I went over to his house. We were going down to the Athenaeum. You know, the art museum in Hartford?"

"We know, Harry," I said. "We've only gone on about a dozen field trips since fifth grade."

"What? Oh, yeah, right. Anyway, when I got to Jimmy's house he wasn't ready. Mrs. Rosen said he had just gotten out of his bath.

"Say what?"

"Jimmy didn't take showers," Harry said.

"Because why?"

"Mrs. Rosen was worried he'd slip, so she asked him to promise not to take a shower. Ever." Harry looked at me to see if I was going to say more.

"Okay," I said.

"Okay. So Mrs. Rosen said I was welcome to come into the kitchen and wait. Of course, she started feeding me. Then Mrs. Rosen told me *she* knew that *I* knew about Jimmy's illness. 'I would never have said anything except for Jimmy told us,' she said.

"Anyway, they both said they had a big favor to ask." Harry stopped as if he expected us to say something, but I didn't know what it was, and I guess Kathryn didn't either. "Can't you figure out the next part?"

Kathryn frowned, then sort of snapped up her head. "Seriously? She asked you to protect Jimmy?"

"Basically, yes."

"And you said you'd do it?" I said.

"Yes again."

"Did Dr. Frank or Mrs. Gerardi or anyone else at school know about Jimmy?"

"Nope. Jimmy wouldn't give his permission. He said it wouldn't be fair."

That piece of information tweaked me in my stomach a little. Somehow, Jimmy's using Harry's idea of fair and unfair like that was the more unfair thing to have done. And something else about that bothered me: I didn't like the idea that Jimmy had known that part about Harry as well as I did.

"Did he know what his parents asked you?"

Harry looked down. "No."

"And that was because...?"

"They asked me not to tell him."

This was getting worse and worse. "Oh, Jeez, Harry. What a mess!" I said.

Then Kathryn asked, "And that's the way things were till the other day?"

"Not really. After that stunt with the snake and then after all that bull about AIDS started, I told Jimmy's parents they had to let Dr. Frank know what was going on. That's how we worked out the plan about riding to school in Mr. Peters' van and me being with Jimmy between classes."

"Harry?" I said.

"What?"

"Why didn't you tell me?" I asked. "Don't you think I would have helped?"

"I couldn't do it, Brian. Jimmy wouldn't let me out of the promise."

I couldn't get a handle on what I was hearing. For as long as Harry and I had been best friends, I always knew he *believed* in things. He *believed* in things more strongly than anyone else, but not ever in a fanatical way. When Harry said things, they always seemed to me to be reasonable. Some I might not get at first, but after he'd explained them, that was what I'd think too. But what I was hearing here just didn't sound right. The words were Harry's words, but the part of Harry that was so special I'm sure I'll never know anyone else like him again – that part wasn't there.

Kathryn stepped toward Harry. "I've got something to say, Harry; then I need to go home.

"I think you made a mistake, not so much about Jimmy, but about Brian and about me. I think you should have told me, maybe, but at least and especially, Brian. You should definitely have told *him* what was going on."

Harry got up off his bed. He stood and faced both of us. He looked funny in a way I didn't know. He looked scared. "Don't you think I wanted to? Don't you think I spent part of every damn day since Broom and that fucking snake – *every single day* – trying to talk Jimmy into letting me tell you guys?" Harry let that sit out in front of us for a moment. "But what could I do? He always said no!"

Kathryn kept right on. "What you could have done, Harry, for Jimmy's sake, was break your promise. Because it would have been smarter, not to mention fairer in a more important way, than letting your freakin' promise threaten Jimmy's life. Sometimes people make bad promises, Harry, or have you forgotten telling me that? I think this was one of those times."

That brought the conversation to a stop. Harry stared past Kathryn and me, as though he was looking out the windows. He moved past us to the window to his left and moved one of the curtains aside. It was dark outside by now, so I think all he could see was our reflections. Then again, probably Harry wasn't looking at anything.

While he stood there, I swear I saw Harry change. I can't say exactly – specifically – what about him changed, but one minute he was the best friend I'd always known, and the next he was somebody very much like that person, but not exactly that person anymore.

"You're right," he said. "That's why I couldn't go to the funeral. If I'd been smarter…" He didn't finish the sentence, but we all knew what it was going to be.

I wanted to tell Harry no, that's not right, that's not so, and I started to; but Kathryn put her hand up in front of my face to shush me.

She said, "It's possible, Harry. It *is* possible." She stood there a moment longer and then left.

I sat back down on the stool. Harry sat back down on his bed. After a while, he plumped his pillow up, drew himself back toward the head of the bed, and lay back. A while longer and I stood up. "I'll see you later, Harry. Call me if you want."

He said, "Yeah. I'll see you later, Bri. Thanks for coming over."

I moved to the door, opened it and was about to step through when Harry called to me. "Brian?"

I turned around. Harry's eyes were very red; in fact, his face was very red. "I couldn't do anything else, you know? You see what I mean?"

I stepped back into the room. "No, Harry. I'm really sorry, but I don't." Tears began to run down Harry's cheeks. I went the rest of the way back over, right beside Harry's bed. "All I see is, Kathryn's right. You should have broken your promise."

Harry covered his face with his hands for a second. His chest shook. He took a raggedy breath and then he pulled his hands down, wiping off the tears as he did. He took another breath that was a little less shaky. Then he took another that was smooth. He started to turn his head toward me, but then didn't. "I couldn't do it, Brian. I *loved* Jimmy." Finally he looked at me. "Do you understand what I'm saying?"

"Yes," I said. "I think that I do."

"That's good," Harry said, but I don't think he believed me.

I went down the back stairs to the kitchen. I could hear Mr. and Mrs. Landis out in the den, watching the news. I didn't feel like saying good-bye, so I just let myself out the back door.

24

Sophomore Year

I don't have much left to say. Actually, I didn't think there *was* anything more to say after telling about what happened in Harry's room after the funeral.

Everything that came before this, I had started to write during our week off in February. I finished just before school started again, junior year. All these pages – basically everything that happened and what I thought about it – sat in the bottom drawer of my bureau for most of a year. Then a few weeks ago, just before Christmas, my mother and I were sitting around in the kitchen waiting for Dad to come home. She'd asked me about my day, and I'd told her. I asked about her day, and she told me. Then we just fell into one of those quiet times where you think your own thoughts, but you're not alone while you do. The quiet had been going on for a pretty long time when she reached over and nudged my arm.

"Brian? Whatever happened to all that writing you were doing last year?"

Up till then, I didn't know she knew about it. I was going to say, "What writing?" but I changed my mind.

"Well, I finished it, I guess."

"May I know what it was all about?"

"It's kind of hard to explain," I began, "but I guess it's basically about what happened last year, about Jimmy and...well, mostly that's it."

"Is it something you mean to keep private?" she said.

I hadn't thought about that one way or another. I hadn't planned it out. I hadn't intended to write so much. It just happened; it just came out, a bit at a time. One day I was sitting at my desk, thinking about Jimmy and the funeral and a couple of times when Harry and Jimmy and I were hanging out. And I started to write about it.

"I don't know," I decided. "Not really."

"May I read it?"

"Sure," I said, and as soon as I had, I was glad she wanted to. I realized I wanted her to know about everything, all the details.

I went up to my room, opened up the drawer, and took out the envelope I'd shoved the pages into. I'd written on the outside in black magic marker **SOPHOMORE YEAR.**

I handed Mom the envelope. "It's not *just* about Jimmy," I said.

"I'm sure it isn't," she replied.

When I got home from the school the next day, Mom was already home. She was waiting for me in the kitchen. She was sitting at the counter on one of those high stools such as Harry has in front of his plywood table. "I finished it," she said, patting the envelope. "I have some questions."

"I don't know whether I have the answers," I said.

"You have them. Some you may not want to give, but you have them."

Some of the questions she asked me were things she said she would have wanted to know if she had just read the story without knowing any of the people. The others were harder to answer. So what comes next is the answers to those questions. They're as clear as I can make them. The easy ones come first.

I said already that Broom was arrested. He was charged with Aggravated Battery, First Degree Sexual Assault, and Unlawful Restraint. A rumor went around school that since Jimmy died, he'd be charged with murder, but that didn't happen. I don't know what happened to him with those charges. He was also expelled from Afton High School. A few weeks after his expulsion hearing, Broom started showing up at school and hanging around in the cafeteria with his old gang. He never got to hang around long, though, because each time he did that, Mrs. Gerardi would call the Afton Police, and the police would send one of their officers over to escort Broom off the school grounds. The third time he did it, Broom was informed he'd be arrested if he continued to break any of the conditions of his expulsion. One of those conditions, of course, was that he not set foot on the grounds of Afton High School. Broom's parents were also informed, and after that Broom stopped coming. I personally haven't seen him again, but every now and then somebody or other would bother to tell me he'd seen Broom at the movies or at Burger King or some other such place like that. We all expected him to return to the high school the next year, but he didn't. The last thing I heard about him was he left home and went to live with relatives in Buffalo, but maybe that was a joke. Anyway, nobody I know of has seen him for a long time.

Broom's father's lawyers kept trying to get Harry's lawyer to persuade Harry and his father to agree to settle the suit out of court. At first Harry's lawyer relayed the offer and said he thought it might be the best thing to do. Then the details of Broom's arrest and the charges filed against him came out. Harry's lawyer told Broom's father's lawyer all that would come up in court. That may have been a bluff because it's hard to see how Harry's tackling Broom's father had anything to do with what Broom did to Jimmy, but if it was a bluff, it worked.

Harry was suspended for ten days. When that happens, you can't come back to school until you come in with your parents for a Readmittance Conference. At the conference, Dr. Frank told Harry and his parents they were responsible for all the damage to the boys' bathroom, and, of course, Harry and his parents agreed to that. I think Harry was also on some sort of probation for the rest of the year, which Mrs. Gerardi explained to him later, was only because according to the policy on "destruction and/or damage to school property resulting in a 10 day at home suspension," he had to be. Nobody, she said, thought for a minute that Harry was the type of person who would ever do anything like that maliciously or willfully.

Harry and I stayed friends, but I don't think either one of us thought we were best friends any more. At first, I still spent more time with him than anyone else, but there was something that just didn't work the same way. I don't believe it was all because of what happened, but whenever we spent time together, I felt a little tight, a little uncomfortable. I guess neither of us was sure he could trust the other one in the same old way, and we didn't know how to go about getting that back. Or maybe we didn't want to. Or maybe we just couldn't even if we had wanted to.

Kathryn and Harry and I would sometimes do things like go skating or go to the movies or just hang out, except now that I think about it, we did that kind of thing less and less as the year went along. Harry went away during both the February and April breaks. He and the rest of his family went skiing way north in Vermont in February, and then Harry and his brother went to Florida during April.

That next summer, we didn't spend much time together at all. In fact, once June was over, we hardly even saw each other. Harry went off traveling again. In July he went on a long cruise in the Caribbean, not on one of the fancy luxury liners but on a sailing ship. I was over at Harry's house one day after baseball practice when his father came in and asked Harry if he'd asked me yet. Harry said, "What? Oh, no, not yet." That was when I found out about the sailing trip and after Mr. Landis had gotten through telling me all about it – he was really excited; you would have thought he was the one going – he suggested I might like to go, too.

Harry said what he was supposed to. "Yeah, that would be great!"

Then I said what Harry wanted me to say, "Sure. I'll check it out with my parents." I was pretty sure Harry was almost scared I'd just say yes. He was home for about a week after the cruise before his whole family went to Alaska.

At the time, I really didn't think too much about how different that summer was. Actually I didn't have that much time to think about it. My dad helped me get a job working for three brothers who had a small construction company. The name of their company was Masters Brothers Builders, Inc. They only worked on what they called "single family dwellings". They were pretty cool to work for even though I didn't make all that much money and didn't get to do anything very complicated. I mean, I couldn't really take you into a house I worked on and point out parts of it that I built, but I could show you the cabinets I helped put in and the closets I helped lay out and the walls I sanded and sanded and sanded and sanded once the sheet rock was taped. In the final analysis, as my father would say, I learned quite a bit about carpentry. Now he never gets tired of asking me how the new bookshelves for the Children's Room are coming along, and I never get tired of telling him they're in the planning stage.

Harry went away to private school his junior year. He told me about it while he was home from the cruise and before the trip to Alaska. A business friend of his dad's had gone to Blair Academy in New Jersey. I guess early in the summer, he took Harry and his parents for a visit. Harry told me he finally made up his mind to go while he was on the sailing trip. He'd e-mail me once in a while. He liked Blair right from the very beginning. He made a lot of friends right away which didn't surprise me at all. In a way I wish he hadn't liked the school so much, or at least I wish he hadn't told me he did. Somehow Harry's feeling so great about his new school made me feel a little funny about going to Afton, but that wasn't Harry's fault, and it wasn't really such a big deal. Anyway, I didn't feel that way for long.

Private school vacations are much longer than the breaks public schools take, and except for Christmas, they aren't even at the same time. So now Harry and I act like old friends who hardly ever see each other anymore, which is pretty much the truth. He brought his roommate from Blair home for a long weekend. He called me up to see if I wanted to go out with them to a movie. I went and had an okay time. His roommate, Rich, was a good guy. Just the kind of person you'd expect Harry to like.

The other day, Kathryn and I decided we were "going out." Actually it was more like a discovery. For a while after Jimmy's funeral, I didn't really see much of her, just to say hello and how are you doing. Then one morning just before the February break I had to go to school early to make up a quiz I'd missed because of having to go to the dentist. I'd arranged to meet the teacher, Ms. Breckley, early, but she forgot. I was sitting on the floor outside her classroom, still waiting for her to show up, when I heard someone walking down the hall toward me. I didn't look up until I realized whoever it was had stopped in front of me. Something about the boots was familiar. I looked up and Kathryn said, "What are you doing here so early?"

I told her. She said it looked like Ms. Breckley was standing me up. Then she invited me for breakfast. Beginning then we more or less picked up where we left off the night I'd eaten dinner at her house, the night Jimmy died. Now it seems as if the less I saw Harry, the more I saw Kathryn. By April or so, I don't think a weekend would go by when we wouldn't spend at least a couple of hours together. Sometimes we'd go out for lunch or some ice cream, or I'd just drop over and visit for a while. But other times we'd take these long walks, hikes really, around Afton's reservoir, or else we'd drive up to the northwest corner of the state, to places like Cornwall and Norfolk. (Kathryn got her license in April. I wouldn't get mine till July.) Discovery tours, Kathryn called them. And of course, we'd do stuff like go to the movies, and we'd mostly go together to school dances, although sometimes I'd just meet her there. Anyway, I know this will sound a little lame, but Kathryn and I never thought of what we did together as having "dates." Basically, we were just keeping each other company. My best friend wasn't my best friend any more, and Kathryn's friend, Melinda, had turned out to be

224

even more of a jerk than anyone, including me, could possibly have suspected. So in a way, it made sense for us to spend time together.

The truth is, the first time we even kissed each other in a way that was any different from the way you'd kiss your aunt or sister or somebody like that was only two days before school started this year.

Last Tuesday Kathryn told me during lunch that Carol Gervaise had asked her how long she, meaning Kathryn, and I had been going out. That's when she realized, Kathryn said, that actually we had been "going out" for almost a year. We decided that this Saturday we'd go out to dinner and celebrate our first anniversary, just for the fun of it.

If you ask if I'm in love with Kathryn and tell me I have to give an honest answer or else I'll be thrown in a huge pot of boiling hot fudge sauce, the best I can do is say I think I am; I think I really am.

The Rosens have moved to California, somewhere around San Diego. I've forgotten the name of the town, but I have their address. Before they moved, which they did the first week in June, they invited Harry and me and Kathryn and Melinda – they didn't know what she'd done and nobody thought it was important to tell them – over for dinner. Melinda didn't go, obviously, but the rest of us did.

We tried to have a good time. We tried to talk about just anything such as what had been going on at school that spring or how hard our exams were going to be or how we were looking forward to summer. And we spent as long as we could getting Mrs. Rosen to tell us about their new home. All of that didn't matter though. Mr. Rosen probably didn't say more than twenty words the whole time we were there, and no matter what we'd bring up, Mrs. Rosen would somehow turn the subject back to Jimmy. After a while we just gave up and let Harry more or less take over.

From then on, no matter what the conversation would start out to be, when Mrs. Rosen would bring Jimmy into the picture, Harry would start on a new Jimmy story. I'm pretty sure at least half of them were about things that never actually happened, but that didn't really matter at all. The Rosens wanted to hear about Jimmy. It must have made them feel better somehow. Whenever I glanced over at them while Harry was talking, in their eyes they looked like they were sad, but their mouths were smiling; and they'd laugh, really laugh, when Harry made something sound funny. So if we helped them to feel better or closer to Jimmy for a while, then I'm glad we went; but it was definitely not a fun night. I was glad when Mrs. Mullen arrived to give us a ride home.

Of course, Mrs. Rosen cooked much more food than we could eat including two different desserts, and when it was time to leave, she brought out packages of cookies for each one of us and a fourth which she gave to Kathryn to give to Melinda. Then Mr. Rosen gave us each a small wrapped gift, and one more for Melinda, which he asked us not to open just then. He said it was from all of them, Mrs. Rosen, himself, and Jimmy. He said, "You were good friends to our Jimmy. We want you to remember that. He loved you all, especially..." He didn't finish that part of what he wanted to say; he couldn't.

Mrs. Rosen went on for him. "Yes, that's right. Jimmy loved you, Brian and Kathryn and Harry, especially." But I don't think that's what Mr. Rosen was going to say. I think the rest of what he had to say was just for Harry. Anyway, he was facing Harry when he stopped.

As soon as we were in Mrs. Mullen's car, we opened the packages. Each one was the same: a small silver frame with a formal photograph of Jimmy and his parents. It's a good picture. You can see what a different kind of person Jimmy was. By the time all that awful stuff started to happen, I'd mostly forgotten to notice that about him anymore. The picture reminds me as much of that as it does of everything else. I keep the picture in my room, sometimes on my desk, sometimes on the bureau; sometimes I set it on a bookshelf in front of some books I don't use much. I'm glad I have it. It's good not to forget.

And that covers everything. Except that we didn't give Melinda the cookies or the other picture. We gave them to Miss Berry instead.

Brian's Vocab Words:

Formal definitions, context, ✦ Brian's definitions.

1   **Allusion** An instance of indirect reference:

*That's when Jimmy Rosen stepped out from the trees. He goes, "How unu-sual to hear literary **allusion** from a runner gasping for breath."*

[Jimmy meant that Harry was referring to Alice in Wonderland by making the remark about the Chesire Cat, which is in Alice in Wonderland.]

2   **Deter** To prevent or discourage from acting, as by means of fear or doubt:

*"No, no," Jimmy went on. "Don't let my humble presence **deter** you from continuing your chat."*

[What Jimmy meant was, "Don't stop talking because of me."]

3   **Aura** A distinctive but intangible quality that seems to surround a person or thing.

*It is my great pleasure to bask in the **aura** of your loveliness in this small portion of the world which enjoys the relative freedom denied so many of our fellow travelers.*

[Jimmy is more or less suggesting that Melissa is surrounded by an al-most supernatural glow that can be sensed but not seen.]

4   **Inane** One that lacks sense or substance:

*That's such a blitheringly **inane** idea, it might just work."*

[That's a Jimmy word for stupid.]

5   **Dissipate** To vanish by dispersion:

We kept having to stop on the way because Jimmy was feeling light-headed. "A moment, mes amis, if you please, to give the fog a chance to **dissipate.**"

[A Jimmy word for go away, like mist in the morning.]

6   **Troglodyte** A person considered to be reclusive, reactionary, out of date, or brutish.

How ever do you think you'll be able to guarantee Master Broom and his pet **troglodytes** *will keep their distance.*

[Think caveman.]

7   **Percipient** Having the power of perceiving, especially perceiving keenly and readily.

And if we were on vacation today, then yesterday, which was, as you point-ed out quite **percipiently…**

[Jimmy was sort of complimenting Melinda by saying how smart she was to know the day before was Wednesday. Actually he was being sarcastic by Melinda didn't notice.]

8   **Hiatus** A gap or interruption in space, time, or continuity; a break:

"In fact, I am too filled with the milk of human kindness and holiday cheer on this the last day before the Christmas **hiatus.**"

[As the definition says, a break. If there was a dramatic way to say something, Jimmy would find just the right word to do it.]

9   **Serendipitous** The faculty of making fortunate discoveries by accident.

My nativity gave my parents **serendipitous** *reason enough to celebrate at a time when all the rest of the world is celebrating as well.*

[A Jimmy word meaning a good thing that happens by chance, not on purpose.]

10 **Indicative** Serving to indicate:

11 **Orientation** A tendency of thought; a general inclination:

*"Melinda, The Nutcracker is a traditional ballet. Consequently, the costumes of the dancers are traditional as well, and as such not a matter of their choice or indicative of their personalities or sexual **orientation**.*

[People used to think, and maybe some still do, that men who wear tights and dance ballet are gay. Jimmy was trying to point out to Melinda that the dancers wearing tights did not mean they were homosexual.]

12 **Obfuscation** To make so confused or opaque as to be difficult to perceive or understand:

*It's too hard to tell with nurses. They're very good at **obfuscation**.*

[Harry may have said it, but it's definitely a Jimmy word. Harry was suggesting that nurses are good at hiding what they think. He didn't really mean it seriously, but Melinda didn't know that.]

13 **Homage** Special honor or respect shown or expressed publicly.

*"My entire. Circle. Of friends, admirers. And well wishers. Come to pay **homage**."*

[As the definition says, honor or respect, but the word is mostly used about someone monumental or epic like a great artist or the President.]

14 **Frivolous** Unworthy of serious attention; trivial

*"May I ask **frivolous** question? What is the time?"*

[Jimmy meant the question might seem silly.]

15 **Poignant** Profoundly moving; touching

*"Not so much boring as terribly **poignant**," said Jimmy. His eyes were red and puffy. He was dabbing at them with a handkerchief. "Sometimes I find the old M*A*S*H episodes appallingly moving, as you can plainly see."*

[Jimmy was trying to suggest that what they'd been watching had made him cry.]

16 **Misanthropic** Characterized by a hatred or mistrustful scorn for human-kind.

*"The second rumor I would prefer to treat in the same fashion as the first, for I feel its creation was motivated by the same **misanthropic** attitude as the first;"...*

[Not a Jimmy word that I know of, but one he certainly would have known. Dr. Frank was saying that only someone who basically hated people would have done that.]

17 **Boor** A person with rude, clumsy manners and little refinement.

*"A small group of unthinking, insensitive, **boors**," my mother said, "are trying to bully a larger group of people..."*

[Mom was saying the people (Broom etc.) who spread the rumors about Jimmy were extremely rude and badly behaved.]

18 **Acronym** A word formed from the initial letters of a name, such as WAC for Women's Army Corps, or by combining initial letters or parts of a series of words, such as radar for radio detecting and ranging.

*"The Afton Committee to Keep Our Schools Free of Discrimination." She heavily emphasized the words that made the **acronym**."*

[Or, KOSFOD for Keep Our Schools Free from Discrimination.]

Printed in the United States
By Bookmasters